**THE VON**

C000024595

By the time he was a mere thirty years of age, Leon Le Grand was a millionaire and the executive director of a multi-national corporation. Then, at thirty-nine, he retired from the world of business to become a full-time writer.

He lives in Melbourne with his wife and three children, and when he is not thinking up new stories of suspense and intrigue, he spends his time travelling the world or engaging in his favourite pastimes — pistol shooting and photography.

THE VON KESSEL DOSSIER

LEON LE GRAND

A Critic's Choice paperback
from Lorevan Publishing, Inc.
New York, New York

Reprinted by arrangement with the Author

ISBN: 1-55547-197-8

First Critic's Choice edition: 1987

From LOREVAN PUBLISHING, INC.

Critic's Choice Paperbacks
31 E. 28th St.
New York, New York 10016

Manufactured in the United States of America

'When a man assumes a public trust, he should consider himself as public property.'

THOMAS JEFFERSON
PRESIDENT OF THE
UNITED STATES OF AMERICA
Remark to Baron Von Humbolt, 1807

THE VON KESSEL DOSSIER

PROLOGUE

Washington was experiencing above average temperatures; the searing midday sun had already taken the mercury above 28°C. Dan Shaw stood in the small departure lounge, overlooking the tarmac. At 1.7 metres tall, his 92 kilograms of body weight spread in monotonous flab around his body while the heavy jowls on his face joined with his overly large hooked nose to form an unimpressive picture of obesity.

The tinted window took little of the glare from Airforce One. The plane stood ready to leave. Two months previously Shaw had been recruited from his internationally renowned investment advisory service to join a presidential sub-committee on national economics. It was charged with investigating corporate bankruptcies.

A civilian-clothed official entered the room.

'Mr Shaw, would you come this way please?'

Shaw swung round to look directly into the face of the man. Raising his voice he exclaimed, 'Do you realize who I am? I am on an important presidential sub-committee. The President of the United States is waiting to see me in that plane.' He pointed to Airforce One. 'I have been here for over ...' looking at his watch quickly, 'an hour and a half. I was due on that plane over an hour ago. I will speak to the President about this ...'

Shaw was curtly interrupted. 'Mr Shaw, would you please follow? Thank you, sir.'

Shaw clasped his small overnight bag and followed the man, puffing and grunting. They stopped at a door marked in bold letters 'Security'. Three uniformed security officers were waiting inside. The small room had a sterile appearance, with its curtainless window and its polished vinyl floor. A plastic topped bench was laden with a variety of electronic equipment.

'Would you mind removing your coat, Mr Shaw, and please open your briefcase.'

The security officer continued. 'This is a routine security search, Mr Shaw. My colleague will do a brief body search and also check you with a metal detector.'

The case was X-rayed and searched. The three pens in Shaw's pocket were dismantled, as was his propelling pencil, then re-assembled and returned.

The door opened and an impressive man in his mid-thirties appeared.

'Mr Dan Shaw?'

'Yes, that's me.'

'When you are finished here I will take you on to the plane.'

Shaw exploded. 'To hell you will. I've got an important appointment with the President. I've been waiting for over an hour. Gross incompetence I call it. And this ridiculous check...'

The stranger broke in. 'Be quiet and let them finish.' He turned and left the room abruptly.

'Who was he?' Shaw enquired timidly.

'That,' said the security officer, 'is the presidential aide. He is blunt but efficient.'

The aide returned some minutes later. His voice was now soft yet firm. 'My name is Brian Thompson, Mr Shaw. If you would care to follow me to the President's aircraft.'

Thompson set a brisk pace as Shaw scuttled along behind him. They reached the end of the passage which opened on to the tarmac. A limousine with darkened windows was waiting and it took them to the stairway leading to Airforce One. Thompson went unchecked on to the aircraft. The two Airforce guards again validated Shaw's credentials before letting him pass.

He was greeted at the top of the stairs by an attractive girl dressed in a blue airforce uniform.

'If you will follow me Mr Shaw, we will be taking off in a few moments.'

The jet was not what Shaw had expected. He was standing in a long corridor which separated a number of cabins. The girl stopped at a curtained opening. Shaw pushed past her and entered a cabin: it only contained twenty-four first class seats.

The girl smiled, slowly gesturing with her hand. 'Please sit anywhere on your left, fasten your seat belt. We will be taking off shortly.'

'The President wants to see me, probably before lunch.'

'Mr Thompson will call you when the President is ready, Mr Shaw.' She looked at his oversized waist, and then smiled again. 'You won't miss out on lunch.'

The aircraft moved down the runway, steadily gaining momentum. There was a small bump as its motors roared and it was airborne. Almost twenty minutes had passed before Thompson returned. 'If you would like to follow me, Mr Shaw, the President is ready for the meeting.'

The President's lounge adjoined his presidential suite. The cabin was tastefully decorated with a distinctly masculine touch. A large timber table dominated the central area, its legs fixed to the floor. Ten comfortable brown leather chairs were set around it, all in fixed positions and equipped with safety belts.

The President was sitting at the head of the table when Shaw came in.

'Pleased to meet you, Mr Shaw,' he said as he shook hands vigorously.

'My honour, Mr President.'

3

The President gestured towards a chair near the centre of the table. 'Please take a seat, the others will be here shortly.'

The first to arrive was Harry Feldberger, Secretary of State. Immediately behind him was Bertram Hillings, President of the Securities Exchange Commission. Seconds later Adrian Telfer of the FBI arrived with Gerald T. Pratt, the President's Personal Advisor on National Economics. Taking adjoining seats, they removed papers from their satchels and placed them on the table.

Thompson broke the silence. 'The President has called this meeting to discuss a new economic problem emerging from the eighties recession. Two months ago Mr Shaw was appointed to a sub-committee investigating the ever-increasing number of bankruptcies which are occurring in the US. Gentlemen, you all have received a copy of his report. However, the President has suggested that we have this meeting to look at certain specific aspects of that problem. Unfortunately his schedule is extremely tight, making it impossible to organize this meeting except on this flight to Paris. Messrs Hillings, Telfer and Shaw will be returning on a special flight arranged for tomorrow afternoon. As you are probably aware, the President has two important conferences coming up: one in Paris tomorrow and then one in Bonn on Thursday.'

'Thank you Brian,' said the President, looking up. 'Gentlemen, during the course of 1982 the Government has been successful in reducing the level of inflation to below five per cent. Generally, the economic recovery commenced then and that continued. The first signs of growth occurred in 1983 and have continued to date. One aspect, however, is extremely alarming. The number of corporate bankruptcies is increasing at an astonishing rate. It is currently at an unprecedented level, even worse than during the depression of the thirties. Mr Shaw's investigations concerning the reasons for this provide little by way of conclusion.'

The President stared directly at Shaw. 'Mr Shaw, is there anything you've noticed that indicates any correlation between these companies' failures? Is there any dominant factor, of which we are not aware, that led to their collapse?'

Shaw flustered through his papers until he reached the conclusion of his report; then he turned it face down on the table. His rubbery lips overformed the words.

'Mr President, gentlemen. The current economic crisis has much to compare with the crash of October 1929. The GNP plummeted from 104.4 billion in 1929 to a low of 26 billion in 1933. Unemployment rose from 1.6 million to 12.8 million in the same period. Mr President, in order to answer your question precisely, it is necessary for me to recap the thirties situation and compare it with this recent recession. And then we can see what we should expect by way of bankruptcies and the possible causes for them.

'The substantial level of investment spending in the booming twenties had inspired intense development and investment. The decline was therefore unexpected. This pulled down American capitalism into the economic chaos from 1929 to the end of the depression.

'Between 1929 and 1933 there was in fact a 70 per cent decline in investment spending. But other factors also, in my opinion, caused the depression. Excess industrial capacity based on the buoyant sales of the years before; the decline in residential construction; the lack of finance and the enormous indebtedness for all people in so many forms, such as consumer credit, housing mortgages, and so on.

'The stock market crash in October 1929 was thus really the spark that set the tinder-dry economy into flames. It was sudden, violent, cumulative. Now the stock market fall during the eighties recession was very similar to that of the thirties. Many purchases had been made on credit. This time it was the spiralling interest rates that added to the fall. In the thirties it was mainly the rush for liquidity that had caused the crash of the shares, and interest rates were never at the levels that we've experienced recently. Possibly, what both the thirties depression and our present recession have in common is the shrinking of the money supply. The climbing price levels is also a factor. This applies particularly to base metals, with the winding down of manufacturing. Both depressions were heralded by spiralling inflation which, I believe, is the inevitable result of spending ever greater sums on a fixed amount of goods.

'Now, in addressing myself to the question...'

The President's lips were taut. His neat, streaked, grey hair glistened in the sun from the window behind. His eyes looked inquisitively from person to person. This was hardly a direct answer to his question. Bored, he commenced tapping a black pencil on the unused white pad in front of him.

Shaw felt all important, but being amongst these senior people was now taking its toll. Beads of sweat were showing on his lips. He continued his misaligned address.

'Ahem... Yes, addressing myself to the question, what did the failing companies have in common?' Feet were shuffled, glances were exchanged, the signs of impatience evident.

'We must look at the first depression and note the number of companies incorporated at that time. The number of companies going under currently must not be compared with the thirties. Less than half a million companies were registered in 1930, and nearly two million companies are currently registered.

'The reason why many companies have gone bankrupt is an obvious one. Manufacturing was reduced to a point where expenses dominated profit. Many companies had borrowed on the basis of increased profit. Substantial losses eventually wiped out their capital as well as their ability to repay higher interest and capital instalments.' He waved his hand with a flourish. 'And then there were also the other usual reasons.'

The Secretary of State spoke for the first time. 'With your permission, Mr President. What you have told us, Mr Shaw, is nothing new. In fact it was more eloquently presented in your report. What we want to know is, is there a common reason why the companies have failed? Are there new sets of circumstances which have not appeared before?'

Shaw coughed again. The President gave an audible sigh.

'Oh, I was getting to that. There is one point, gentlemen.

In the sample of one hundred companies which were investigated, twenty-three of them lost money through mismanagement. All twenty-three had changed their directors shortly before they went under. In each case they made disastrous acquisitions which cost the company enormous amounts of capital, and, in some extreme cases, all their available cash.'

Adrian Telfer interrupted. 'If someone else made a profit, then all the money is still in the States, isn't it?'

Shaw continued. 'Now that's the strange thing, sir. Invariably we note that the money has gone off-shore, I mean...that is...the cash has gone to Europe or another country.'

The President snapped irritably. 'We know that. Get to the point, Shaw.' But before allowing Shaw to continue, he looked straight at Bertram Hillings. 'Bert, you've read this report, wouldn't you have checked these company directors to see they're clean? Is there any possible chance of a Mafia tie up?'

Hillings answered directly. 'No, sir. There appears to be no crime link with the directors involved. I checked that out immediately I received Shaw's report. The men have impeccable characters and backgrounds, and no tie up with the mob.'

Telfer spoke again. 'I, too, have checked their connections, sir. None of the directors of the fallen companies in the one hundred samples taken by Shaw have any Mafia connections, and certainly not with any other underground or semi-illicit organization.'

The President was annoyed. His voice tensed. 'Shaw, could some of these bankruptcies have been inspired by overseas interference, possibly Russian?'

'You want me to answer that question, sir?' Shaw said nervously, a waver in his voice.

The President directed ... 'Proceed ...'

'Well sir, as far as we know the Soviets are not involved in corporation building and never have been. There seems to be basic philosophical reasons for this. Their ideas are not set for private enterprise as we know it.'

The President rose. 'Thank you, Mr Shaw, that's all for now.' And looking towards Thompson, he continued quietly. 'Please show him out.'

Shaw stood up hastily and shoved his papers into his bag. When the door closed after him, the President exploded. 'Who brought that bum in here? Who suggested he head that sub-committee? Even if he found anything, that blabbermouth wouldn't hold his tongue anyway!'

The Secretary of State responded. 'I am sorry Mr President. I was told he is the best available. He falls a little short in the flesh doesn't he?'

The President's resentment rose.

'That asinine fool — sack him. Let's work harder on the mob.' Looking at the representatives of the SEC and the FBI, the President outlined the force of his new attack in this direction. 'And find out where in the hell those profits went.'

Adrian Telfer rose to his feet when the President had finished. He was a clever, articulate and handsome man, with a clean-cut face and soft brown hair tinged with grey at the temples. He was known for his old-fashioned courtesy and was always punctilious.

'Mr President, sir. Gentlemen. I regret that our President and this meeting today had to suffer that bag of wind. However I think he made two points which are important; failure through mismanagement and the fact that the ailing companies lost their capital to foreign companies. I pledge my complete support in finding the reason for the corporate failures and in seeking an answer to why losses were sustained by American shareholders ostensibly to the benefit of foreign countries.'

Telfer's body inched back down to his chair as if in slow motion. All at the meeting nodded in agreement. Without rising the President spoke. 'It is bad enough that a company goes bankrupt in our country, but to think of another country profiting from it is intolerable. Gentlemen, I want answers! Lean on the expertise of our business leaders and specialist staff. The CIA can provide assistance in foreign investigations.' Turning towards the Secretary of State he continued, 'Advise all our foreign agents to watch for any suspect investment organization.'

'Excuse me, gentlemen I would like to thank you for coming today. Now I would like to have a word with our Secretary before lunch.'

When they had left he wagged his finger at Harry Feldberger.

'You know...I've got a gut feeling the Russians have a hand in this. How, I don't know. But we sure need help.'

HAGBRIN AA364807A1 TURN.L.

21 FEB.

ATTN: R. BRIN

TURNSTILE INVESTMENTS LTD. HAVE
PURCHASED 22 PER CENT CONTROLLING
INTEREST IN TRALAS ENTERPRISES LTD.
NOTIFY STOCK EXCHANGE WE HAVE
9 PER CENT ONLY. REST HELD HERE IN
NOMINEES NAMES. CONTACT THEIR
MANAGING DIRECTOR MICHAEL BERRESFORD
AND ARRANGE MEETING, WE WANT BOARD
REPRESENTATION LATER CONTROL. SUGGEST
COLLERITI ITALIAN FINANCIER SUITABLE
AS OUR DIRECTOR.

THE TELEX

4819607 TURNL

HAGBRIN   AA364807

TRASENT AA446348ZI TURN. L

21 FEB

ATTN: M. BERRESFORD

MANAGING DIRECTOR

TRALAS ENTERPRISES LTD.

OUR COMPANY TURNSTILE INVESTMENTS
LTD. HAS ACQUIRED 9 PER CENT OF
YOUR COMPANY ON MARKET. STOCK
EXCHANGE HAS BEEN NOTIFIED. REQUEST
EARLY MEETING WITH OUR ACCOUNTANTS
IN MELBOURNE MR. BRIN OF HANG AND
BRIN TO DISCUSS TURNSTILE BEING
GIVEN BOARD REPRESENTATION.

REGARDS

ANDREW MOFFATT

DIRECTOR

4819607 TURN L

TRASENT 446348

H. O. LONDON

DECODED MESSAGE FROM TURNSTILE MAIN
 FRAME COMPUTER

MESSAGE — FILE ASILTOR

CODE 4471930

21 FEB.

ATTN: M. BENINI

PROCEED TO MELBOURNE AUSTRALIA
TRALAS ENTERPRISES LTD. SHARES
PURCHASE COMPLETED. PROCEED
TO ELIMINATE 2 DIRECTORS PATTERSON
AND HERON IN ONE HIT. MUST BE DONE
WITHIN 3 MONTHS FROM NOW. BUG THEIR
HOMES AND OFFICES. TAKE IMMEDIATE
ACTION IF PROBLEMS OCCUR. LOW
KEY PLEASE. LEAVE BERRESFORD FOR
LATER.

THE TELEX

BOOK ONE

CHAPTER 1

It was late May and a week away from the official start of winter. The cold wind lashed the driving rain against the windscreen of the station wagon. Its motor was still running and its lights shone on the boats bobbing in the marina.

George Patterson had just turned sixty-seven. He was stocky and thick set and the Germanic features of his face often led the uninformed to believe that he was years younger. From under his floppy yellow waterproof hat his two blues eyes kept staring out at his moored boat. He turned to his colleague and co-director, Brian Heron to offer some reassurance.

'It's five in the morning, windy, and pouring with rain. You must think I'm mad, but I promise you my barograph doesn't make mistakes. The weather will abate within an hour. When it does, Brian, you're in for a treat. We'll have some of the biggest snapper seen in years on the ends of our lines.'

'You're the expert, George, but I take it you won't leave the mouth of the river until this wind slackens?'

'Of course not. I'll tie up under the bridge until it's a bit calmer. The smaller waves won't hurt. We might be the only one out there. I reckon we'll be on our spot when the tide is coming in. Okay?'

'You're the captain,' Heron replied respectfully.

By the time they left the mooring the wind had dropped to a steady ten knots. Not another boat stirred in the marina. The southern sky was still pitch black. The boat spotlight lit up the narrow flood gates, opening into the Patterson River. It proceeded down the river past the public jetties and launching ramps, towards the mouth of the river.

Heron's voice boomed over the sound of the motor. 'We're not the only one. Look there's a small light burning in that cabin cruiser up ahead.'

The light went out as suddenly as it had come on. As they passed the fibreglass cruiser with the large twin outboards, the white running light on Patterson's launch revealed the shadows of two figures moving in the cabin.

A few minutes later one of the two motors started. The boat followed in their wake, lightless and out of sight of Patterson's launch. As it edged along the river the crewmen engaged in urgent conversation.

'What's he doing?'

'I can't quite see. He's stopping under the bridge. Quick, cut the motor!'

As they did, they could hear the motor of Patterson's launch cut out.

'What the hell's he doing?'

'Might be going to fish under the bridge,' replied one of the crewmen, an Englishman with a harsh accent. 'I think it's more likely he's just waiting for the wind to die down.

'We'll just drift — the tide's coming in.'

The bow rope secure, Patterson climbed through the forward hatch, his weatherproof plastic clothes dripping with rain.

'I'm glad we've stopped here, Brian. We'll have a cup of coffee before we brave the elements.'

Patterson poured the hot black coffee into two china mugs. Heron sniffed at the hot vapour.

'A drop or two of brandy in there, George?'

Patterson laughed, a happy laugh. 'Yes, it's one of

Helga's specials.'

Heron, too, was jovial. He was thoroughly enjoying the outing, despite the cold weather.

'I suppose the next thing you'll tell me, George, is that the river was named after you?'

Patterson gestured. 'Of course.' Then he corrected himself. 'Well, you know that can't be true; that wasn't my name when I immigrated to Australia in 1946.'

'What was your real name, George?'

'Gunter Schmirer. Good old German stock ... there was more than one reason why I changed: firstly, this was my new home so I thought I'd anglicize it in some way; secondly and I really don't like talking about it, I was an officer in Hitler's army. Actually, I had a desk position in Corporate and Financial Investigations.'

'Oh, really? That's where you got involved in accountancy?'

'Involved, yes, but I got my qualifications in Australia; did it part-time through a technical school. Then I had my lucky break — I met Michael Berresford. His father was the American Ambassador then. Michael was not sure whether to return to Boston or start a company here. Well, all that's nearly ten years ago, when he first floated Tralas. He was looking for a company secretary and didn't want to pay much.'

'It suited me fine, and I was glad to get the job.'

'And now you're a director, a wealthy one at that.' Heron smiled.

'Comfortable, I wouldn't say wealthy.' Suddenly Patterson's tone changed. 'Brian, there's another reason I asked you to come fishing. What do you think of the new director we've put on our board?'

'Colleriti? He's a genius. His reputation is longer than the Nile. Damn good luck finding him, if you ask me ... Why? Don't you like him?'

Patterson sighed deeply. 'There's something about him, or perhaps more precisely about the company he represents, that Turnstile crowd.'

'What do you mean?' Heron was becoming quite interested.

'As you know, Helga and I came out from Germany virtually penniless. You could carry our useful possessions in a child's school bag. As I said, I was working in Corporate and Financial Investigations for the Third Reich. Towards the last few days of the war I took a bundle of files with me and stored them in my cellar. After an air raid a bomb wiped our house out. We lost everything. Even valuables in the cellar were stolen by looters, but the old files remained. Some of them are very interesting. Since I had little to bring to Australia I fossicked through them and took about fifty dossiers to bring with me.'

'What's that got to do with Turnstile?'

'That's what I'm coming to. I'm not sure, but I think there's a connection between a fellow we were investigating at the time and Turnstile. His name was Von Kessel. It's only a hunch. I'll tell you more about it next week when the latest findings come back from Berlin.'

'Berlin?' Heron said with surprise.

'Yes. I have an old professor digging up information; following on where we left off. I think there may be a connection. If it's the same man, we've got trouble. Von Kessel's mob stole millions from shareholders of German companies just before the war.'

Heron whistled. 'What would that be worth today?'

'Exactly. More coffee?'

'I think I will.'

Patterson opened a small forward hatch. 'The rain's stopped and the wind's definitely quietening down. It'll be rough at first, but this old bus'll plow through it. It beats the hell out of fibreglass junk.'

'Right, George, let's go. I'll get the bow rope.'

The old timber displacement hull began to plug steadily across the bay. Periodically a short chop crashed across the deck; the bow dipped and caught the next wave, then it righted itself for several minutes until it hit another breaker. It took almost an hour to reach their spot in the main shipping channel.

The fibreglass boat had followed them. Patterson's mooring light was not strong enough to cast its beam on the blacked-out cruiser, standing off almost a quarter of a kilometre away.

'How long will we leave them, Englishman?'

'About ten minutes.'

The Italian looked at his watch, pressing the light switch near the band. Their anchored boat was rising and plunging violently in the short steep waves of the bay.

'Fair enough.'

'Switch the navigation lights on, I'll pull the anchor up and we'll mosey over.'

Heron was first to bait up and cast into the bay.

'Look, George, we must be in the right spot. Here's another boat.'

As the boat approached Patterson remarked, 'That's funny, Brian. I'd swear that's the same boat we saw in Patterson River.' The German thought quickly. 'The bay is too big for both of us to end up in the same spot accidentally.'

'Do you think he followed us?'

'No, why should he? He wouldn't even know where we're going. Probably headed for much the same direction and homed in on our lights.'

Heron laughed. 'Perhaps he's heard of your reputation as a fisherman, George.'

'Rubbish. Hang on, I think I've got a bite.' The rod kicked, Patterson jagged, and the line went dead.

The fibreglass boat approached cautiously. A boat's length away the Englishman called. 'Can you help us? We've got problems.' He yelled through the wind, his hands cupped like a megaphone. The words were lost over the sound of the motor.

'What?' Patterson yelled back.

The Englishman tried again. 'Throw us your stern rope. We're in trouble.'

'He says they're in trouble, George. Throw him a rope.'

Patterson deftly gathered up a coil of rope, and fastened one end around the stern cleat on the leeward side. 'I'll wait till they're a bit closer,' he mumbled. Seconds later he cast the rope towards them.

The Englishman caught it, almost falling overboard, then hitched it to the bow and pulling in on it until he was alongside, he climbed aboard the timber launch.

'What's the trouble?' Patterson enquired.

'We've got a loose fuel line. I need a screwdriver, a medium-sized one.'

'Let's have a look,' said Patterson, as he opened a small timber compartment on the port side and removed a metal box containing a number of tools. The Englishman's torch focused on the contents. The three men's eyes searched the box for the required tool.

Patterson and Heron didn't notice that the Italian was on board until he spoke.

'Stay where you are, both of you.' In his hand was a Colt .45 automatic pistol. 'You,' he commanded pointing to Heron, 'Move back.'

Patterson and Heron, shocked, moved to the end of the tiny cabin. The Englishman suddenly went mad, grabbed a large spanner, and bashed it into Heron's head. Heron was still focusing his attention on the Italian and the attack was totally unexpected; he collapsed to the floor, blood flowing profusely from the wound. Patterson was stunned, wide eyed.

He remained silent, crouching in the corner of the cabin, his hand gripping, vice like, on the bulkhead.

'You've got something that belongs to us. Where is it?' the Italian rasped.

Patterson was shocked, yet strangely fearless, as if he

knew it was the end. 'Nothing. I've got nothing. What do you want?'

'We've got no time for pranks!' the Italian roared. 'The Von Kessel dossier, where is it?'

Patterson's eyes opened, owl-like, his jaw dropped. 'You'll never get it!' he screamed, waving his fist. 'It's in the bank, you'll *never* get it out.'

'We'll see about that.' The Italian spat in his face. 'Grab him!' he yelled, putting his gun back in his shoulder holster. From his pocket he took a syringe and he removed the protective head.

Patterson, cursing, lashed out with his foot, catching the Englishman on the shins. The Englishman returned the kick, knocking his feet from under him. He fell to the floor with a resounding thud. The Englishman grabbed an arm, thrusting it up his back, and Patterson screamed in agony.

'Pin the bastard down!' the Italian bellowed.

Patterson yelled, 'You'll never ... get it ... dreckiger dieb!' The Englishman pinned him down with his knees. Patterson's face lay against the floor. The Italian jammed the needle into his neck and squirted the contents into the flesh; seconds later Patterson lay motionless.

'Come on, we've got to hurry, it'll be daylight soon.'

Already faint traces of light were beginning to appear in the eastern sky.

The Englishmen took one of the two five-gallon fuel tanks and soaked the two bodies on both sides. Then he tipped the remaining fuel inside the boat, covering the seats, the bunks, and everything that he could see. He repeated the action with the second five-gallon tank.

'Come on ... give me the delayed ignition device.'

The Italian passed him a small box. He threw the packing overboard. He forced the metal skewer carefully through a narrow opening in the phial, until it penetrated a second chamber, then he pulled the skewer out and threw it away.

'That'll do it,' he yelled. 'That'll leak through in about five minutes. Come on, we'd better piss off, sometimes they go off prematurely.'

Safely aboard the cruiser the two men cast off from the timber craft, fired both motors and sped away.

They watched the riding and navigation lights bobbing in the distance. At first, bright yellow flames appeared inside the cabin and spread quickly to the afterdeck. The flames on the pyre developed into a large orange ball in the early morning mist. Then two explosions occured; one following shortly after the other.

'The last bit of gas in the fuel tanks,' the Italian remarked.

'There she goes. Whacko! Let's splice the mainbrace!' the Englishman yelled as the flaming hull began its slow descent to the bottom of the channel.

CHAPTER 2

Two days later the tragedy was confirmed. The television media were the first to report it on the morning news cast. Cala Berresford rang and broke the news to her husband. The news flash only confirmed their worst fears as both men had been posted as missing the previous day.

Michael Berresford, the thirty-six year old Managing Director of Tralas Enterprises Limited, was sitting at his office desk opening the morning mail when his wife called him on the phone. He called in his secretary Jan to dictate a telex to be sent to his only other surviving director in Rome. Jan had turned twenty-eight the week before. The two dead men had taken her to a birthday lunch. Her eyes were swollen and tears were rolling down her cheeks as she started to record the message.

A mood of gloom hung over the office of the oil exploration company the following morning.

Mrs Patterson had been taken to hospital suffering from shock.

The Italian director, Colleriti, had not replied to Berresford's telex. Berresford was therefore very surprised when Jan announced that Colleriti was in the foyer waiting to see him. Berresford did a quick mental calculation. Colleriti must have left within an hour or so of his sending the telex.

'Show him in, Jan. Take him into the Board Room and put on some coffee, please.'

Colleriti's manner was charming, gentle. Berresford found the man intelligent and most cooperative. His qualifications included a Master of Economics from Cambridge University, and his reputation in banking and finance was worldwide.

He greeted Berresford with a smile and a handshake. 'Michael,' he said enthusiastically. 'It's good to see you, despite the shocking circumstances.'

'Yes, it's good to see you too, Aldo. But how in the hell did you get here so quickly?'

'Everything is fed into the Turnstile computer, including telexes. The machine has the capability of ringing my number at home. It gives a recorded message for me to plug in to my small computer terminal and I can search the memory banks for messages. I probably received it within minutes of you sending it off.'

Colleriti slumped back on the couch, exhausted after the long flight. 'How did it happen? They must have been together.'

'They were out fishing. Evidently a fire started in the boat; the poor devils were burnt to death.' Berresford continued. 'Helga Patterson is in hospital with shock.'

Colleriti shook his head. 'I suppose, Michael, you realize that you and I have some tough decisions to make. We must get some replacements. We can't have our shareholders thinking we are falling apart. Do you have any suggestions?'

'Yes, Aldo, as a matter of fact I've made a shortlist of four. Would you like to have a look at the resume I've made on each of them?'

Colleriti fitted a pair of pince-nez glasses and perched them half way down his nose. 'Good work, Michael, good work. They all appear most suitable.'

'What about you, Aldo? Any ideas?'

'Only two things have been occupying my mind on the plane; my colleagues' deaths and the possible replacements.' Colleriti withdrew a number of typewritten sheets from his inside coat pocket.

Strange, thought Berresford. How could he have had that information typed up on the plane?

Colleriti was tired, but his eyes were sparkling. He anticipated Berresford's question before it was asked. 'I suppose you're wondering how this information was typewritten?'

'You're right,' was the curt reply.

'Here are the rest of them.' Colleriti withdrew from his inside pocket an even larger bundle of papers. 'I've got six here for you to look at. I started off with thirty. They are directors I am associated with in other companies. I keep them in a file in Rome. I know all six would accept the position. Have a look.' He stuffed them into Berresford's outstretched hand, his grin widening.

Silence reigned for several minutes as Berresford read the detailed account of the six directors. Two were British, two Dutch and two American. All six names were known to him. In addition, he knew they were held in the highest esteem in their respective professions.

'Christ, Aldo. They're top of the tree. Are you sure they'd join a board on *our* company?'

'Not a doubt.' Colleriti's smile was continuous. 'Pick one.'

'This fellow, Dan Shaw, he's the most highly paid Economic Consultant in the world. I think he charges a thousand dollars an hour. I don't think we could afford him, Aldo. Our directors' fees would be too low for him.'

'Leave that to me, Michael. He's a personal friend of mine. If I ask him to do it, he'll do it. You'd be lucky to get him to more than half a dozen meetings a year, but his name and contacts would be of enormous value to you. Most prestigious for a company of your size.'

'You're on, if you can get him at five thousand

dollars a year.'

'It's done.' Colleriti said softly, almost mockingly. 'And now, for the second one. Your choice, Michael. These people are totally independent.'

'This man Bradford looks good. I read an article about him in the *New York Times* recently.'

'Well he's your man.'

'But are you sure he'll come on? Five thousand a year is not much.'

'You want him or not?'

'Sure, Aldo, I do. How soon can you get a confirmation on them? I'd like to make an announcement as early as possible. The shares dropped twenty cents yesterday when it was announced our two men were missing. I reckon this would put them up fifty.'

'I'll have an answer first thing in the morning.' Colleriti yawned loudly while patting his mouth politely with his hand. 'If you don't mind I think I'll call it a day and we'll leave it till tomorrow to continue our discussions. I'm all in.' He was still yawning as he went out the door.

St Vincent's Hospital was only a short distance from Berresford's office. Mrs Patterson's doctor had arranged for her to have a private room.

The Pattersons kept very much to themselves. They had no relations in Australia and only a few friends, except those at the Chess Club or at the Australian German Association.

Helga Patterson was sixty-five, but her hair was stark white and made her look older. Her English was not as polished as her late husband's.

Tears rolled down her plump cheeks when Berresford came into the room. She beckoned him over to her and they kissed each other on the cheek.

'How are you, Helga? Anything that Cala and I can do for you, you know we will. Would you like to come and stay with us for a while?'

'No, Michael, thanks all the same. I have told them at the hospital I am going home already. Today sometime. I would like to be alone. I will look at pictures of my dear man, he was all I had.' She started crying again. 'I can't believe that it happened. He is always so meticulous and careful with petrol. He has never forgotten the war. Anything explosive he treats with great care. The police say it was a fuel leak. I don't believe it, Michael. He always checks the fuel tank and lines everytime he goes to the boat. No one is allowed to light a cigarette or a pipe until he has done his checking. And it was raining, so I don't see how it caught on fire. I think he was murdered.'

'What!' Berresford said loudly.

'Shhh!' she put her finger to her lips. 'He had been doing some investigation into your shareholders. He found an old Nazi folder which he had brought from Germany. He thought that there could be a connection. He told me that if anything happened I should give it to you. Unfortunately it's in German.'

'Look, Helga, don't worry your head about the papers, you leave it there until you feel better, we can do that anytime.' Berresford thought, she's cracking up, the old bird's nuts, she's hallucinating.

The nurse came in with some long-stemmed roses and with a card from Cala and Michael. She cried, thanked him for them. Berresford excused himself and left.

CHAPTER 3

The stock exchange posted the announcement just before the close of morning trading. Dan Shaw, investment advisor from Chicago, and Clifford Bradford, senior partner in the firm Bradford, Thompson and Kennett of Dallas, Texas, had been appointed as the new directors in Tralas Enterprises Limited.

Aldo Colleriti and Berresford had a luncheon meeting at the board table. The menu was simple, mixed sandwiches and coffee.

'Well, Michael, what do think of it?'

'Tremendous. It's a brilliant move if we can pull it off. To have our own off-shore oil rig is something beyond my wildest dreams, even if it is a small one. That drill ship is ideal for shallow waters. It will go a long way in assisting us in getting off-shore exploration concessions from the Government. When we're not using it ourselves we'll lease it out. At seventeen million dollars we'll make a fortune out of it.'

'Well, it's up to you to get the engineers to Borneo and make sure the equipment's up to scratch. It's also up to you to devise the cheapest way of bringing it to Australia.'

'Leave that to me,' Berresford said enthusiastically. 'I had an early morning meeting with our two geologists this morning. They'll look after things at home; I'll head off to Singapore tomorrow and commence negotiations. I'll organize a team of engineers to check it out and make sure it is as good as they say. Aldo! It's an absolute bargain. My guess is that its real value is nearer to twenty-three or twenty-five million.'

'And you can afford it?' Colleriti smiled.

'Of course, you know our balance sheet? We've got 30.9 million dollars in the bank or on short-term deposit. We're one of the best dressed companies money-wise in the country — I mean in the oil exploration business,' Berresford said with a laugh. 'With the combined funeral out of the way this afternoon I'm free to get going. I'll have Jan book me on the first flight out tomorrow.'

The flight to Singapore was pleasant and uneventful. Only five people occupied the first class cabin between Melbourne and Singapore. Berresford used the opportunity to calculate once more the profit and advantages of the off-shore rig. The file which Colleriti had given Berresford included photographs, detailed specifications of the ship, a recent marine survey, a diagrammatic view of the ship and rotary drilling rig, and a lengthy engineer's report on the components. The inventory of the equipment and its condition again surprised Berresford. The drill string, drill collars, and bits were in far better condition than he expected. It was definitely a bargain. Support craft were also included in the purchase. Berresford figured out the overheads and if his calculations were correct, the rig would pay for itself in only one year, making it a very sound investment.

The plane touched down on schedule at Changi Airport. After clearing customs and immigration Berresford was met by a representative of the Malay Star Oil Exploration Company.

The first meeting brought some disappointment, but still the proposition was a good one. It quickly became clear that a new appraisal would have to be conducted, so as to establish the exact condition of the rig, the ship and the equipment. Berresford realized that it would take some weeks to finalize the negotiations.

The Shangri-la Hotel was one of the world's best. The balcony of Berresford's suite overlooked the swimming pool and small golf course. The beautiful bougain-villea spilled over the balconies, abundant with green leaves and magnificent magenta flowers, in a simple yet spectacular statement of design. After his first meeting with Malay Star, Berresford rang Colleriti to report his progress. It appeared that negotiations would take longer than anticipated. Colleriti urged Berresford to stay and conclude the transaction. He assured him that all was running smoothly at the Melbourne office. Colleriti offered to remain until Berresford returned and told him, blithely, to stay until the sale was consumated.

Three weeks passed. The delaying tactics of Malay Star were annoying Berresford. No matter how hard he pushed, the languid sellers found new excuses for putting off signing an offer which Berresford needed before committing his company to the expense of a detailed appraisal.

In an effort to mollify Berresford's frustrations Colleriti suggested that Berresford take the engineers to Brunei, inspect the ship and rig, and then finalize the deal on his return to Singapore.

The inspection proved that the purchase was a bargain. Berresford telephoned Malay Star. They agreed to finalize the transaction and sign the sale documents on his return to Singapore. Colleriti was ecstatic, he confirmed board approval for the purchase.

Berresford booked on the first flight available to Singapore. On his arrival back at the Shangri-la Hotel there were a number of messages. Berresford stuffed them into his pocket. He couldn't be bothered reading them; he would do that at dinner time. He had enjoyed a number of celebratory drinks on the plane from Borneo and he wanted a rest before returning to business.

The alarm on his watch buzzed loudly. Berresford struggled out of bed and staggered to the bathroom, letting the cold water from the shower revive him. Quickly shaven and cleaned up, he dressed for dinner — wearing a new suit, one of the three that he had ordered the week before from a local tailor.

Berresford was disappointed that Cala hadn't joined him on this trip as she often did. He was also upset that she did not ring him once during the three weeks although he'd rung her several times. Not like her, he thought.

He looked at his watch again. Five minutes left to keep the appointment in the main foyer with John Wong, the Malaysian business man he had met on the plane. He grabbed the messages, which he had intended to read while waiting for his guest. 'Oh well, I'll read them later,' he said to himself.

The food was delightful. After coffee his guest excused himself and left. Berresford stayed on for a cognac. 'It's time I read those messages,' he thought.

The third message almost stopped his heart beating. A sweat broke out all over his body; his fingers trembled.

'God,' he thought. Then aloud. 'My God, what have they done?'

A Tralas board meeting had been held in his absence. The new directors had entered into an agreement for just on thirty million dollars in purchasing rights to oil exploration in Argentina and Nigeria. The purchase had been made under great protest from the two company geologists, who believed that the sum was extraordinarily high. But the deal had been consumated, the Reserve Bank's approval had been given and the money had been paid. Tralas Enterprises Limited was now devoid of funds.

He couldn't believe it. Stunned, shocked, he beckoned the waiter. 'Double cognac,' he ordered, shoving the glass away from him.

He hastened to open the other messages. Two messages down, the next bombshell erupted.

The board had decided not to proceed with the purchase of the rig from Malay Star. What in the hell had happened? What have those idiots done? But they're not idiots. I've been robbed, he concluded. Turnstile's a hoax. A gang of thieves.

Not waiting for the bill he pushed his chair out and left the room, the messages clutched in his hand.

I'm ruined, he thought. He stopped in the foyer, he hadn't read the other two messages.

One was three days old and from the company secretary.

'Michael, contact me urgently.' It said. 'There's been a spate of share selling. Seven million shares have been turned over. The price has gone from $2.67 to 7¢. Turnstile has sold all their shares. I suspect their mates have done the same. They sold through different brokers, but I suspect they're connected. When the Stock Exchange was informed that we had used our total cash resources on the purchase of the Nigerian and Argentinian oil patches the market wrote us off. Considerable share selling occurred before the announcement, subsequently they didn't lose. The selling was probably connected to Turnstile. I'm sorry Michael. I think the company's finished.'

The rain started again; within seconds it developed into a downpour. The humidity was awful. Berresford stood at the sliding door opening to the balcony. Rain drops splashed against his face, his suit and on to the carpet, but he didn't notice. His career was ruined. Lightning struck a short distance away; the brilliant white-blue flash coinciding with a thunderous explosion.

Berresford's mind kept oscillating from the problems associated with Turnstile to conjecture about his wife, Cala. Where was she? Over the last two months tension had developed between them. The feeling was unconscious. Why hadn't he realized until now? How long had it been since they had gone to bed together? Strange, he thought, that's never happened before.

He had left Melbourne three and a half weeks ago. The night before he had called her on the hour from 9 p.m. until 2 a.m., when he had fallen asleep. He had resumed his attempt to contact her at 8 a.m. He looked at his watch again, 11.30 p.m. The phone rang. Suddenly he was aware his clothes and the floor were getting wet. He closed the sliding door and hurried to the phone.

The Malaysian telephonist was apologetic.

'I am very sorry, Mr Berresford, your person-to-person call to Mrs Berresford was unsuccessful, there is still no answer.'

'Okay, I'll cancel it. I'll catch a plane to Melbourne on the first available flight. Thank you.' He slammed the phone down. 'Where in the hell is she?' he said aloud. Everything seemed slanted against Berresford. Even the planes to Australia were fully booked until next morning. He couldn't contact Cala. It appeared his world had shattered without warning. The man felt bereft and humiliated not only because of his own loss, but that of his shareholders. Sleep would not come until the first rays of sunlight appeared in the sky. The torment of recent events did not hamper his self determination. He would fight them to the last.

Berresford placed the hotel account on his American Express card. He went to the counter where the messages were kept.

'Excuse me, Miss. My name is Berresford, I was staying in 401 for three weeks. Is it possible that messages were left here for me and I didn't get them?'

'Oh no, Mr Berresford. I remember your name. You got all your messages. Your wife regularly called in to pick them up.'

'What? I'm not here with my wife,' he said in disbelief.

'I'm sorry, sir. Your girlfriend called herself Mrs Berresford.'

'I was not with anybody,' he said indignantly. 'What did she look like?'

'An Australian girl, with long blond hair, I'd say about 22 years old. I'm very sorry Mr Berresford, we weren't to know.'

'Forget it,' Berresford said irritably.

'You're welcome,' she said politely, smiling.

He stamped towards the main entrance. The rain was pouring down, the gutters were awash. And that was not the only problem; at least twenty people stood in a queue waiting for a cab. He beckoned the concierge.

'I'll miss my plane, I need a cab urgently.'

The dark skinned man spoke with a decisive Indian accent. 'I am very, very sorry sir, there is nothing I can do. You must wait your turn.'

Two more cabs pulled up. A Dutch couple and their teenage daughter had the first one. The second cab moved to pick up its passenger at the main entrance. It was John Wong.

Berresford's eyes lit up. 'John!'

He did not even have to ask. 'Take his bag,' Wong instructed the driver. 'Hop in, Michael, I'll take you to the airport; you'll never get a taxi.'

Berresford slammed the door.

'Thanks for the lift, are you going to the airport too?'

'No, as a matter of fact, I'm going to a meeting. But I am early, I have plenty of time to return.'

'That's very kind of you, I'm extremely grateful.'

Wong looked at Berresford. There was genuine concern in his eyes. 'You look worried, Michael, is anything the matter?'

'Oh, just the usual business problems and a break-down in communications.'

'Oh...? I do hope you get over your problems soon,' Wong replied slowly and meaningfully.

The hint flashed through Berresford's brain. My God! It's showing already, he thought. I'm finished, broke and any man in the street can see it... No, I won't let it happen, I'm master of my own destiny, I've got a problem and I'm going to fix it. I mustn't over-dramatize the situation.

His Chinese friend spoke softly. 'You know, Michael, business problems can be like having your motorcar stop. So you lift the bonnet. Your first impression is to be overcome by the sea of wires, pipes, metal boxes, bolts and fittings. If you keep your cool and break the problem into parts and attack them sequentially you'll find a simple answer. Most people look at the complex mass, are overawed with what they see, slam the bonnet shut and call for a tow truck.'

The little man started laughing; then, turning towards Berresford, he remarked. 'It has always amused me that the first thing people do who know nothing about cars and are placed in a situation of motor failure, is to raise the bonnet, look at the motor for a few seconds and slam it shut. I wonder why they do it. I've often thought, maybe it's to satisfy themselves the motor is still there.' And he burst out laughing.

Berresford found it amusing too. That's better, he thought, I've got to keep my cool to beat those Turnstile thieves.

The flight home gave Berresford time to think. He made a number of calculations on the plane. His house was mortgaged to the hilt. The money was invested in Tralas shares; and he had expected them to rise when the oil price increased again. The oil price war was supposed to be temporary; in the medium to long term, with the increase in demand and a lowering of supply, the prices should return to the OPEC bench price set in 1981. But now Berresford's finances had tumbled from millions of dollars to perhaps a nett two hundred thousand dollars. And that meant selling all his shares without any further drop in the market and selling his home.

He eased the tension by enjoying his favourite drink, a Jack Daniels whisky. At last he was looking forward to his return. Home... there's nothing better than sleeping in your own bed, he thought.

He needed help, and one man he could rely on was his old friend Ian Garreau, whom he had met at the time when his father was American Ambassador. Garreau was six feet tall, sandy haired and pink-faced. He had a keen intellect and a methodical brain and his resources seemed unlimited in investigating people. He had come to Australia working for the CIA. With the consent of the American Government he had then joined ASIO — the Australian intelligence organization.

The four huge motors of the giant 747 screamed as the plane touched down on the tarmac. Cala wasn't expecting him for a few days yet; it was the first time she hadn't met him at the airport after an overseas trip. It took him twenty-five minutes to clear immigration and customs. Then he set off to make a series of calls.

His home number answered.

'Is that you, darling?' Berresford said affectionately.

'Michael! Where are you honey? You sound as if you're home. Are they planes I can hear in the background?' Cala's voice was blurry, hesitant. Berresford was perturbed.

'Have you been drinking, Cala?'

'Whhat's... that?'

'Oh, all right, never mind. I won't be home for a while; I'm going across to Ian Garreau's. If you can pull yourself together come over and have coffee.'

'No, I think I'll toddle off to bed,' she said.

'Maybe you had better, I won't be home till late. 'Bye darling.'

'Bye bye, Michael,' the phone clicked.

Berresford dialled Garreau's phone number.

'Hi, Mandy, it's Michael Berresford. I'm back in town, is Ian there?'

A few seconds later he heard a familiar voice.

'Michael, old buddy, where are you?'

'I've just arrived at Tullamarine Airport. I need to see you urgently; I'm in a real bloody mess. What are you doing tonight?'

'I was going down to the RSL Club, but that can wait. Come on over, I'll see you when you get here.'

'Sure you don't mind?'

'Not at all. Tell Cala to come over. Mandy would love to see her.'

'No, she's gone to bed. She's been out with the girls I think.'

'She hasn't been out with Mandy; we've hardly seen her at all since you've been away.'

'No, I think she might have gone up to the snow. There's still some left isn't there?'

'Search me, I had enough snow in the States to last me a lifetime.' Garreau laughed.

'I'll be there as soon as I can.' Berresford hung up.

Frankston and the Tullamarine Airport are on opposite sides of the city. It was ten minutes to nine when Berresford's taxi pulled up in Garreau's drive. Berresford was just passing the signed cab charge voucher to the driver when Garreau greeted him.

'Hi there, old buddy,' Garreau said with a grin, extending his hand to shake Berresford's firmly, a welcome smile on his face.

'Good to see you, Ian.' Berresford tried to smile.

'Hey, you look all in. Come on, I'll get you a drink.'

Two hours and half a bottle of Jack Daniels later, Garreau had the whole story.

'Now let's get this straight. You *never* got the message that there was a board meeting?'

'Correct.'

'How can the two overseas directors vote at a board meeting if they're not there?'

'They flew in for the meeting and left the same day.'

Garreau nodded his head pensively. 'And the money's changed hands already?'

'Yes, and with Reserve Bank approval. They had time.'

'Was the drill ship offer genuine...?'

Berresford did not reply for a moment.

'I've had plenty of time to think about it. On the surface it appeared to be so, but now I have grave doubts. Anyway, even if Turnstile engineered it, that doesn't return the money.'

'How can we get it back?'

'Unless there is some flaw in the agreements, and I very much doubt that there is, I'll have to prove fraud; and I can't see for the life of me how it could be done.' Berresford's eyes were wild, his voice angry. 'I tell you, Ian, those accountants are in this up to their necks.'

'What do you mean?'

'Look at the facts. They're the accountants for Turnstile. All the negotiations for the Italian director were done by them. Their instructions, I believe, come by telex from London. I can see what they've done; they've carefully engineered control of the company.'

'Be fair Michael. They didn't engineer the accident which killed Patterson and Heron.'

'I haven't excluded the possibility,' Berresford replied.

Garreau stood up, pushing himself out of the huge lounge chair. He started pacing around the small room. 'Be reasonable, Michael. For God's sake man, pulling a share stunt and selling the company some crappy leases is a long way from murder.'

Berresford was annoyed. Perhaps it was the drink.

'I'll be the judge of that when I see what those leases are worth. I know our geologists tried to talk them out of it. It's the oldest stunt in the book.'

'Cross your bridges when you come to them.'

'I haven't spoken to Rick Thompson, our chief geologist, yet. I'll ring him now.'

'Do you think you should? It's nearly eleven o'clock.'

Berresford walked over to the phone, resting on a small table in the corner. He stopped for a moment while he recalled the number.

'Rick, it's me, Berresford.'

Thompson broke into a torrent of words. 'Those new fellows have ruined the company, they've stuffed it completely. What they've sold us is damn near worthless...Sure you could find oil on the areas that we've purchased, but where's the money to explore it? Even if we had the money to explore it, I'm not too sure that I'd pick those areas anyway...The reports look tremendous, but it was the greatest lot of doctored up crap that I've seen in my life. I pressed for an independent appraisal; but they scrubbed it.'

'Well, didn't they have any geological reports?'

'Of course, they did. But their reports were meaningless and certainly not good enough to make that sort of decision...Why didn't you contact me?' Thompson yelled.

'I never got the messages,' Berresford answered.

'I must have rung you a hundred bloody times!'

'Well, I got nothing. The first indication came when I returned from Borneo. That was yesterday. There were several messages then.'

'Christ, Michael, we're in a mess. When we advised the Stock Exchange that we had spent virtually all our available cash on those areas the arse fell out of the shares...they're down to six cents today...Stuff you.' The attack was personal.

Berresford took a deep breath. 'I know. I think it about wipes me out.' The line went dead.

'What's he saying? What's he saying, Michael?' Garreau asked inquisitively.

'He just hung up. You can't blame him, we'll have to retrench most of the staff. We're finished.'

'What did he say?'

'Crap, it's all crap.'

'What is? Look, I can't help you if you don't tell me what's going on,' Garreau said with annoyance. 'Sit down for Christ's sake, I'll get you a drink.'

Garreau listened to the account of the phone call to Thompson.

Berresford was shaken. His worst fears had been confirmed. He pulled out his cigarettes and offered one to Garreau.

Berresford puffed the smoke audibly towards the ceiling, watching it float aimlessly around the room. Something was beginning to take shape in his mind. He drew hard on the cigarette and puffed again at the ceiling before speaking.

'When my father was alive, and you were working for the CIA you guys did some pretty shifty things...'

'What are you getting at?' Garreau asked quietly.

'Remember when you broke into the Communist Party headquarters? They were planning to blow up the Pine Creek satellite tracking station. It never got out, did it?'

Garreau looked at him and smiled. 'No...neat wasn't it?'

'I don't know how to ask you.'

'Come on, give. What do you want me to do?'

Silence. Berresford drew heavily on his cigarette again.

'There is only one way we can nab them, right on their home ground.'

Garreau hit it in one. 'The accountants' office, eh?'

'Right on... If I could lay my hands on a copy of the telexes and communications between Turnstile and Hang and Brin, I think there's a damn good chance I could wrap that lot up.' Shaking his head,despondently Berresford moaned. 'But I couldn't ask you to do that. What'd happen if you got caught...? All hell'd break loose.'

Garreau spoke softly, slowly. 'I'm not so sure. What sort of security arrangements do they have? Have you been to their offices?'

'Yes, I've been there. I don't think they've got any sort of alarms at all. But it's a new multi-storey building in Bourke Street. The security would be pretty tight at night I guess.'

Garreau laughed. 'It would be a push over. I could empty the whole bloody office if I wanted to.'

Berresford took a serious note. 'I don't want the whole office. All I want is a photostat or copy of the communications between Turnstile and them; there'd have to be some incriminating instructions, unless they do it all by phone, which I doubt. I've heard Brin talk about the telexes between them...' Thinking aloud Berresford continued. 'That's right, Turnstile do everything by telex.'

'Consider it done, Michael. I'll look the building over tomorrow and do it tomorrow night. I'm trained at doing this. I'll get a pencil and paper, I want you to draw a layout of their office.'

It was almost 3.30 a.m. when Berresford arrived home. The lights in the drive and front entrance were burning. Cala was sound asleep, so he didn't disturb her. Tomorrow he'd explain everything.

CHAPTER 4

Cala pulled the curtains back, sunlight streamed into the bedroom. Slowly Berresford roused himself from a distorted dream. He sat up and rubbed his eyes, yawning. Cala was dressed. She had a breakfast tray with a large plate of scrambled eggs and bacon.

'Good morning, darling.'

'What time is it?' he said, endeavouring to focus on his watch.

'About half past nine. I thought I'd let you sleep in; you looked so tired.'

'Cala, where in the hell have you been the last three weeks? It's been a hell of a job to try and get you on the phone.'

'Oh, I've been staying over with Myra Johnson. She's been sick. I didn't think you'd mind.'

'Oh no, no, I don't mind. But you could have told me where I could contact you.'

'Forget it,' she said, and left the room.

Berresford got dressed and went downstairs. The garage door opened in response to the depressed button. He looked at his new Rolls Royce and shook his head. Unless he could recover the money squandered by Turnstile, the Silver Spirit would have to go too.

The drive to work was pleasant. It was a beautiful sunny day. He took the usual route around Beach Road. It normally took a fraction longer, but the drive along the cliff tops was very pretty. He dreaded the thought of returning to the office. However, it had to be done.

The staff greeted him with anxious faces. Berresford called for the agreements on the thirty million dollar deal from the Company Secretary. An hour later he was convinced; there was no need to call the lawyer; they were watertight. Why would the new directors pay such a ridiculous sum of money for these, he thought? There was only one answer; they had some scheme to bleed the money off at the other end.

Berresford then went through his messages. Most of them he farmed out to the other members of the staff. One, however, puzzled him. Helga Patterson had left a strange message. She had asked Berresford's secretary, Jan, to ring her when Berresford returned. Berresford himself was not to ring her, or to call and see her; she would contact him.

'Do you want me to ring her, Michael?'

'By all means, do what the lady said.' Lunch would be a bore, he thought, but I can't stand this office any longer.

He arrived back at the office at a quarter to two, feeling somewhat refreshed. Jan had a message from Helga Patterson.

'She's in town, Michael, and she says it's urgent. She's calling you at two o'clock.'

Berresford was describing the enjoyable parts of his stay in Singapore to his secretary when the old lady rang.

'Hello, Helga.'

'Michael, listen,' she whispered. 'I am in town. I have the Von Kessel Dossier for you.'

Berresford had completely forgotten about it.

'I've got it out of the bank already. I'll meet you at St Francis Church. How soon could you get there?'

'Whenever you like.'

'Can you come now? It is not safe to keep it at home.

You must put it in the bank.'

'Are you sure this is necessary?'

'Yes, yes,' she said with some urgency. 'I'll meet you on the steps of St Francis in ten minutes.'

Berresford arrived a few minutes late. The old lady was beside herself.

'Michael, take this with you now. Put it in the bank and get it translated. Be careful you are not followed; don't trust anyone. They killed my husband you know.'

'Who did?'

'These Von Kessel people. They have a legacy: *Life will never be the same.*'

The old girl's nuts, thought Berresford. But it's only fair to humour her. He looked at the ancient document. On the top right hand corner there was a complex of file numbers. Underneath it the name Rudolph Von Kessel was written in capital letters. Underneath that, also in capital letters, was a tongue twisting German name and the word for bank. In the centre of the brown cardboard cover was the German swastika. On the left hand side of the cover were numerous dates, which had obviously been entered when entries had been added to the file. The first date was January 1917; the last was October 1944. In its entirety the document was meaningless. It was in German. Ah, well, one day I might get it translated, he thought. And I bet she asks me to produce the receipt from the bank. 'Yes, I'd better put it in the nearest bank I can find,' he said aloud, to the complete amazement of the passers-by. He was standing right at the financial heart of the city, on the corner of Queen and Bourke Streets, and his own bank was staring him in the face.

The rest of the afternoon Berresford spent with his solicitors. After considerable discussion they reached the conclusion that he had dreaded all along. He was well on the way to insolvency. The mortgage on the house was a fixed term and did not have to be repaid for six months. He could last that long, but after that his assets would topple over, domino style. Little would remain after his shares were sold to cover his debts.

He returned home a despondent and broken man. Cala had left a note on his pillow. She was at her girlfriend's, who had taken a turn for the worse, and she wouldn't be home until ten o'clock. He fixed himself a cold meat salad and went to bed; it was a deep sound sleep.

At the same time Garreau was busily engaged in breaking into Hang and Brin. Berresford had an accurate memory. Garreau had little difficulty in finding the telexes and documents. He used the office's own copying machine to copy most of the telexes and correspondence. And he also took a handful of original telexes. They appeared to be incriminating; and they wouldn't be missed he thought.

In the early hours of the morning he deposited them in a locker at Flinders Street Station. The key would be delivered to Berresford at the office in the morning. He made a mental note to ring Michael at the office.

CHAPTER 5

The rain increased in intensity, whipped up by the chilling south westerly wind. Mario Benini turned up the collar of his expensive leather overcoat. He cursed the cold wintery conditions. Ten weeks ago he had been enjoying summer in his native country, on the Italian Riviera. Then an urgent message was sent to him to cross the equator to the Australian continent and Melbourne. Benini stealthily skirted round the seaside parking lot. His trained eyes never kept still. It was his third check for witnesses. But his assumption had been correct; the parking lot was deserted. The foam-tipped waves pounded on the rocks with a resounding crash, the process continuing with monotonous repetition. The smell of rotting seaweed permeated the dampened air. A solitary light shone from the public telephone box. And as he approached it Benini could just make out the faded letters which had been painted on the notice board. He dutifully read them.

> City of Brighton, North Road launching ramps. Motor vehicles and trailers must be parked in the areas designated. Launching ramps must not be obstructed.
> Penalty: $50.
> By Order Town Clerk.

Benini sought refuge from the rain in the brightly lit telephone booth. He was neatly dressed in his dark brown suit and matching hand-made shoes. He prided himself on his fitness, which few men of his age could better. At last he focused his dark brown eyes on the gold Omega wrist watch, thinking aloud. 'It won't be long now.' He ran his fingers through the wet dark brown hair. His fine olive skin was uncreased by any blemish or wrinkle and women found him handsome. But as he flexed his overly large hands, the knuckles on his fingers revealed themselves to be wider than usual. They had been tempered and strengthened by the rigorous karate exercises. In fact, the edge of his little finger and palm was completely calloused through the constant breaking of timber, tiles and bricks.

In the distance a flashing yellow light was coming in his direction. Minutes later he could distinguish the lettering on the side: 'Tony's Tow Truck.' It slowed down as it neared the telephone box, and stopped a few yards short of it.

Benini approached the driver at the open window.

'My car is down the other end of the car park.'

'Get out of the bloody rain, jump in.' The short tubby driver had to yell above the scream of the huge motor.

Benini closed the door with a resounding bang and pointed through the windscreen in the direction of his Mercedes. Seconds later they could see Benini's car in the truck's headlights.

'I thought you told the base it was a yellow Renault?'

Benini gestured, with his hands uplifted. Shrugging his shoulders, he apologized.

'I must have mixed it up with my wife's car.' The lie was deliberate, calculated.

The driver spoke with a strong Australian accent. 'What's wrong with it anyway?'

Benini was vague. 'I think I've picked up a stick and put it through the radiator. Maybe you can fix it?'

The driver nodded. 'Let's have a look,' he said as he climbed out of the truck.

Benini joined him and assisted by opening the

bonnet. The driver took a flashlight from his pocket, the beam casting its light on a mass of wires, pipes and motor components. A gust of wind increased the intensity of the rain. The driver shivered in his dirty white overalls.

Benini moved closer. His eyes measured with absolute precision the distance between him and the driver. He placed his feet in position, his right shoulder twisting slightly as he extended the fingers of his right hand stiffening their muscles. His lips tightened. In a split second his body uncoiled like a maddened animal, his hand slashing its way through the air, crashing with deadly accuracy on a spot just below the unsuspecting man's hairline.

From the corner of his eye the driver saw what was happening. His eyes opened owl-like in horror, his mouth gaped and his body froze in anticipation. The knife edge of Benini's hand struck its mark, instantly snapping the man's neck at the second cerebral vertebra. The driver's head arched back from the body, with a crack which was quite audible. His tongue was partially severed by the reflex action of his mouth snapping shut. His body contorted violently during the next few seconds and then he fell against the mudguard.

Benini grasped the man on his shoulders and held him until the trembling stopped. He heaved the dead body over his shoulder and returned to the tow truck, shoving it into the driver's seat. He hurried back to his car and slammed the bonnet. The rain had already washed away the splattering of blood.

From the boot Benini took several large foam-filled boat fenders. He carefully placed them in a cushioning position between himself and the dashboard of the truck. Some newspaper was lying on the seat. He grabbed it and covered the head and shoulders of the dead driver, whom he had wedged between himself and the truck door. Next he familiarized himself with the truck controls, the hand throttle would be useful later, he thought.

Benini fired up the motor. It responded with a roar to the staccato presses on the accelerator. As he drove it down North Road the truck looked ominous with its red and black colours, and its teeth-like chrome grille. A heavy metal frame, wrapped all around the front fenders, created added protection against any collision. And the winch mast, in its erect position, gave the vehicle the appearance of an enormous wasp poised ready to strike.

Benini reflected that his training with the Italian Secret Service had not been wasted. He switched the two-way radio on, and changed to the first channel as arranged. A message would come soon.

As Benini sat pensively behind the wheel of the truck he recalled the string of events which had brought him to Melbourne. He was born in Rome, in late 1944. His mother had died giving birth to him. His father, a fearless fighter in Mussolini's army, died the same year through war injuries. His father's eldest brother and his wife had brought him up. They had no children of their own and had lavished the best of their humble earnings on him.

Benini's uncle died when he was eighteen. The following year his aunt was diagnosed as suffering from terminal cancer; she died in agony some months later. On his twentieth birthday he joined the police cadets.

Over the next two years his progress was excellent. From time to time, the Italian Secret Police recruited new agents from the most promising cadets. Benini was selected as a potential candidate. He accepted the proposal and spent the next three years training in the martial arts, in karate, and in all matters pertaining to covert and undercover activities. Throughout the next years his talents had led to considerable success in the

Italian Secret Service.

He had started to live beyond his means. He began to need the money. Mario Benini would enjoy the good life: cars, women, clothes, wine and food. Only the best would do. And this had been his downfall.

In 1972 he ruined his career. He had been selected to investigate one Antonio Montala, an Italian electronics engineer engaged in the production of a secret guidance system for ballistic missiles. Montala had arranged to sell the plans to a Russian KGB agent for 100,000 Swiss francs. Benini went to Montala's flat. He shot both the Italian and the Russian agent and took the money. He staged the scene so as to make it appear that Montana and the KGB man had in fact killed each other.

Unbeknown to Benini, a fellow agent had planted a listening device in the flat. The theft was uncovered, although the murders could not be proven. Word leaked out that Benini was responsible. The Italian Secret Service decision was rapid and irrevocable. He was sacked.

He was now a wanted man, out of a job, with little hope of escaping the tentacles of the KGB. It was therefore much to his surprise that an offer was made to him only ten days after he had been dismissed from the service.

The surprise call had occurred at seven one evening. The caller knocked twice before Benini answered. 'Me lo scriverebbe per favore?'

The caller had replied in English. 'I don't speak Italian. You don't know me, my name is Moffatt. I've come to offer you a job.'

Benini had been very cautious. 'I will open the door, walk in please, with your hands on your head.'

Benini had opened the door carefully. The man entered with his hands on his head.

'What is your business?' Benini had frisked him.

'May I put my hands down now, please?'

'You may. Your business please?'

'Wait a minute, don't be so edgy. Here is a letter, read it and everything will be explained.'

The typewritten letter was unsigned. Benini had read it while the man waited.

Attention Mr M. Benini —

The gentleman before you is Mr Moffatt. He is a Senior Representative of Turnstile Investments Limited, the holding company for some major share investments throughout the world.

We are aware of your present dilemma. You no doubt realize that you are on the KGB death list. If you grant us your services for cash, we can terminate the order. We will do so on your acceptance of employment with our company. Our terms are $100,000 US per year, payable quarterly in advance. You will be required to work at any hours as requested by us and travel to any country of the world which we choose. Any assassination selected by us will be low-key and therefore attract little risk.

There will be other duties from time to time. Your work requires services to us for perhaps no more than five to six weeks per annum. You are to be on call at all times except for a thirty-day holiday period. Should you reveal the existence of our contract, or provide us with unsatisfactory service, your life will be terminated forthwith.

Others of your calibre are in our employ. At all times you are to communicate through the small computer terminal modum connected to a telephone line. All equipment is provided. You will check in daily; the main frame computer memory will advise you of our requisites (if any). The small terminal has a keyboard similar to a typewriter. Send all messages in telex form. The supreme head of the organization always signs

'The Telex'.

Speak to no one other than the man in front of you, Mr Moffatt.

Instructions for use of the computer terminal are contained in the bag which Mr Moffatt will give you if you accept. The code language must be memorized within two hours and then destroyed. The telephone numbers you ring to connect you to our computer terminal must also be memorized in the same time.

Should you accept our offer a cheque will be given to you forthwith.

If you reject it there are two Russians waiting in the street who wish to have words with you.

The Telex

Benini had raised his large brown eyes and focused them on Moffatt before speaking.

'I accept Mr Moffatt.' He had shrugged his shoulders and extended his hands, his palms uplifted. 'There is no alternative, is there?'

Moffatt had then given a brief forced smile. 'Your cheque for $25,000 US payable from a Swiss Bank.'

Benini, his hands on his hips, had spoken contemptuously. 'Put it on the table.'

Moffatt was seething with rage. 'Listen you thief. One warning only.' He hissed through his teeth. 'You break with me and you're dead.' Opening up the bag he had taken out a smaller case which contained a small computer terminal. His voice had returned to normal.

'This needs to be plugged into main line voltage. It is adjustable for 110, 220 and 240 volts. Make sure you adjust it to the correct voltage. Dial one of these London telephone numbers. The phone will stop ringing but no one will speak. Place the handset there, pointing to two holes surrounded by small rubber collars. Make sure the microphone goes in this end.'

He had pointed to the right hand orifice. 'It is called a

51

computer "modum". You will read your instructions and learn to address our computer. When you key in the correct entries, it will give you messages in typographical form on the paper previously fed into the roller.' Moffatt had gone on with a flourish. 'You can address only the memories in our computer which we allocate to you. You will have the facility to recall considerable information. At all times keep your passport and travel documents in order. We will advise you what visas you will require as there are a number of countries in which we have interests. Our address is Knightsbridge London, where the Turnstile Investments offices are situated.' He had handed Benini a card. 'You may, from time to time, be brought there to see me. You are never to discuss anything with any of our staff. You get cash bonuses for good work.'

Benini had been intrigued. He had killed before; why not for money?

In the years that followed, he had carried out many assignments. Now, only a few months ago he had been sent to Melbourne by 'The Telex'. During the morning he had patched in his computer terminal to the main frame computer and had received the following instructions.

Subject: M. Berresford. Code: M.A. Carry out above this evening if possible. Confer with Farwood on tactics. Advise on completion.

The Telex

Eight miles away a second Tow Truck from Tony's was racing to another call, its destination South Melbourne. Standing on the corner of Morey and Banks Street an isolated dark figure was waiting impatiently. John Farwood looked at his watch. It should have been here twenty minutes ago, he thought. Benini would be furious.

Farwood too was following orders, just like Benini

— orders that he and Benini were forced to execute if they were to remain alive. The roar of a large V8 motor, followed by a squealing of brakes, drew his attention to the tow truck as it turned the corner into Morey Street. The truck slowed down as it reached the Bank Street intersection. He waved the driver down.

The driver's voice had the distinctive timbre of gravel sliding down a metal race.

'Did ya ring, mate?'

The answer came in a sharp English accent. 'Yes, I did.' He had to shout over the roar of the engines. He slid into the passenger seat and continued. 'Pleased to meet you.' He stretched out his hand. 'I've got a rather odd proposition for you tonight. I haven't got a car to be fixed at all.'

Stunned, the driver looked at him. In an angry voice he turned on Farwood, his harsh accent rising to a crescendo. 'What in the bloody hell did ya ring for. Do you think this is a taxi service for Christ's sake!'

In a quiet voice the Englishman muttered.

'Listen, I've been in Australia for some two years. I'm on a monthly remittance from my family in England to stay out here. Back home I was always in trouble gambling.'

The driver's brow creased as he struggled to comprehend. Why had he been summoned?

'My mother and father have just arrived in Australia on a holiday. I want them to think I own a tow truck business here; I just need to drive them around for a few minutes, then I'll return it.'

The driver looked at him with absolute amazement. 'Look here, I don't give a stuff what you want to do, mate. As far as I'm concerned I'm running a towing business. I said before, a tow truck is not a bloody taxi.'

'All right, all right,' the Englishman said. 'How does one hundred dollars suit you?'

'You're crazy, what for?'

'Simply, I need a loan of your tow truck for one or

two hours.'

'No mate, forget it. Even the tools in the back of this thing are worth two hundred dollars.'

'All right,' the Englishman sighed. 'I'll give you five hundred dollars for the loan of the truck for two hours.'

The driver was silent for several seconds. 'O.K.' He nodded. 'You must be mad . . . let me see the cash first.'

Putting his hand deep into his trouser pocket the Englishman counted out five hundred dollars in crisp red twenty dollar bills.

The driver was completely wide-eyed. He nodded as every note was counted out and placed in his hand. Without hesitation he alighted, shouting out as he opened the door. 'Ya got me.' The Englishman slid across into the seat.

'I'll tell you what. Drop me down at the corner pub. I'll have a couple of beers while I'm waiting.'

Farwood replied. 'You'd better direct me there. I'll mark it on the map.' Following directions he drove carefully to the hotel, fumbling with the unfamiliar controls. A few minutes later he stopped in front of a round, quaint, Victorian building. A modern blue and white fluorescent sign displayed the locally brewed beer.

'Look, mate, you get back within two hours, or I'll call the cops and say you held me up and stole me truck . . . all right?'

Indignantly Farwood protested. 'I wouldn't pay you $500 to steal this heap, would I? I'll be back.'

The driver turned as he shut the door and jerked a thumbs up sign to Farwood as he walked through the hotel swing doors.

Farwood manipulated the unfamiliar controls hesitatingly as he drove toward Kerford Road in South Melbourne. The arterial road linked Freeway One to South Road. Peak traffic was still streaming from the city. Farwood stopped his truck in Kerford Road, and positioned it in a spot where he could study the outflowing traffic. His fingers felt for the metal switch that turned on the two-way radio, tuning into channel one. Picking up the microphone he pressed the talk button and, imitating the voice of a child C.B. operator, he began speaking in the highest pitch possible.

'Breaker, breaker, this is Beefy Charlie, are you out there Big B. Come on, come on.'

Eight miles away, in the tow truck parked near Beach Road, Mario Benini replied by pressing his black button. His voice similarly disguised.

'Affirmative, affirmative. You in position?'

The reply came quickly. 'Still waiting for Big Silver. I'll give...' Farwood was interrupted by an irate voice.

'Get off the channel. This is a private channel and no place for kids like you with your stupid antics. Come back on this channel again and you'll be in real trouble. Get off!' The radio speaker reverted to a low hiss.

Almost fifteen minutes had passed when Farwood saw the Rolls Royce. He checked the numberplate, it was Berresford's. Immediately he revved the tow truck motor and set off in pursuit; and he eventually manoeuvered to a spot twelve cars behind it. He depressed the microphone switch again, the voice childlike.

'Have Big Silver in sight, am following, see you shortly. Give you a call as I cross Martin Street.'

Benini was ready to proceed. He pushed the driver's lifeless limp body into position: the head pushed forward on the dash and covered with a sheet of newspaper, a second and third sheet over the shoulders. As he twisted the ignition key the motor sprang to life. He moved down the street and stopped short of the intersection. The corner of North Road and St Kilda Street was only yards away. As the lights turned green, he changed gears with some difficulty, then built up speed, pulling out the hand throttle.

Benini had a clear view down St Kilda Street. It was a straight section. He blurted on his two-way radio 'crossing Martin Street.' Three-quarters of a mile down the road he focused on the flashing yellow light of the other tow truck, in which Farwood was following Berresford's Rolls Royce. The next lights were altering from green to yellow.

He pulled the throttle out further as he crossed the street. The lights were turning red but it didn't matter any more: the commitment had been made. His safety belt secure, Benini adjusted the foam boat fenders so as to cushion him from the dash and windscreen. The traffic in his direction was negligible; but the flow of city traffic was heavy against him, packed into three lanes. The Rolls idled sedately twenty feet from the car in front, and made his job easy. Thirty feet from the Rolls he swung the steering wheel and aimed for it. The Bedford's motor roared on. He braced himself behind the padded boat fenders.

The Rolls Royce driver did not see the metallic monster until the last second. It ripped and crashed through the hand-made stainless steel grille, thrusting it and the radiator into the motor which in turn was torn from its mounts and thrust into the cabin. Windscreens were shattered, lights extinguished and the squeal of brakes from the cars following ended in a reverberation of crashes as cars piled into each other. A Volkswagen rammed the rear of the Rolls Royce and burst into flames, its forward fuel tank succumbing to the intense pressure. Its occupants' screams joining the sounds of tearing metal and the tinkling of glass.

Benini unsnapped his safety belt. Leaping through the hole left by the passenger door, which had been torn from its hinges, he hurried off from the scene of the carnage towards the second tow truck stopped in the line of damaged vehicles. He climbed into the passenger seat of Farwood's tow truck.

'Are you O.K., Mario?'

Between short breaths he replied. 'O.K. . . . but out of breath . . .'

The panic of the road scene was to their advantage. Farwood reversed the tow truck several feet. 'I'll have to go on the wrong side to get clear. Put on your seat belt and hang on!'

Farwood drove over one hundred yards on the wrong side of the road, until he passed the scene of the accident. Concerned motorists had opened the door of the damaged tow truck only to close it immediately. The broken windscreen had decapitated the driver. And no one was attending to the Rolls Royce driver either, since there was no sign of life left in the body.

Farwood passed the scene of the debacle, then he hastened down Beach Road in the correct lane until he reached the intersection of North Road. Oscillating blue and red lights were flashing some distance ahead. Sirens screamed. He turned right and proceeded to the car park where Benini had left his car. He skidded to a halt next to the dark blue Mercedes.

Benini rubbed his arm and shoulder cursing in Italian.

'Can you drive now, Mario?'

Benini was recovering his breath. 'Fine. I'll follow you back to South Melbourne, I don't want to be too late collecting the telexes from Berresford's place.'

Whilst Benini and Farwood were returning the tow truck to South Melbourne, Michael Berresford was being sedately driven home in a Ford LTD limousine. Torrential rain thrashed down on the windscreen. The chauffeur increased the speed of the windscreen wipers.

'What an awful night, Mr Berresford.'

'It is and it isn't, Brian. The weather's rotten, I agree, but the parcel you picked up from the locker in the railway station has made my day.'

Berresford turned on the personal reading light and opened Garreau's canvas bag. He took several telexes off the top. The first few were originals, the ones which Garreau had felt were the most incriminating.

Berresford read the top one, dated 21 February. Turnstile Investments, it said, have purchased a controlling interest in Tralas...

'They've broken our security laws,' he said aloud.

'What was that, Mr Berresford?'

'It doesn't matter, Brian. I was thinking aloud.'

The telexes to the two new directors, Shaw and Bradford, were also very interesting. Turnstile had not asked them, it had told them to accept the position. This was proof that they were on Turnstile's payroll. Berresford skipped through the other telexes in his hand, reading them quickly.

'Got them!' he shouted, brandishing his fist and shaking it at the unseen corporate thieves.

The telex that he had just read was the very thing that he was looking for. It was prime evidence and would entail police action against Turnstile for fraudulent conversion. The feeling of elation surged through Berresford's body. He felt the urge to leave the car and run a block or two, shouting, 'I've done it! I've done it!...'

He wished the car could clear the traffic and get home quickly. He wanted to tell Cala that his problems were over. The money would be returned to the company and all would be well. It was still not clear to Berresford how the money had been syphoned off overseas. But now it no longer mattered. He'd know eventually.

The journey home seemed to take longer than usual. The car had barely stopped when Berresford slid out of the rear seat, dragging the bag of telexes behind him.

'Can I help with those, sir?' The chauffeur disappointed that he could not open the door or assist.

'No... no, it's quite all right, Brian,' Berresford said excitedly as he clambered up the front steps.

He was searching in his pocket for his keys when without warning the front door opened. The part-time maid, a reliable helper in her mid-fifties, stood there smiling.

Berresford was surprised. Mary normally finished at 5.30 p.m. unless they had a function on at home. 'I didn't expect to see you, Mary. I thought you would have gone long ago.'

The neatly dressed grey-haired woman didn't mind working overtime whenever she was asked.

'Mrs Berresford asked me if I'd stay on a little later, sir. She changed her plans and will not be coming home late as she told you this morning.'

'Oh ... why is that?'

'She's not going to her girlfriend's tonight. Apparently she's feeling much better. Mrs Berresford tried to contact you in the office but couldn't seem to get you. Your secretary, Jan, told her that you were coming home in the hire car. She should be home shortly Mr Berresford. She wanted me to stay and give you the message. Mrs Berresford has booked a table at Carlo's restaurant, also she was concerned that you wouldn't have your car to go to work in tomorrow.'

'Oh, that was kind of her,' Berresford said warmly.

'Oh, I don't think she minds, sir. She loves driving the Rolls Royce.'

CHAPTER 6

The Mercedes was some distance from the crash, heading for Berresford's home. The rain had eased slightly. Benini put the wipers on a delayed sweep, causing a silky haze between each wipe. Farwood shivered and turned the large black knob on the heater. It was a freezing night.

Farwood eased himself back in the seat and began in his harsh nasal accent.

'This sort of business makes me thirsty. It'll be three hours before the Berresford woman gets home. Let's stop and have a couple of beers and a quick bite.'

'I'd prefer to get the business done first.'

'It'll be too late, Mario. Hotels close at 10 p.m. and we've got hours. Let's stop for a counter dinner and a couple of drinks.'

'Very well, but not for long, and only two drinks, Farwood. This is an important assignment,' Benini warned.

Berresford dismissed the maid and made his way to the library. He sat in the soft leather armchair which dominated the whole room of fine furniture. He kicked his shoes onto the Persian carpet. Its muted colours complimented the red gum parquetry floor.

The blackwood shelves housed a handsome library. The books covered a wide range of interests. Berresford felt jumpy, excited. In this room he could normally relax. He rose and went to the bar where a small collection of bottles, the ones he used most frequently stared at him.

He took a short stubby crystal glass from the shelf. From the fridge built into the bar he grabbed two blocks of ice and dropped them into it. He poured a good three fingers of Jack Daniels over it. He rested his left elbow on the corner of the bar and looked through the window to the patio. The rain had abated, but the wind had grown stronger. Gusts of wind momentarily rustled the drapes at the windows and whistled through small cracks under the doors opening to the balcony. The events of the last two days had made him feel insensitive and withdrawn. But now he could face the world with renewed vigour. He sipped his drink. His contemplative eyes fell on the canvas bag of telexes left on the floor.

Suddenly the phone rang. It's shrill message thrust Berresford back into action.

'Michael it's Ian Garreau here.'

'Great to hear your voice, Ian.'

'Before you start, Michael, draw the curtains.'

'They're drawn, Ian. What made you say that?'

'Your place was bugged! I removed four devices this afternoon.'

'You've got to be kidding.'

'No, they've had you tapped. Cala rang Mandy and I took the call. I keep a special device hooked up to my phone which indicates when a line is bugged. I don't always use it, just spot check occasionally. To my surprise it gave a positive signal. Cala asked me to come over and see.'

'Is it all right to speak now?'

'Yes, but I mentioned to pull the curtains in case they've got a device focused on the windows.'

'How's that?'

'I'll explain later.'

'Do you think ... Turnstile?'

'Yes, I think so and I wouldn't mind betting they've

got your office bugged too.'

'Does that include the office telephone?'

'Sure.'

'Then they'd know I've got the telexes?'

'Good chance. That's the reason I rang. You can't take the risk of having the only copy of those telexes. I didn't have time to photocopy them.'

'What'll I do?' Berresford's voice now indicated concern. He drained the remains of the whisky and began rattling the ice.

'Michael, you've got a copier at home. Is it working?'

'Yes, I'll run a copy off tonight.'

'Send a copy over to me as soon as you've finished. It's not safe to leave the only copy in your home.'

'Thanks. By the way it's great stuff. It's a clear case of fraud. We will get the money back and see the lot of them behind bars.'

'Good. Don't forget, copy them tonight.'

'I'll speak to you later.'

'Cheers, Michael.'

Berresford was unnerved by Garreau's revelation. He reflected on the conversation that had taken place both at home and in his office over the last few days. What had he said?

He couldn't remember. The strain had been enormous. He hadn't slept for more than three hours in the last two days.

He looked at his watch. This is as good a time as any to have a rest, he thought. Cala would be home shortly and wake him up. Half an hour's sleep before dinner would certainly revive him and make the evening more enjoyable.

He turned off the light and shuffled himself into the most comfortable position in the large leather chair. It was as if a huge weight had been taken off his shoulders. The business animal was being tamed. A languid feeling spread over his body. His eyelids flickered, his head nodded forward, his mind drifted aimlessly for a number of minutes, and then settled into a deep peaceful sleep. The rain resumed, heavier than before, drumming a hypnotic monotone note on the glass windows.

A telex was sent during the same night from London to Hang and Brin, the accountants for Turnstile. It gave explicit directions for the disposal of all telexes, correspondence and records that may incriminate Turnstile. Hang and Brin completed the assignment in the early hours of the morning.

Hang stuffed the last of the shredded paper in the incinerator shoot as he turned to his partner. 'Seems a waste,' he said, 'all this work destroying records when a photostat copy has already been stolen.'

Brin was a little man but his mind was sharp and devious.

'Don't worry, pal. If my guess is right the Turnstile men will burn the copy to-night too.'

CHAPTER 7

The dark blue Mercedes drove quietly out of the Hotel car park and headed toward Berresford's home in Beaumaris. Benini now sat in the passenger seat. The smell of garlic from the steak which he had just eaten caused Farwood to sniff audibly and to open his window a few inches.

Benini scowled in response. He plunged his right hand deep into the pocket of his leather coat and withdrew his shiny black pistol. He checked the magazine. The brass-cased bullets glistened in the half light.

Farwood gripped the wheel, his face taut, determined. 'We're not going to need that tonight are we?'

Benini counted the bullets as he replaced them in the magazine. He replied in a soft modulated voice. 'I can assure you; complacency is not one of my virtues.'

No reply came, the only sound emanating from the tyres on the wet road, through Farwood's window.

Farwood kept within five kilometres of the speed limit. The mercury lamps illuminated the stark white railing fence which separated the road from the cliff tops. A police car came into view in the rear vision mirror. Farwood moved over and reduced speed. The police car accelerated past. Farwood exhaled loudly. Benini continued though some minutes had passed since Farwood had asked the question.

'There's no permanent staff at night, but I don't want to take any chances.' He placed the heavy gun in his shoulder holster. 'Are you sure the telexes will be there?'

Farwood was agitated. 'That's what I heard in one of the recordings we tapped today...he was going through the telexes tonight with his friend, "Ian"... whoever he is. His secretary ordered a hire car to pick them up but I didn't hear her conversation. I didn't tap her phone.'

Farwood pulled up at the red light. 'He must have stolen them last night or early this morning. Think he might have photostated them?'

'He wouldn't have had time. I watched him up till 5 o'clock.' Benini undid his seat belt. He leaned over the back seat and grabbed a small brown case.

'What if he's already given them to someone else?'

'Please...I know this man...I don't think so.'

There was a silence before Benini continued. 'When he was talking to his friend Ian, on the phone, he said repeatedly that he was going through them tonight.' Benini was sick of Farwood's endless questioning. 'We've got him and we'll get those papers. Don't concern yourself.'

'What if he had them in the Rolls Royce?' continued Farwood, indifferent to Benini's agitation.

'They *were* to be taken home by hire car, weren't they?' Benini said impatiently.

Farwood threw his cigarette butt out of the window; Beaumaris was only a few minutes away.

The Mercedes slowed at Berresford's drive. The large trees blocked out much of the grand house. There were no lights in the drive or in the house. Farwood stopped a short distance around the corner. Benini fingered his gun as Farwood adjusted the rear vision mirror to sweep in an arc from left to right. Benini checked the street in front, his trained eyes looking for any movement; no one was about.

The rain increased in intensity. Benini cursed the

heavy shower. Raising the collars of their coats the two men walked down the drive past the main entrance. They casually approached the side entrance to the library. Weak light filtered through to the trees and native shrubs from the double fluorescent lamp on the street corner.

'You stay here.'

Farwood ducked between the wall of the house and some thick shrubs and returned quickly. 'All clear.'

'What about burglar alarms?' Farwood whispered.

'None.' Farwood smiled. Yet at times he hated Benini, who treated him with contempt.

A dog began to bark over the fence next door. Benini bent lower and removed his pistol, wishing he could silence the animal. He took out the small brown case from his coat pocket as he approached the library door leading off the narrow pebble path. Gloves on, he inserted the picking device into the lock and with the other hand, he inserted a small L shaped lever to turn the tumbler. The dog continued barking, and another neighbour's dog joined in. Farwood could see its nose through the crack in the palings. The white teeth flashed in a narrow shaft of light.

The barking dogs aroused Berresford from his groggy state. The room was not immediately familiar. He rubbed his fingers into his eyes until they stung, then he sank back into the chair not wanting to stir.

Opening his eyes he accustomed himself to the ambient light. His attention suddenly sharpened when he saw a human shadow on the curtains. He sat up, the adrenaline racing through his body. The dog barked aggressively. Sweat broke on his brow.

He waited for the tumbler to turn. There was a click. The handle moved and the door opened. Berresford pressed himself against the curtain behind the door. At the same instant a light from the intruder's torch beamed on the opposite wall. Berresford drew back a clenched fist for a surprise punch. For an instant the two men faced each other. Benini lurched back like a coiled spring. The torch light blinded Berresford.

Berresford's punch missed its mark by an inch. Benini's pistol landed on the floor. He crashed his fist into Berresford's solar plexus. Berresford reeled over on the floor, momentarily crippled by the impact. Reflex energy tossed him to his feet. He threw his whole weight at the intruder, using his shoulder as a ram. It knocked Benini down, Berresford landing on top of him. Benini swung another blow to Berresford's face with his rock-like fist, then he sprang to his feet before Berresford had recovered. His reverse karate kick lunged at Berresford's head.

The timing, a split second short, caught Berresford in the chest. He cried out with pain. The blow thrust him across the room, his body crashing into the glass cabinet which shattered with a resounding explosion. Berresford buckled over, blood streaming from his head. He could see the silhouette of Benini's body between him and the window. Desperately he rolled to escape the shoe aimed at his head. His arm outstretched, he grabbed Benini's leg, and twisted it with all his might, tripping him over. Benini screamed, the pain intense. It maddened him to a frenzy.

Benini sprang at Berresford like a wild animal, landing a karate blow to the nearest part of Berresford's body. Berresford's ribs cracked. He gave out an agonizing yell. Each man kept struggling for supremacy. Both rose to their feet again. Berresford threw himself at the intruder. He tripped over an unseen foot stool and landed at Benini's feet.

'Got you!' Benini yelled. In an instant he had grabbed his pistol from the floor and bashed the butt on Berresford's head; two vicious blows connected and Berresford dropped limp to the floor, unconscious. The library door filled with the silhouette of Farwood.

'What happened?' Farwood peered in, his eyes not

yet adjusted to the limited light cast from the torch, which had rolled on the floor. Benini picked it up and searched for the light switch. The dog continued barking. The lights lit up the blood over Berresford's face. Smashed pieces of the porcelain collection and pieces of the glass case flashed like diamonds over the floor and carpet.

'Figlio di puttana!' yelled Benini, kicking glass off Berresford's open bag.

Next to the large leather chair were the remains of the drink and half a dozen telexes. Benini, bewildered, grabbed at them and crumpled them in his large hand.

'This man . . . this man,' he stammered. 'Berresford?'

'Sure that's him?' Farwood put his gun away and looked at Benini.

'Farwood, how in the hell is he alive! I thought we killed the bastard . . .'

Farwood looked over the crumpled body.

'We've killed somebody, but it certainly wasn't Berresford,' said Benini, still thumbing through the papers.

Farwood jerked his head back. 'That's Berresford alright.'

Benini didn't see the astonished look on Farwood's face.

'Better fix him now,' Benini continued. 'Grab a few things and make it look like a burglary. Take some of those ornaments up there. Get his watch and wallet, while I finish packing the telexes.'

Farwood took out his gun.

'You going to crack his head open, or put a bullet through him?' asked Benini.

'I don't want to use the silencer; it would look too much like a professional job.'

'Do what you like.' Benini put the telexes into the case.

'I'll give him one really good bash on the head.'

'Good.' Benini strapped up the overstressed bag with

Berresford's belt. Farwood took Berresford's wallet and watch and went over to the shelf for some expensive ornaments. He was studying Berresford's body on the other side of the room when Benini suddenly turned off the lights.

'Quick!'

A car revving in a low gear was entering the drive. It skidded to a stop. Streaks of light darted across the curtains — a flashing blue light.

Farwood panicked. 'Fuck . . . it's the police!'

Benini crunched over the glass, the bag in his hand. A car door slammed. 'Get out, leave him for later, quick . . .'

The front door bell rang. Outside the library the two men listened, their hearts racing. They heard footsteps. 'Quick, the garden,' whispered Benini.

Stealthily they crept through the foliage, towards the entrance to the side street. 'Run!' They raced between the trees. A small gap gave them momentary exposure; they made the gate, and within seconds they were out of sight.

The two police officers returned to the front door. They rang the bell for the third time.

'Maybe they're out,' said the tall officer, holding his hat.

'The front light's on, and there are no lights along the side or back.'

'Try the door.'

'It's open.'

'Call first.'

'Anyone home?' came the yell. The two men looked up the drive. Only the dog next door broke the silence. It was still barking furiously.

'It's a very big house,' said the sergeant wiping his feet.

'Must be filthy rich.'

He put his plastic clipboard under his arm and

pushed the door open.

'Walk up the hall and give another yell. He might be asleep. We can't let the poor bugger wait any longer, he might hear it on the radio.' With that the sergeant cleared his throat and called again.

The officer found the light switches and flicked them on.

'Try some of the rooms, Jack,' called the sergeant from the door.

The officer tried all the rooms to the end of the passage where it turned right. His heavy boots sunk into the thick carpet. Knocking first he opened the door and flicked the light on in the library.

'Sarg! Over here.'

Berresford lay motionless, his forehead bleeding. The two officers scanned the room, then rushed to his side.

'He's still breathing. It's just happened I think.'

'I'll check the front,' yelled the sergeant, spinning round and running towards the back door which he found locked.

The senior constable bent over the injured man. He felt for the pulse.

'He's O.K. Sarg, he's been knocked out.'

The sergeant came back through the hall. The two men then lifted Berresford carefully and laid him on the couch.

'Could be a burglary job, Jack. The younger officer got a handkerchief and wiped the blood from the cut on Berresford's forehead.

'Don't touch the door: there could be prints on it.' The sergeant then ran out to the driveway and radioed headquarters.

When he returned, Berresford was sitting up. He was feeling his head with his fingers. His head was throbbing. He could taste blood in his mouth. Trying to focus on the police sergeant made him dizzier.

He tried to get up, bewildered. 'He hit me, I can't ...'

but the sergeant eased him back. Berresford was responding quickly. 'See if you can find him,' Berresford moaned.

'I'm sorry sir, we've already done that. There is no one ... I've put a call through to headquarters to see if we can get a squad car to search the streets. Have you got any idea what he looks like?'

Berresford was still dizzy. Benini's features, real and unreal revolved inside his head. 'About six feet tall, dark brown hair.' Again he went blank.

'We'll get that description out. Do you know what's missing?'

Berresford looked around. His eyes struggled to focus on the objects surrounding him; the fragmented stool, the smashed cabinet. He noticed papers near him which had blown off the bar next to the phone. It hit like an electric shock.

'The telexes ... they're gone!'

'What telexes?' asked the younger officer.

Berresford moaned. 'I'll explain later. Who gave the alarm?'

The sergeant stood up and closed the door. 'There's another reason why we called to see you tonight.'

Berresford was puzzled. 'Why *are* you here? How long have I been lying here?'

'We don't know, probably not long.'

Berresford looked for his watch. It was gone. 'What time is it?'

The young officer became anxious. He strode over to the door and went up the hall. The sergeant stepped around the broken glass and sat next to Berresford. He was fumbling with his hat. Berresford's eyes had cleared and the cuts had stopped bleeding. His top lip was swollen and painful when prodded with his tongue.

'Your name is Michael Charles Berresford?' said the officer. Berresford barely registered the question.

'Yes.' He asked himself again who had phoned them,

and how they knew about the break in. But his thoughts were cut short.

'Mr Berresford, your wife was killed in a car accident this evening.'

The room was silent. The younger officer walked in with three cups. The sergeant continued to stare at the carpet. 'In a head on collision,' he added.

Berresford caught his breath. Then he gushed the words out in a coarse whisper. 'Oh my God . . . I don't believe it . . . I can't believe it.' He sat bolt upright, grabbing the officer's arm and shaking him violently. 'She can't be dead.'

'Please, Mr Berresford, we know it's a great shock.'

'How did it happen?'

'Tow truck ran into her in your Rolls. The truck's driver died too. I am very, very sorry, sir. It was a terrible accident. Take it easy; we know what a terrible shock it must be.' It was, Berresford lay back in shocked silence.

The officers were at a loss. 'The others should be here shortly,' said the sergeant as he sat next to Berresford on the couch looking at Berresford with genuine sympathy. 'Is there anyone else I can notify for you; close family?'

Berresford felt his swollen lip. 'Could you ring Ian Garreau, please?'

Garreau, grim faced, hurled his car around the last corner into Berresford's street. The tyres squealed momentarily. Braking the speed back he entered the long drive into Berresford's home and parked behind two police cars.

An ambulance straddled the portico. It's red warning light flashed a message of urgency. Maybe he's snapped and gone into shock, he thought first. The hell the man's been through the last few days would test any ordinary man. But Berresford was far from ordinary, he considered. He was not a subscriber to 'the Peter's' theory; accepting that the worst that could happen, would happen. His determination to succeed would make a strong man's resoluteness pale. Those against him would face a vehement, tenacious aggressor.

The front door was ajar. Garreau pushed it open without knocking and strode confidently down the hallway towards his closest friend whose voice was audibly dominating a conversation at the end of the hall.

'Look, I'm O.K., sore yes, but O.K. I don't need hospital attention...Please!' Berresford insisted. He waved his hand in an airy dismissal of the two paramedics.

'Oh Michael.' Garreau said warmly.

Berresford turned to greet Garreau, his hand plastered with band-aids extended towards him.

'Michael, I'm terribly sorry.'

'I can't believe it, it's like a bad dream.' Berresford said softly shaking his head. 'Come into the den Ian, I must talk to someone who understands.'

Garreau followed his friend into the dimly lit room full of game fishing trophies. The stuffed shark's head with glassy eyes seemed more ominous than usual. The two men seated themselves, a small coffee table in between.

'Cala was murdered.' Berresford said grimly. 'It was the Turnstile mob. They knew I had the telexes, the evidence to nail them. I'm going after them.' He thumped a fist into the palm of the other hand then flinched with the unexpected pain.

'Come on Michael. It will look different tomorrow.' Garreau fumbled for a cigarette and offered one to Berresford. The smell of the antiseptic on Berresford's bandages lingered in the air.

Seconds later Berresford continued. 'It won't look any different tomorrow. I'm going after them, bring them to justice, make them pay for it.' The hate, the fury was building up in the man.

'What in the hell can you do?' Garreau exploded,

endeavouring to jolt his friend back to reality. 'Leave it to the police. Do you *really* think it's your job to track them down, collate the evidence, prove the case and clap them into durance vile?'

'Ian, the police won't listen. They say Cala's death was an accident, a simple case of a head-on collision.'

Garreau decided to take a softer tack, his voice changed to a kinder tone.

'Come on old pal, we can discuss this later. Go and pack a few things and stay over with us for a few days. I'll go and talk to the police. Maybe you're right, they may need a nudge in the right direction.'

The men rose, Berresford heading upstairs to his bedroom, Garreau making for the voices in the back of the house.

Garreau pushed the door opening into the kitchen to find the two police officers who had discovered Berresford unconscious.

'Mr Garreau,' one said, extending his hand.

'Detective Sergeant Allan Bradley.' The tall man shook his hand, gripping it firmly. 'Berresford got quite a dose tonight,' he said.

Garreau refrained from responding.

'What's this about murder, any substance to it?' The man bit on his bottom lip, studying Garreau earnestly.

'No, the man's in shock.' Garreau's mind raced, let them reach their own conclusions. It was too early to involve Turnstile in the investigations.

'Seemed adamant to me,' the sergeant said cautiously.

'Berresford has no enemies that I know of. Up until last week he had everything.'

'Had everything?'

Garreau realized that he had made a slip. He quickly corrected it. 'Yes, wife, house, a good business.' He lit a cigarette.

'I can't see any connection between his wife's death and tonight.' The detective looked across the room before he continued. 'He said some telexes were stolen; know anything about them?'

'Nothing.' Garreau crossed his arms.

'Nothing?'

'That's what I said.' Garreau was agitated. The detective knew it.

'Business fraud, maybe?'

'I don't know. I just arrived here,' Garreau said emphatically. 'Berresford is always carrying telexes around.'

'Important ones?' persisted the policeman.

'I've no idea,' was Garreau's laconic answer. 'If you've finished with the questions I'd like to have another word with him.'

'Sure, go right ahead.' Gesturing with his open hand the policeman pointed to the library where he had last seen Berresford.

Garreau entered the bedroom expecting Berresford to be resting. Instead, he was packing two large suitcases. His passport and cheque book lay on the small bedside table. Garreau became genuinely concerned for his friend.

'Michael, what in the hell are you doing?' His tone lifted on the last two words.

'I'm not sure myself yet, Ian, but I'll take you up on your offer and stay with you for a few days.'

'What's the passport for?'

'For God's sake Ian, don't bug me. I'm trying to get a range of clothes, I'm not coming back here,' Berresford said emphatically.

'Christ, Michael, what are you packing summer clothes for?' Garreau thought as he asked the question that Berresford might be suffering from concussion.

'While you were out I had time to think. My head is filled with ideas, facts and suppositions. But despite that, some conclusions are obvious.'

Good old Berresford, Garreau thought; the break-in, the brutal attack and the news that his wife had been killed in an accident would immobilize most people and reduce them to a crying heap. Berresford continued packing, neatly folding the various clothes as he put them into the suitcases.

'Come on old buddy ... give.'

'Listen, Ian. Those telexes indicated conclusively that Turnstile and their fancy directors are engaged in a major corporate fraud. No doubt a good chunk of that thirty million has been syphoned off into their pockets. If I can prove it, the millions they'd lose, the fines and jail sentences they'd receive, is good enough reason for me to believe that they'd not stop at murder. I think they intended to kill me tonight but were disturbed when the police officers came to tell me about Cala.' As he mentioned her name something stuck in Berresford's throat. He coughed and started packing again.

'And what's with the passport and the clothes, the summer ones?'

'I've no doubt these goddamn thieves have done this before. From reading those telexes it is obviously a repeat performance. The operation is too smoothly contrived. The first Turnstile director, that smooth talking Italian Colleriti must be in it up to his ears. The same for Moffatt, the Managing Director of Turnstile in London. Colleriti is involved with two Turnstile companies in Italy. Before I went to Singapore and Borneo my secretary, Jan, received a few telexes from Rome for him. She passed them to me. I read them and then told her to give them to Colleriti when he came in. There was one hell of a similarity between the content of those telexes and what's happened to me.'

Berresford stopped packing and turned to Garreau, who had taken a seat on a velvet chair. His eyes were angry.

'I'm going to get those Turnstile thieves in Rome, or London, or wherever in the hell they are. I'll track them, investigate them, pursue them, until they pay for what they've done.'

His finger pointed accusingly at Garreau. 'And they did kill Cala. How they did it I don't know; for that matter I don't care.'

The anger in Berresford ran hot and cold. The animal in him had been uncovered. The beast would stalk his prey until he could take them one by one. He called Garreau from the dressing room.

'Here Ian, I've got a job for you.'

Berresford went down on his knees, peering into the bottom of a wardrobe. He pulled out a small panel, revealing a built-in floor safe. He quickly flicked the tumblers to clear it and applied the combination. He pulled the door open.

'Empty the lot out, Ian. Put all the cash in the suitcase.'

'Hell, you have $50,000 here.'

'Yes. Get a plastic rubbish bag from the kitchen. They're on the top shelf in the pantry. Put all these papers in. You can go through those at home. There's Cala's will and a few other things; I'd rather you read it, I'm not quite up to that yet. Then let's get out of here.'

'What about a doctor?'

'I don't need any doctor. I need Moffatt behind bars,' Berresford said bitterly. 'I'll spend my last cent getting him.'

By the time Garreau had packed the contents of the safe in the plastic bag, Berresford had showered and changed into a pair of neatly cut denim jeans, a light blue shirt and a heavy wool navy blue jumper, the royal crest and flags of the Royal Brighton Yacht Club stood out impressively on the right hand side of his chest.

'Come on Ian, let's go.'

Garreau insisted on carrying the two heavy suitcases, much to the protest of Berresford.

CHAPTER 8

There was pandemonium at the Garreau household when Garreau and Berresford arrived. Garreau's wife was crying as she opened the front door. A child was bawling in sympathy in the bedroom down the hall. Garreau's wife threw her arms around Michael. His large arms and wide shoulders enveloped her.

Garreau interrupted. 'Come on Mandy, I want to get Michael to bed, he must be all in.'

He shuffled down the hallway carrying the heavy suitcases to the spare room.

'Would you like a cup of coffee, Michael, or perhaps a drink?' he asked.

Berresford smiled. 'If you don't mind, I'll take you up on both.'

'Come on. We'll go down to the living room.' Garreau muttered.

Mandy hurried off to the kitchen to make the coffee.

'Cognac?'

'Love one.'

Garreau took two large balloon glasses from the shelf. He held them up to the light.

'A bit of dust won't hurt anyone,' said Berresford with a smile.

'They're clean anyway.'

Garreau looked at him, his mind elsewhere. 'I'll do the identification and make all the arrangements for the funeral tomorrow.'

'Thank you, Ian. I still can't believe that Cala's dead.'

'What about Thursday?'

'What for?'

'The funeral.'

'Make it a closed one, Ian. I don't want all the onlookers ogling around the place. I couldn't think of anything worse.'

'Anyone you want to ask?'

'Neither of us have any relatives here; make it just you, Mandy and myself. Arrange the service in the Catholic Church in Mentone. Tell Tobin Brothers we have a family burial plot in Springvale; I arranged that when Dad died.'

Garreau could see Berresford was on the point of breaking. He changed the subject. 'Come on old buddy, sit down and tell me what you're going to do in Rome.'

It was four a.m. before they went to bed.

Berresford's plan makes sense, thought Garreau, but he'll need some tuition to cope with the human jungle. He sighed deeply. I wonder which'll go first, he thought, the hunter or the hunted.

It was still raining next morning when Garreau left to identify Cala's body. He left two manuals on undercover investigations and surveillance for Berresford to read.

Berresford sat all day reading the books in the kitchen while Mandy prepared dinner for the family.

The evening meal consisted of roast rib of beef, vegetables and crunchy roast potatoes. The succulent aroma drifted through the house. Bright lights flickered outside the kitchen window. The clang of wrought iron gates preceded the revving of Garreau's car as he drove into the carport.

Garreau pushed the back door open and entered carrying a box of assorted drinks and chilled beer. On top of the box a large brown paper package balanced precariously. He rested the lot on the sink.

'Everything's fixed for Thursday,' he said grimly.

'Oh, this is for you Michael.' He passed Berresford the package.

Berresford opened the bag and checked the contents. A piece of card held three rings: Cala's engagement ring, her white gold wedding ring and a large blue sapphire ring which he had given her last year.

He took out her leather handbag. Opening it he removed a combination purse wallet. He saw the bottle and smelt her favourite perfume. Fresh pangs of anguish leapt up in his stomach. He thumbed through the rest of the contents — a bottle of foundation creme, eye liner and eye shadow.

His eyes focused on a roll of paper tied up with a small blue ribbon. The roll consisted of a number of handwritten letters. He untied it.

The letters were not Cala's. He couldn't recognize the writing. He began to read the top one. 'My dearest Cala.' He then rushed to the last line. 'Your most darling love.' The signature: 'Sig. B.'

'What in hell?' he exclaimed, sitting upright and pressing his cigarette into the glass ashtray. His face became ashen, his stomach nauseous.

Ian Garreau noticed the sudden change.

'I'm terribly sorry Michael. How foolish of me, I shouldn't have given these things to you now!'

Berresford didn't hear him. He coughed violently and left the room, his eyes holding back his tears. After he had closed the door of his room he read the whole letter:

My dearest Cala,

Every week that goes by my love is stronger, more wanting. I hate to leave you when I go away. The last weeks have been heaven, sleeping with you every night.

I keep a pair of your pants in my pocket to remind me of your loving body.

Have you told Michael you are leaving him yet?

Now he's broke he won't care anyway. Don't mention we leave for overseas next week. Make sure your passport is current.

Your most darling love,
Sig. B.

Berresford's hands were shaking. He was shattered. Tears streamed down his face. 'Oh God, oh God,' he moaned softly. 'How could she do it to me?'

Thoughts raced through his head. Memories flashed in random fashion. Everything crashed upon him in a hurricane of disbelief. Cala. Her face was clear in his mind, but only ugly lewd pictures reared up — imaginary scenes which ripped open his illusions.

Outside, through the white cotton curtains, branches knocked like impatient strangers on the window. Berresford buckled over. He wanted to scream, curse, wake up and believe it never happened. And then the self pity was slowly replaced by anger; the spirit in the man lashed out.

'How could she do it to me? Why did Turnstile choose *me*?'

A feeling of guilt came over him. 'Am *I* to blame? I'd been giving her little attention in the tiresome months since Turnstile bought into my company. Business worries affected me, but I'd give up any business to change this. Oh God, if only she knew, I could have beaten Turnstile.'

Garreau knocked again, jolting Berresford from his agony.

'Michael, can I get you something?'

'No ...' louder 'No.' Then 'Yes. Please Ian. Get me a bottle of whisky and a glass. I need a drink.'

Garreau returned with two glasses, a bottle of scotch and some ice.

Berresford sat sullen on the bed.

'Come on buddy, you can do better than that. I'll join you.' Garreau was decidedly uncomfortable. He felt pushy, yet determined to stay.

'I think I'd rather be alone!' Berresford felt the closeness of the other man: it made him feel tense.

'No you won't.' Garreau sat himself opposite Berresford on the bed. 'Pull yourself together, I'm your friend, remember.'

Berresford wiped his eyes on a handkerchief. He wanted the other man to leave. The letters were still in his hand; he crumpled them up and gave them to Garreau.

'Please put these in the fire.'

Garreau was silent.

'*Now* Ian,' he said raising his voice.

Garreau felt the awkward tension; he put the glasses on the dressing table. Taking the letters he went to the lounge room and threw them into the fire. He watched the paper burst into flames. It gave him some satisfaction; he guessed that whatever had been in them, was killing Michael.

When he returned, Berresford had poured two drinks and already had drunk a three finger scotch. 'I don't know where to start . . . I've got to get Turnstile.'

Berresford was completely devastated. 'Why in the hell is this happening to me? What have I done to deserve this?'

'Come on, Michael. Let's talk about something else.'

'I'm finished, Ian. Those rotten murdering thieves at Turnstile, they've ruined my life.'

He suddenly felt guilty, aware of Garreau's efforts to comfort him, his friendship and the trouble he had gone to on his account.

Garreau poured another drink . . . then more drinks until the bottle was finished. Berresford relaxed; Garreau changed the subject, they discussed fishing trips together, films, the CIA, the KGB.

Yet the seed of vendetta had been planted. Berresford's mind raced away to fanciful confrontations with Moffatt and the other Turnstile crooks. He sank back in his chair. Garreau's muffled conversation kept floating past him without meaning as the darkness closed in.

After breakfast the schooling began. Garreau covered a variety of subjects from practical application to surveillance equipment to shaking off a tail on foot or in a car.

Berresford was a willing learner. The fact that he had been a member of the exclusive SAS during the Vietnam war was a help. He retreated to the back verandah when Garreau left for his office. He sighed deeply and brushed a few crumbs from his jumper as his eyes unconsciously focused on the paling fence. Two willie wagtails were perched on the top rail, and were using this vantage point to spot small insects. They kept darting off in unique mid-air manoeuvres and returning to the fence to await their next prey.

Berresford considered his present predicament. He had plenty of questions but few answers, a lot of assumptions but no proof. Was the tow truck accident meant for him? Why hadn't the thieves who stole the telexes killed him? Perhaps they were interrupted by the police. How could he get evidence against Turnstile now? Was his co-director, Patterson, killed or was it an accident?

A small blue wren joined the wagtails. Suddenly a new picture emerged in Berresford's mind. The police had stated that there were no suspicious circumstances. They had put the fire in the boat down to a careless fuel leak. But this was not consistent with Patterson; and his wife didn't believe it either.

Recent events had overshadowed any importance that the report she called the 'Von Kessel Dossier' might have had. But it was now time to reconsider the possible importance of the document which she had left in his charge.

His concentration was suddenly broken when the back door squeaked open.

'Getting some sun, Michael?'

Garreau had come back early. He seated himself on the verandah edge. Berresford bent his knees and leant forward in his chair. He looked intently at Garreau, who was studying the ground near his feet. The tone of his voice changed to a more serious note.

'Helga Patterson gave me a report. She said it was connected with the death of her husband. I told you briefly about it, remember?'

Garreau turned and looked at Berresford. 'You did . . . just briefly. You thought the old lady had lost her marbles. She blamed the Nazis or something.'

'No, that's not quite right. She tied the report to Turnstile and maintained that Von Kessel's men murdered her husband.'

'Go on.' Garreau requested.

Berresford lay back in his chair and pulled out a packet of cigarettes. He lit one and puffed before speaking.

'I'll tell you all I know about George, and what she told me a few days ago.'

Garreau moved from the verandah step and sat in the chair opposite him. Berresford gave a detailed resume of all that he had learned of the Von Kessel dossier. Garreau didn't interrupt until he was finished.

'What could it possibly have to do with your company? You've only been in Australia for a little over ten years. What effect could it have on you? It goes back sixty or seventy years doesn't it?'

'Yes, 1917 to be exact. There is certainly no Von Kessel in Tralas, so I really can't see any relevance in Helga Patterson's plea.'

'Well, did she tell you what was in the report?' Garreau questioned authoritatively.

'Not entirely, she said her husband knew there was a connection between Von Kessel and Turnstile and that he was continuing investigations through some fellow in Berlin. I really can't see the connection.'

'Well, let me have a look at it.'

'I've put it in the bank. Anyway it's all in German and I haven't had it translated yet.'

'What's it called again?'

'An enquiry into something or other Von Kessel, and some German bank, one of those long complicated German names. In passing it over to me you would think she was giving me the plans to an atom bomb. And I'll never forget her remarks: "My husband was insistent that I give these to you. These people are all powerful; they'll seek you out anywhere in the world, once they know you have got it ... *Life will never be the same again.*"'

'Sounds a bit dramatic,' Garreau said disbelievingly.

'I'm not so sure ... after the events of the last few days, I'm inclined to believe anything.' Berresford blurted out.

'Well obviously, Michael, there are two things to do. One, get it translated; two, get back to Helga Patterson and find out what else she knows.'

'Yes, she told me to come back after I had read the report.'

Garreau did not reply. He was concentrating on something else. His face showed obvious signs of concern, his eyes staring into space. He spoke deliberately and slowly. 'We must be careful. You discussed this report with her on the phone from your office; if those bugs were working, then you can be sure Turnstile knows you've got it.'

Berresford, panic stricken, studied his watch and ran back to his room. It was only ten minutes past four. He dialled his bankers.

He knew the managers personally.

'Bill ... It's Michael Berresford here. About a week ago I deposited a large brown envelope, contents "German report". I'll drop you a note this afternoon confirming you release it. Could you send it back to me urgently this afternoon by courier?'

'Sure, Michael, my condolences on the loss of your wife, terrible thing.'

'Thanks . . . thanks, I appreciate that.' He hung up. Immediately grabbing the phone book, he looked up the list of consulates and dialled the second number. A woman's voice replied.

'West German Trade Commission.'

'Mr Stefan Holst please.'

'Hello? Holst speaking.' A high pitched and heavily accented German voice came on the line.

'Michael Berresford here. Remember you kindly translated a technical document on oil drilling rig parts; in particular, the drill collars that one of your German companies exports?'

'Oh, yes. I remember, you were in a great hurry, sure.'

'I was wondering if I could stretch the friendship a little and ask you to translate a twenty-page document for me? It's been passed down in the family, old records from the war.'

'When can I have it.'

'Within half an hour.'

'I can translate it this afternoon, throw it on tape, and you can have it typed up by ten o'clock tomorrow morning.'

'Many thanks. I'll send it to you as quickly as possible by courier and ring you tomorrow at ten.'

Berresford sat on the bed, relieved.

CHAPTER 9

Benini and Farwood had safely retreated from Berresford's home. They had done well to avoid detection. It was the first time that they had muddled an assignment.

They returned to a small cream brick veneer villa in Beaumaris, which Farwood had rented. It was only a short distance from Berresford's home; and was a most suitable location for their high-frequency radio receivers and voice recording equipment.

Benini decided to remain there until next day; until they were certain that their car had not been seen near Berresford's home.

Upon entering the house, they immediately went to the recording room and switched on the receivers. It took less than two minutes for them to realize that all the bugs at Berresford's office and house had been removed or destroyed.

This deepened their concern. What would they report to Moffatt?

Farwood proposed that they play down the whole affair. He suggested they leave out the incident at Berresford's home. Benini would not agree, untrustworthy assassins are not fired, he argued, they are eliminated. So they had to report the facts.

It was almost 11 p.m. before they had connected the computer terminal to the overseas telephone line and dialled the telex office at Turnstile Investments Ltd in London. Communication was complete and accurate.

Benini advised the car accident and the incident at Berresford's home. He believed that retrieving the telexes would soften the blow.

They then retired to the sparsely furnished bedroom — the sheetless beds and curtainless windows. Benini was annoyed.

He had no change of shirt or underwear, and Farwood's electric razor was incompatible to the skin of his blade-shaven face. Despite all this, he decided to stay until they had received a message from 'The Telex' in the morning.

It was almost seven o'clock when Benini awoke. He looked at his watch, anxiously awaiting nine o'clock when he could telephone London and hook up his portable computer modum. He turned to Farwood who had just come out of the bathroom.

'I don't want you to leave any mess, John.'

Farwood snapped back. 'What about your mess, Mario. It's hardly what I call a clean job!'

Benini felt anger mount in him. He grabbed a handful of telexes and stuffed them forcefully into the fire. 'It was not my fault he wasn't in the car...'

Farwood sensed his fury and forced a smile.

'Let's not fight about it, Mario. You finish burning these telexes. I'll pack up the equipment and put it in the car. We won't need this house any more. Well, you'll miss fucking the Berresford woman. Why did you take up with her in the first place?'

'Had too; I needed her to gain access to the house and his office. I've been in Australia three times in past months and was taken with her.'

'Go on, you can't resist the skirt.'

Benini didn't answer. He resumed feeding the telexes in small handfuls into the roaring fire.

A few minutes after nine, Benini placed a telephone call to the Turnstile Office London. He entered the coded instructions.

The small printer began; lines of writing flashed across in sequential order.

'You have connection to mainframe Turnstile.
1. What is the priority of your message?
2. Designate persons for immediate, delayed or random access.
3. State your name code, location code, and operation code.
4. Quote in Greenwich Mean Time your availability for a reply.
5. Enter code for record on your individual file or additional persons' files if a joint communication is desired.

Benini entered the information sequentially. As the correct encoding was entered, line after line disappeared until the screen was clear. A new line of type appeared in front of him.

Proceed with message. At end of transmission await acknowledgement. Then transfer for messages.

Benini reported abandoning the house in Beaumaris, packing up their equipment and his request to proceed to Rome to his next assignment while leaving Farwood behind to carry out any additional duties required in Australia. At the end of the message he entered the appropriate code and requested the computer to search for messages left for him.

Attention M. Benini, J. Farwood —
E.L.6 Berresford. E.L.6 his friend Ian. $100,000 US bonus on completion. Farwood responsible these matters. Benini return to Rome to complete assignment previous advised.

The Telex

Benini and Farwood had both been reading the electronic printer as it rapidly traced the letters across the perforated edged paper. Farwood broke the silence.

'My God, Mario. That's a first. Highest priority assassinations! They really must be flies in the ointment. Moffatt's usually not that blunt either.'

Mario was still staring at the printed message. The machine signed itself off, the printer silent.

'He's never offered such a bonus before. Must want them badly. Well, that reward will no doubt be yours. I'll be heading off to Rome tomorrow or the next day.'

Benini removed the telephone handset from his computer terminal and hung up. The line had already been cut off at the London end. He tore off the message, took a lighter from his pocket, set fire to it and placed it in the open fireplace. When it was burnt he crushed up the cinders. This was hardly the time for mistakes.

It was ten minutes past ten when Berresford dialled the Department of Trade. Holst said that he had translated the Von Kessel Dossier. Pick-up was arranged.

Berresford then rang Mrs Patterson. The phone rang for some time. She had been in the garden, she explained. Her voice still showed signs of nervousness. However, she agreed to see Berresford around 11 a.m.

Garreau was in the kitchen making a cup of coffee. The smell of the freshly ground beans in the percolator permeated the air.

'Smells good!' Berresford exclaimed as he bounded into the room, a hearty smile on his face. 'How about running me over to the West German Trade Commission? That document's translated. Then let's speak to Helga Patterson.'

'Sure Michael, sounds great. It's good to see a smile on your face again.'

Garreau drove quickly but skilfully. It took barely twenty-five minutes to get to the West German Trade Commission. Some minutes later Berresford appeared carrying two envelopes.

His face showed considerable anxiety. Garreau could

judge by his hurried gait that something was the matter. He was barely seated in the front passenger seat before he gushed the information.

'Ian, it's incredible,' he said excitedly.

'Holst's just told me. Millions of dollars involved, illegally removed from Germany, now it's in the U.K. I wonder if it's connected with Turnstile.'

CHAPTER 10

The old grey-haired lady was in the front garden; her long hair was neatly wound into a bun, speared by two ornate pins. Her face exuded kindness, yet there were lines of tragedy above and below the light blue eyes.

The garden was neat, with small beds of roses and other flowers set in precise rows. The manicured lawn was neatly trimmed along the concrete path which led to the door. Hearing the visitors unlatch the gate, she looked up.

Berresford smiled as he walked towards her — a smile which she returned, but it changed when she saw Garreau. Berresford spoke confidently.

'Mrs Patterson, may I introduce Ian Garreau, a close personal friend.'

Her index finger beckoned Berresford towards her and whispered.

'Why did you bring him? The less who know the better.' Her strong Germanic accent was difficult to understand.

'He's all right Helga. He's helping me in my investigations.'

'You remember what I said, Michael. To investigate this file, *life will never be the same again*. And that goes for him too,' she said louder, looking towards Garreau. He nodded as if he understood.

'Come in, come in,' she said beckoning them both towards the door.

They followed her into the loungeroom.

'Well, have you read it already, Michael?'

'I haven't read it yet. I only picked it up this morning, that is, the translation; but I must say I was stunned with the amount of money!'

'This is what George found to be most exciting. You see, it was the file name that made him look into this matter more carefully. An old friend, a professor in Berlin did the further investigations. He found the London connection. One minute, I will give you his card.'

She returned and gave a small visiting card to Berresford. It was obviously old. The white card was now grey, the edges pitted with brown spots.

'He is still at that address, but the phone number is different. Please, you will go and see him?'

'I might do that too, Helga. Tell me, what other investigations did George do, other than those carried out by the Professor? Is there anything else in writing?'

'No other investigation and nothing else in writing, Michael. He never even left that report in the house again. I had to get it from his bank. He kept the rest in his head. Whenever he received a letter he read it and burnt it. I can recall quite a deal of it. Perhaps I should write it down tonight and you could collect it tomorrow morning? It would be easier that way. Less likely that I forget anything, understand?'

Michael nodded.

'Did Von Kessel go to England?' Garreau asked, speaking for the first time.

'Ya, yes ... He had six names to choose from, six stolen identities. I will give them all to you tomorrow.'

'Is he still alive?'

'Yes, Rudolf is the son of the thief. He inherited the fortune.' Her voice dropped almost with a tone of sadness. 'He is a very bad man, Michael, he will kill both of you. I am sad I have involved you, but I promised my husband to give it to you if anything happened to him. Then Von Kessel's men killed him.'

'How can you be sure of that?' Michael asked politely.

'The Professor believed he had found Von Kessel's identity so he went to London to confirm his findings. He was searching old company records when he discovered he was under surveillance. The following day someone tried to kill him.' She stopped, shivered nervously, her lips whitened, drawn back in a rictus of terror.

'A car ran him down on the footpath. He lay in hospital on the brink of death for days.' Her voice was soft in cogent explanation.

'The Professor went underground and completed his search with perfervid drive. He wanted Von Kessel more than ever. The search completed, he sent a copy to George. It arrived the day before he was killed.'

Berresford sighed. 'I should have read it sooner,' he said, referring to the Von Kessel dossier.

Her lips thinned, her eyes squinted. 'If they trace you Michael, you are as good as dead. He has enormous wealth, beyond imagination. The report will tell you. He took millions with him, our German people's money. Loaned it to the Bolsheviks for their revolution and recovered it with interest. Blood money if you ask me.'

'He must be old,' Garreau remarked quizzingly.

'He is eighty-two, and still as dangerous as ever. In a way I hope you never find him, though I want revenge for what he did to my husband.' The last words acidulous. With this her face contorted and tears came into her eyes.

A cacophonous whistle came from the kitchen. Mrs Patterson rose quickly from her chair.

'Follow me,' she said. 'I will talk as I work.'

A large pressure cooker on the stove was letting off excess steam, hissing, squealing. She continued her conversation.

'George thought it was most likely that he would be

using the knight name.' '

Berresford was confused. 'How do you mean, the night name?'

'In killing that poor English boy he stole that too.'

'Stole what?' Her back was to Berresford, who shook his head in bewilderment.

Without speaking she turned off the gas and they returned to the loungeroom.

'Please Helga, write this all down.' Berresford pursued.

'Yes I will, but you need more, see our friend the Professor. He is a good man, Michael, and can be trusted. But please be careful.' She shook her finger at him.

It was nearing twelve noon. She rose from her chair. 'Gentlemen, if you go now I will start writing my recollections. If you come this time tomorrow morning it will be ready for you. Keep the documents safe, Michael. There are no copies.'

Berresford and Garreau rose and followed her to the front door. As she opened it she smiled and turned to Berresford. There was great kindness in those eyes.

'Aufwedersein Michael, thank you for chasing my husband's murderer.'

Berresford returned the original German dossier to his bank, and gave new instructions restricting its release only on *his* written authority. That night Garreau and Berresford studied the report and discussed it in detail.

The first entry in the dossier was dated May 1932. It fully described the work of the Die Drehkreuz Bank A.G., how nearly all of the bank's money had been transferred to support the Bolshevik revolution in Russia.

The agreement which had been made between the Russians and Von Kessel was that the money would be repaid with interest and paid in any currency in any country at the expiration of fifteen years. Sole recipient of the return of funds was to be either Rudolf Von Kessel or his successor, who would identify himself with a given code.

The document then gave a complete account of the son and heir Rudolf Von Kessel. It traced all his connections and relations in West Germany. The report indicated that by the end of 1944 none remained. They were executed by Hitler, who hated revolutionaries.

Von Kessel had obtained six false passports. There were no names in the report, and they had not been discovered. A Von Kessel had left Germany in 1932 and had illegally entered England under a false name.

'Turnstile,' Berresford recounted, 'does not necessarily tie in with the German bank. There is no indication or proof that there is any connection between the two. Secondly, there appears to be an enormous amount of money involved. Eleven million pounds sterling in 1932, what, it would be worth say 100 million today, wouldn't it, Ian?'

'Easily, Michael. If it was put to good use between then and now, maybe a lot more.'

'There are no names in Turnstile to my knowledge that sound anything remotely like Von Kessel.'

Garreau then came up with an important assessment. 'It's quite possible that George Patterson stumbled upon this ancient German's fraud, and discovered Rudolf Von Kessel's whereabouts. That in itself may bring down the wrath of Von Kessel; maybe he was killed for that reason.'

Berresford agreed. 'You're right, Ian. I can't see that they are connected, they can't be. We might have got ourselves into another jam and stirred up ants in another nest. I'm fairly sure they're not connected. But perhaps we should reserve our decision until we see what Helga Patterson gives us tomorrow morning.'

CHAPTER 11

While Garreau was driving to the ASIO headquarters, Berresford had set off to see Helga Patterson. He arrived around the same time as he had done on the previous day. Somehow the house looked different, he thought.

He walked up and rapped on the front door with the brass knocker. Standing there waiting for a reply his eyes focused on the loungeroom window, less than ten feet away. It suddenly struck him.

The blinds were drawn. Yesterday they had all been open. He rapped again, the noise echoing down the hall.

He walked around the side path. It led him to a neat back garden, almost fifty foot square. Areas were divided up for fruit trees, vegetables and flower beds. The watering hose was neatly coiled up near a tap just outside the back door. He knocked again. No reply.

Berresford began to feel uneasy. He tried the back door knob. It turned and he opened the door a few inches.

He called. 'Is anybody home? Helga are you there?' Nothing.

He opened the door a little wider.

'My God!' he exclaimed loudly. The room looked as if vandals had broken into the house on a rampage. All the kitchen drawers had been removed and their contents littered the floor. Flour, rice and sugar tins had been upended, their contents tipped into the sink or onto the floor.

Berresford put his hand under his coat and clasped firmly the .38 Smith and Wesson revolver which Garreau had lent him. He pulled it from the shoulder holster and kept the gun well in front of him as he searched from room to room.

The pictures and etchings which had been on the walls were now all torn from their mounts, the backing of the pictures ripped off. The loungeroom too had been similarly disturbed. There was a pattern: someone had searched the house.

There was a door opposite the loungeroom, which was obviously that of the first bedroom. The door was ajar. He pushed it open slowly, sweat coming from the pores of his hands. With his right thumb he pulled the hammer of the revolver back so that it could be fired quickly from a single action. Then he saw her.

'Oh God!' he yelled, his eyes transfixed on the naked body of the old lady on the bed.

She had been horribly mutilated — no, he thought, tortured. The fingers on one hand had been cut off, the detached appendages lying on the floor.

Bile rose in his throat. He went back into the hallway, ran to the bathroom and vomited into the toilet. He forced himself to think. Her blood had already dried; so they must have left hours before.

He went to the phone. It was still connected. The telephone handset rattled as he started dialling.

He stopped. He looked at the mouthpiece. It had been tampered with, it was loose.

He started to screw it up, tightening it on its thread. Then Garreau's words came to his mind. *'Telephones are easy to bug, always check the handset. Screw off the earphone and the microphone and check for inserts.'*

He hastily unscrewed the mouthpiece. He pulled out the microphone and peered inside. He saw two small connecting wires leading nowhere. They had been snipped off, and this phone had been bugged. I bet the rooms were too, he thought. Whoever bugged the house knew that she would be giving us more information on those reports.

Replacing the microphone and screwing on the cap he got the dial tone again and called 000.

A girl's voice replied. 'Emergency services, police, ambulance or fire department, please.'

'Police thank you, homicide.'

Seconds later a stern male voice responded. 'Homicide, CIB. Sergeant Johnson speaking.'

'I am calling from 17 Sugargum Drive, Glen Waverley. I have just called to see a friend of mine, Mrs Patterson. No one answered the door, so I went to the back door and found it open. The house is in a mess, obviously ransacked. I searched through the house and I found her on her bed; she has been horribly mutilated.'

'What is your name and address sir?'

Berresford hung up. There was nothing for him here. He hurried to the loungeroom to pick up a serviette which had been thrown on the floor from a drawer of the credenza. He removed the fingerprints from each door he opened. Quietly he retraced his steps to his car and drove away sedately. Her last words flashed through his mind. 'Life will never be the same, once you have that report.'

Garreau found Berresford in the loungeroom.

Berresford went to the bar. 'Drink?'

'No thanks.'

'I think you will need one. Helga Patterson has been murdered, tortured.' Berresford said grimly.

Garreau gasped. 'Tell me what happened.' Berresford gave a detailed account, at the end of which he said impatiently.

'Anything on Cala's crash?'

'Nothing, I don't think we will ever know the truth.'

'Ian, I know in my heart it was Turnstile — in time I'll prove it. We've got to get some concrete evidence, files, telexes, anything that incriminates them.'

Berresford and Garreau guessed the same; it was a tough assignment.

'If I can lay my hands on their prime records,' he kept repeating to himself, as he returned to pour them another drink.

'What about other companies that Turnstile invests in?' said Garreau, sipping the cognac.

Berresford said in a challenging tone. 'Just name one.'

'Airline industries.'

'They've got shares in one I believe. Overheard Brin talking to his partner one day.' Berresford was an astute businessman and considered nearly any company could be related to Turnstile. He reflected again before he spoke.

'Corporate fraud in an airline company would be a pushover. A moderate to small airline company would have a market capitalization of about $50 million.'

Garreau interrupted. 'That's something to do with share value, isn't it?' The two men sat opposite each other.

Berresford hated repeating himself.

'Yes market capitalization is the share price multiplied by the number of shares in the company. If the shares are widely spread, that is if there are mostly small shareholders with small parcels of shares; and say if ten per cent was held by one person or company, then this small percentage could control the company. For example: a five million dollar investment may give you control of a fifty million dollar company. This would only occur when the other major shareholders together were holders of less than ten per cent. As a rule, if you hold the majority of the shares held by the top twenty shareholders, you have effective control.'

Sounds reasonable, thought Garreau.

'Most airways lease or hire their aircraft. The value of their aircraft and parts is usually many times the market capitalization; say the fleet is worth 300 million dollars,' Berresford was getting excited. 'Imagine the deals that a dishonest director could engineer. They could set up a small company on their own behalf; say in Hong Kong, Lichenstein, Switzerland, any of the tax havens. This company then approaches an aircraft manufacturer: "we have a customer for 300 million dollars worth of aircraft. We want ten per cent commission for the introduction." In one deal they could rip off 30 million dollars; the public never being the wiser.'

'That sort of thing went on in the States, didn't it?'

'It's likely going on everywhere, but to what extent, we'll never know. You have to prove it. Getting the prime records from Turnstile's head office would not only give us *their* holdings of the *public* companies they control; it would give us also all the internal workings of their companies.' Berresford stubbed his cigarette. 'That's why we need evidence.'

'You'll get it in Rome, I'm sure of it Michael. But never mind: if you fail to get the evidence there, you still have their headquarters in London. And don't forget my London contact if the going gets tough.'

CHAPTER 12

Garreau's arrangements for Cala's funeral were handled with the utmost discretion and secrecy. The unannounced funeral went smoothly, with only the Garreaus and Berresford present.

While the service was being held in the empty church, John Farwood was searching Berresford's telephone recordings for a surname to fit 'Ian.' Hours later he found one: Ian Pendel. Even better he also knew the day of the week and venue for a small luncheon club where Berresford often met Pendel for a drink. He decided to move quickly. It was almost lunchtime anyway.

Farwood climbed the front steps and entered the main foyer of the hotel. He followed the sign to the Cricketers Bar. The inside was decorated with bats, shields and cups, giving the bar name some authenticity. Seated at the top end was a man who fitted the description which the cashier had given him at the entrance. Farwood strode up and approached the man cautiously.

'Mr Ian Pendel, I believe.' The stout man was trying to recognize him. His eyes squinted as he tried to place the face.

'Yes.' He replied in a rather cultured Cambridge accent, placing his beer glass on the bar.

Farwood began his lies. 'My name is Brian Thompson. We have a mutual friend, Michael Berresford.'

Pendel did not speak and remained indifferent. He did not wish to have the company of strangers.

Farwood changed the subject.

'Did you hear about the tragic accident?'

The older man stopped and turned, facing Farwood. 'Yes, I did. Absolute tragedy.' Pendel's heavy, rounded, polished voice boomed.

Farwood knew that Pendel's accent was inconsistent with the Ian he had heard in the wire tappings, but he continued. 'Last time I was here with Michael he had another friend named Ian with him. I just can't remember the name.'

Pendel replied, looking down earnestly. 'The only other Ian I know that comes here with Michael would be Ian Garreau.'

'Oh really, yes, I just couldn't put my finger on the name, it could be him. May I buy you a drink?' Farwood continued.

'No, please join me, my pleasure.' said the portly man, now willing to have the company.

Some minutes later Farwood again introduced the subject of Garreau. 'What does Ian Garreau do? What's his job?'

Pendel looked at him rather surprised, over his heady framed glasses and then said.

'Well frankly, I don't know. Some sort of sleuth or something, although at times I thought he might be a travelling salesman.'

Farwood pressed further. 'There couldn't be many Garreaus around, does he come from Berresford's suburb, Beaumaris?'

Pendel looked at him wondering the reason for this questioning and replied simply, 'No, he lives in Frankston.'

In typical Australian tradition Farwood completed the round of drinks, patted the man on the shoulder, muttered something about a meeting, and left.

Back in Benini's room, Farwood slumped in a chair.

'Much better than I thought.' His voice was relaxed. 'His name is Ian Garreau and he lives in Frankston.'

'Have you checked the phone book?'

'There is no listing, obviously a silent line.'

Farwood took out his papers and jottings.

'I suggest you check the electoral rolls, go to the suburb and try all the newsagencies. Someone will know who he is. You should find him fairly quickly.'

Benini was pacing the room anxiously. 'I'm getting out of here as soon as possible.' He had dialled his travel agency to book the 2 p.m. flight to Rome.

Melbourne's Tullamarine Airport was buzzing with excitement. Television sets were flashing out digital information, while loudspeakers were playing restful music and armed federal police stood as speechless sentries. Airline checking counters stood like islands in the ocean of carpet and tile. Garreau watched the rows of impatient travellers.

There was only an hour and a half before the 2 p.m. flight left for Rome. Berresford picked up his passport and checked his papers. He discussed the final details with Garreau.

'With your own set of papers and passports, you now have two identities.' Garreau handed them to him.

'Please be careful, when arriving in Rome, to use your own name in the Hotel. Over the next few days I will use your solicitors and check on the Turnstile directors in Tralas, I'll find out what other director-ships they hold in Australia and elsewhere.'

Berresford felt the full weight of his suitcase. He wanted to leave, anxious to begin the search. 'I wouldn't be surprised to see more than two companies involved with the same directors in Italy and perhaps other companies in England.'

Two hundred feet away Benini stood at the Qantas check-in counter. The final boarding call appeared on the screen for passengers travelling to Rome via Hong

Kong on the 2 p.m. flight with Qantas Airways. Three minutes later another final boarding sign appeared for the Alitalia flight to Rome, via Athens. Garreau turned to Berresford.

'Your final call, Michael. Best of luck.'

Their hands met, shook vigorously.

'Let's hope we can wrap this up quickly.' Garreau said unconvincingly as he turned to leave.

Berresford felt confident when he arrived at the customs counter, Benini was already seated in departure lounge number 2. After being cleared by immigration and customs, Berresford proceeded to departure lounge 6. Suddenly Berresford caught a fleeting glimpse of Benini, who turned away sharply. He seemed vaguely familiar.

CHAPTER 13

The streets of Frankston were bustling with shoppers.
Farwood could find no trace of Garreau's name at the
post office on the electoral roll; he would never know
that ASIO operatives were exempt from registration.

He returned to his car, opened the glovebox and took
out a writing pad and pencil. He commenced writing a
shortlist of addresses and phone numbers of newsagencies, schools, shops and chain stores where he
might trace Garreau's address.

With a little luck he might be able to trace the home
delivery of daily papers to the Garreau household. The
glare of the sun strained his eyes as he pencilled out the
possibilities, using the dash board to rest his pad.

By the time Farwood finished he had listed nineteen
places.

He relisted them in order of priority, according to
street name and number. He wound through the
impatient traffic. In order of precedence, the first call
was to a newsagency in Station Street, opposite the
railway station.

It was a typical newspaper shop. Wire gridded
posters depicting news headlines rested against the
front window. Young teenagers milled around outside.
On entering the newsagency he searched for the person
who would be the most senior on the staff. The walls
were lined with books, mostly paperbacks. He
approached with forced humility.

'Excuse me, Miss, I was wondering if you could help

me?' The girl continued stacking a new batch of books on the shelves. 'I have just arrived on the train . . . on my way to see a friend of mine, Ian Garreau and, unfortunately, I have left my address book behind and I can't seem to find him in the telephone book.'

She turned around and caught his eye.

'You wouldn't happen to know him, would you? Garreau. Ian Garreau.' He spelt out the name.

The girl was most helpful. She went and asked the proprietor the same question. Farwood could see him shaking his head.

'Never heard of him,' said the impatient man. 'Not a customer of ours.' Farwood turned to leave. Another shop attendant called, 'Wait a minute.'

Farwood stopped and turned to hear what the young man said.

'Although I don't know the address, I have met Mrs Garreau. She comes in with the children.' He turned to the girl shop assistant. 'You know her, blond, attractive, we keep their newspapers for them. For some reason they don't want them delivered. Garreau, Garreau, it's such an odd name.'

'Would you have her address?' interrupted Farwood.

A small crowd gathered behind the counter. 'No, she just has her name in the order book. She always pays cash.' The young man said.

'Are the children school age? Perhaps I could ring up the schools and work it out from there.'

The lad behind the counter sensed the urgency.

'Yes they are. The boy was wearing a Peninsula Grammar uniform, and I think the two girls go to the state school.'

More people entered the shop. He turned to serve them.

'Thank you very much. That will help me considerably.'

Farwood hurriedly left the shop. A short distance down the road he stopped at a group of telephone boxes. One telephone call to the secretary of Peninsula Grammar was sufficient. She was only too pleased to help and gave him the address.

Two hours later, sixty feet away from Garreau's house in Frankston an old battered van parked close to the kerb. A pencil-like beam was focused on the loungeroom window. The source of light emanated from a small box inside the van. The laser beam device could detect voices from the changes in vibrations on the window. Farwood sat listening to his earphones, with a tape recorder turning.

BOOK TWO

CHAPTER 14

The roar of the jet engines gradually diminished as Berresford drew further away from Leonardo Da Vinci Airport.

He leaned back in the rear seat of the taxi. Rome was less than an hour away.

Berresford was suffering from jet lag. The flight plus stopovers had taken over twenty-three hours. But it was not the jet lag that caused the frown on his face. The last few weeks had been the most difficult and trying period of his life.

He pondered over the German money that Von Kessel had shifted to England in the thirties. Was there any connection between the Von Kessel file and Turnstile? Berresford still didn't know. Mrs Patterson may have known the connection, if any, but she was dead. Berresford felt the dossier translation in his pocket.

His thoughts raced back to Ian Garreau's break-in inside Turnstile's accountants' offices. The documents and telexes had conclusively indicated that Turnstile had fraudulently converted funds from his company for their own use. His ribs ached, he felt the bruise on his skull and shuddered when he recalled how the next round was won by Turnstile when they recovered the documents.

His one hope now was to obtain similar documents from the accountants' offices in Rome. Otherwise there was not a piece of evidence for a police investigation.

Everything rested on the success of the Rome operation. He believed they certainly would kill him if he was caught.

The false passport provided by Ian Garreau had worked perfectly. Berresford had flown in under the alias of Michael Forrest. The accommodation at the Hotel Excelsior was a different matter. There he would use his own passport. If he was being pursued, then they would not trace his name on any transport out of Rome.

The taxi passed two bus loads of passengers from the Leonardo Da Vinci Airport. The agitated taxi driver honked his horn at the bus driver, who had failed to give him sufficient space to pass.

The driver yelled over the roar of the car and bus engines. 'The Excelsior you want to go to is in the Via Veneto, signore?'

'Yes, that's the one,' he confirmed.

As the taxi pulled up in front of the hotel two stunningly attractive young women sauntered by, dresses too short, make-up overdone. As they casually walked past, one winked at Berresford; the slightest form of acknowledgement would result in them offering their bodies — at a price.

Berresford followed a wealthy Arab and his entourage through the main entrance. He had stayed there before on holidays and occasionally on business trips. The magnificent timber in the mirror-polished reception desk complimented the staid atmosphere of the hotel.

The formally dressed concierge was engaged in an animated conversation with the Arab businessman. Some minutes later he turned his attention to Berresford.

'Parla inglese, tedesco, o francese?'

'I speak English,' was the quick reply. 'My name is Berresford.' He spelt it to ensure that the young man understood. 'I have a suite booked on the first floor.'

The young man flipped through a card index system. 'Ah, here we are. Half of suite 3. Signore, I must explain. We have let 3a, which is half the suite, and 3b is reserved for you.'

'Who's in 3a?' Berresford asked.

'An American named Mr Nixon. If I can explain. The whole of Suite 3 comprises two state rooms, two bedrooms and two bathrooms. When we let it as two suites you have one state room, bedroom and bathroom. The doors between them are locked from both sides.'

'I know,' said Berresford. 'I've stayed here before.'

'Of course you have separate entrances. The entrance to 3a is the first left at the top of the stairs. The entrance to 3b is at the end of the small hallway.'

Berresford sighed. He was tired and worried. He had already said that he'd stayed there before and that he knew the set-up. I'm talking to a dullard, he thought. The young man passed the key to another formally dressed attendant. 'Show Mr Berresford to his room, please.'

'The porter has already taken your bags up, sir. He'll unpack for you if you wish.' Berresford left and followed the hotel attendant to his room.

His tired brain was concentrating on Garreau's suggestion. *'Endeavour to swap rooms with the adjoining guest. Offer to pay their accommodation, but leave the hotel records in the original guest's names.'*

I'll try in the morning, he thought.

The two room suite was elegantly furnished. Berresford left the porter to finish unpacking and went into the living room. The small timber bar caught his attention. He poured himself a whisky with ice and water.

He returned to the bedroom and tipped the porter. His body was hot and sticky after the long plane trip. He ran a bath. He felt exhausted but there was more to be done. A plan had been made, and it was essential that he adhere to it.

The bath, the shave and the drink did something to revive him. He changed to a light-weight fawn suit, which was more appropriate for the climate. As he opened the door to the hallway he glanced momentarily at the other door, the one that connected 3b to 3a when the whole suite was occupied under one booking.

I wonder if the American guest snores, he thought. He shrugged his shoulders, the heavy timber doors should be soundproof surely. The one flight of stairs proved faster than the lift. The doorman whistled a taxi as he went outside.

'Where to, sir?'

'The airport.' Berresford lied. When safely in the taxi he told the driver the true destination. 'The Hotel Quirinale, please.'

'Don't you want the airport, signore?'

'No, I've changed my mind.'

The driver nodded and drove off in the opposite direction.

Berresford had never stayed at the Hotel Quirinale before, but he was assured that it had a good reputation and that the cuisine was excellent. The hotel would be used in an emergency, an emergency he hoped would never occur. He was following Garreau's suggestions to the letter.

He registered using the name Michael Forrest. He filled out the reservation card, signed it and explained to the clerk.

'I've booked the room for seven days. It looks like I may be staying over with friends and won't be using the room everyday.'

'Shall I cancel it, sir?'

'No, please listen.' Berresford was tired and irritable.

'Certainly signore.' The desk clerk wrinkled up his

face trying to understand Berresford's request.

'Let me make it clear. I want to pay for seven days, please don't let it to anyone else. I'm not sure which days I'll be using the rooms. Is that clear?'

'You want the room for seven days sir, whether you use it or not, who cares?' the clerk said lifting his hands, shrugging his shoulders.

Berresford gave a deep sigh. 'Thank you.' He collected his key and returned by taxi to the Hotel Excelsior.

Berresford went to his room. There was one phone call to make before turning in. He sat on the bed and thumbed through the Rome telephone book. He stopped when he reached the American Embassy.

The phone buzzed for several seconds. A girl with a familiar accent answered.

'United States Embassy.'

'Is Mr Tom Brady in please?'

'I'm sorry sir, he's not in at present. Can I take a message?'

'Yes, I'm a friend of his. My name is Michael Berresford. Would you ask him to call me. I'm staying in 3b at the Hotel Excelsior. Will he be back today?'

'No sir, is it urgent?'

'Not really. Please ask him to ring me in the morning.'

'You're welcome.'

He hung up and climbed into bed naked. There was something familiar about the fragrance he could smell; it was the room deodorizer. His eyes closed, his mind drifted to a holiday he had had with Cala in Honolulu. She was parading in a new dress she had bought. She was laughing.

His thoughts drifted. He was lying next to Cala on Waikiki Beach, the sun beating down on their suntanned bodies, the waves crashing on the sands behind him.

It was at this moment he lost consciousness.

The shrill ring of the hotel telephone stirred Berresford from deep sleep. He grabbed at the source of disturbance and strained to read his watch. It was 8.45 . . . hell is it night or morning, he thought.

'Hi, is that you Michael?' The cheery voice of Tom Brady sounded through the earpiece.

'Yes Tom, good to speak to you.'

'Sorry I didn't get your message 'til this morning. How long are you staying?'

'Not sure, couple of days, maybe a couple of weeks.'

'Great, we'll have to get together.'

The tone in Berresford's voice changed. He knew he could trust his old friend, who had once worked with his father at the American Embassy in Australia.

'Tom, I'm in trouble. I need you to help me.'

Brady was suddenly serious. 'Of course Michael, anything I can do?'

'I'm staying in 3b at the Excelsior. Could you come over and have a chat.'

'I'll be over around midday.'

'Good. Thanks Tom, much appreciated.'

'Good. See you.' The phone went dead.

Berresford had a quick shower and dressed. He pulled the ten foot long curtains to each side and tied them back. Bright shafts of light streamed into the bedroom.

A rattling noise followed by a door being slammed broke his attention. He hurried to the door and looked up the hall. A portly middle aged man dressed in American western clothes was checking the lock on the door. Berresford hurried towards him and greeted him politely.

'Hello there, I'm your next door neighbour.'

The Texan beamed, with a broad smile. 'Hi there, glad to know you,' he said cheerily.

'I checked in last night, how long are you staying?'

'About three days, partner, how about you?'

'Not sure yet, I'm here on business. Would you like to

join me for a coffee?'

The Texan was delighted. 'Surely!' he yelled, the emphasis on the 'ly'.

Over coffee the Texan explained. 'I'm over here on my own business too. Bit dull without my wife. Left her back home in Texas. Won't travel with me when the trips are shorter than seven days.'

He was a friendly man, wearing an open-neck, western-style shirt, with fancy pleated and scalloped pockets.

Berresford replied. 'I can't blame her. No sooner would you be over the jet lag than you'd be travelling home again. Anyway, my name is Michael Berresford.'

'Bill Nixon. Pleased to meet you, partner.' Nixon's large head suited the short crew-cut hair. His ruddy complexion fitted a man fond of liquor.

'Never stayed in a hotel before with such fancy bathrooms . . . decked out more like a church altar than a bathroom!'

He bellowed loudly, causing guests nearby to look around. Berresford felt obliged to laugh with him, yet he was a little embarrassed by his noisy acquaintance.

'Rather like it myself. Bit of a change from the drab old hotel chains. I usually stay in 3a, but I settled for 3b instead. My wife and I,' the night of the accident stung his mind. 'We always booked into 3a.' Silence. 'I lost her just recently.'

'Divorce,' the Texan yelled, grinning ear to ear.

'No, killed in an accident,' Berresford muttered.

The Texan was uneasy. He didn't want to be dragged into a crisis, yet he was obviously embarrassed.

'I'm terribly sorry . . . I mean, I never thought . . .'

Berresford relieved the tension.

'Mind if we swapped suites?'

Nixon was caught unawares. His sympathy gushed out and he gave in immediately.

'Not at all, old buddy, anytime you like. Should have asked earlier. You say when.'

'Whenever it suits you. What about you join me for lunch while they change them over?'

'Love to.'

Berresford continued. 'To save messing around with the accounts, I'll pick up the tab. The company pays all my bills so don't worry about it.'

'I couldn't do that...' Again the Texan wanted to please. 'If you want...'

'No, no, think nothing of it. The company can pay and I do appreciate your kindness. By the way the suites are very similar and you won't be disappointed by the change.'

'Course not.'

They finished their coffee. Berresford returned to his room and repacked his suitcases.

When Brady arrived just before midday they greeted each other as long lost friends. The camaraderie rekindled. Brady had had a great regard and respect for Berresford's father, and he had sadly missed him after he died from a heart attack some years before.

Tom Brady was a tall, handsome negro. He was highly thought of in the CIA. Both intelligent and thorough, he was clever with words. Some of his felicitous sayings had remained pleasant memories in Berresford's mind. Yet for all his cleverness the adroit Brady had an insatiable yearning for adventure.

After they had exchanged pleasantries Berresford told Brady of the events which had brought him to Rome.

Brady's handsome black hulk sprawled out in a comfortable chair. He listened intently. He was trained to.

'Then you want someone to break into their Rome accountant's office and photograph those telexes?'

Berresford was surprised that the other man had understood him so quickly.

'Either photograph or photostat, it doesn't matter;

117

but I want a copy of them all. We need proof — evidence.'

'I hope you weren't considering doing it yourself, Michael?' laughed Brady, confidently, trying to relieve the tension.

'No,' replied Berresford. 'I thought you might know of someone.'

Brady knew Berresford had an intense antipathy for violence and corruption.

'For break-ins, eh, far cry from Company Director.'

Brady sat composed, his mind rapidly assessing the situation. 'I must warn you, Michael, this is not a CIA affair. We have diplomatic immunity to protect us. So my first concern, my friend, is to caution you. You're not biting off more than you can chew, are you?'

'Tom . . . Tom, *you* know *me*; I'm fighting corporate crooks, murderers, thieves, and doing it single-handed. This time I need help. Help like I've never asked for before.'

Brady walked to the bar.

'Mind if I have a drink?'

'Go ahead. You'll find our old favourite there — you still go for it don't you?'

'Sure do Mike.'

A term of endearment which had been almost forgotten. His father had always called him 'Mike'.

Brady passed Berresford the drink.

They raised their glasses and drank.

Brady began to lay out a plan. 'I've got the very man for the job. We use him occasionally for this sort of thing. He's a private investigator; a one-man show. He's efficient, charges a reasonable price and you can count on him to keep his mouth shut.'

'Is he competent?'

'Yes, he does one hell of a good job. He's quick; if you brief him today, you'll have those telexes on your table tomorrow morning.' Brady slapped his hand on the table demonstratively.

'How do I get in touch with him?'

'You sure your phones are cleared here?'

'No problems.'

Picking up the phone Brady dialled a local number.

'Anto Capriglo.'

'Yes, who's speaking?'

'Tom Brady, how you going Cap?'

'Good Tom, what can I do for you?' Capriglo spoke fluent English.

'I've got an assignment for you. You'll be briefed by a friend of mine called . . .' Brady hesitated. 'Mr Michael.' He winked at Berresford. 'Could you meet us down at the Excelsior Hotel in twenty minutes? I'll meet you in the foyer, we'll go up to his room and I'll fill you in. O.K. Cap?'

'Ah huh.'

'Cheers.'

'Well that's fixed. Anything else?'

'No, not yet. But I'm not sure what's going to happen next. I'm worried they'll catch on to what I'm doing. In that event, I'll have to move out of this area immediately and certainly keep away from public transport. If things get hot, could you drive me to Paris?'

'Sure thing. I'm not doing much this week anyway. Will it be this week?'

'I've got no idea. I'm just playing it by ear.'

After Brady left the room, the telephone rang.

'Hello.'

There was a slight delay and then a few beeps, and then the voice of Ian Garreau came on the line.

'That you, Michael?'

'Sure thing.'

'Everything O.K.?'

'Yes, just fine. Are we on a safe line?'

'Yes, I'm ringing from home. It's a silent line and it goes through a different telephone exchange.'

'I met a good friend of mine over here. Do you

remember a black guy, Tom Brady?'

'Big fellow, I remember.'

'He managed to put me on to a real hot shot investigator. He'll break into their accountants' offices and photograph those telexes tonight.'

'That'll be tomorrow morning, our time, Michael?'

'Yes, that's right.'

Garreau continued. 'I got the first reports back from the solicitors doing the searches today. The Turnstile directors in Tralas have directorships in a number of companies. In fact, we've come up with quite a list.'

'I suspected it. How many.'

'So far we've identified thirteen companies in Australia, which apparently have similar Turnstile share holdings and directorships. Sometimes a company secretary is a director of another and vice versa, but all in a position of power, enough to control it. Looks like we have a larger operation than we anticipated.'

Berresford had guessed that the companies would be spread out. It would take a while to know exactly where to search. If they knew that he was investigating, every door would be locked, and all evidence would be destroyed.

'Listen,' Garreau continued, 'before you left, I gave you an envelope, the contact in London if anything goes wrong. If things get hot, it's your only hope. When you read my note you'll know what to do.'

'Looks like there is no turning back,' said Berresford, his hand sweating as he held the handset.

'I'm still trying to organize the telephone scramblers. I should have them by the end of the week.'

'Ian, have you had any luck with the investigations over the car accident yet?'

'No, drew a blank. Nothing new at all. When you get the telexes, Michael, ring me then bring them home. We'll process them here, then return to Rome to piece the whole thing together. I'll go with you.'

Berresford broke in. 'I'm expecting the investigator to arrive any minute, so I'd better get clear.'

'Cheers Michael, and best of luck.'

'Thanks Ian.'

Berresford put down the phone, put his hand into his coat pocket and felt the envelope that Garreau had given him. His last hope, he thought.

Brady returned, bringing Anto Capriglo with him. He was a short, plump little man with big brown eyes and a balding head. When he spoke he smiled constantly.

'Very pleased to meet you, Mr Michael. My friend Tom Brady here tells me you've got a job for me.'

Berresford didn't like the man, but it was business.

'There is a firm called Napoli and Napoli. They are accountants.' He handed him a small piece of paper. 'Underneath are two company names. I want you to search their office and find these company's files and then photostat all the telexes and any correspondence from Turnstile Investments Limited in London. If you draw a blank, it means they probably have a master file for telexes. Usually it's kept near the telex machine.'

Capriglo was making notes.

'Take care, these are most unscrupulous people.'

'I'm used to trouble, Mr Michael.' Capriglo smiled at Berresford's impulsive display of the arcane. It was meant to impress his new client but only received an impassive grunt from Berresford, whose face soured as he considered his own encounters with Turnstile.

CHAPTER 15

Ian Garreau had never considered himself to be a man of commerce. Berresford had placed him in an invidious position: Turnstile Investments Limited probably headed a web of companies. How would he unravel the complexities? He was sitting at the small desk in his study, tapping his pen on his personal telephone book. Suddenly he recalled a face, then a name: Richard Joiner, a retired accountant. He would know whom to contact and give him an introduction.

The phone call brought immediate results.

Garreau picked up the phone. 'Hello, 787-3639, Garreau speaking.'

'Tom Crowley from Financial Services International Limited.' The voice clipped, precise, continued.

'I've just heard from Richard Joiner. You evidently want some international company searches, Mr Garreau.'

'Yes, that's true. How soon could you do a search on the companies?'

'If it's urgent, two days. If you give me the names now and indicate the type of search you require, I will telex for the information immediately.'

Garreau gave him two Italian companies controlled by Turnstile.

'I would like to find out what other boards the directors are on, not only in Italy.' He gave a list of several countries to check.

'I'll include that in my search. If you are prepared to

pay the extra, I can have it sent back by facsimile copy. It will be far more detailed and faster.'

'Go ahead,' Garreau ordered.

Meanwhile, a message was being transmitted to a memory bank in the main frame of a London computer.

Att. M. Benini —
Located Berresford's friend, Ian, known as Ian Garreau. Have just intercepted conversation between Berresford and Garreau. Berresford in Rome staying at Excelsior Hotel, has instructed private detective to break into our Rome accountants' office tonight. Garreau engaged in searching all companies. Suggest all controversial telexes in all centres be destroyed immediately.

Farwood

At 4 p.m., Benini rang the Excelsior Hotel and asked for the manager.

'My name is Bartoni. I am the manager of the travel agency which booked your guest Michael Berresford from Australia. I must protest formally that you have not given him rooms up to the standard to which he is accustomed.'

'One moment Signore, please.'

Mario Benini smiled sardonically.

The manager went hurriedly to the desk.

'Mr Berresford is in Suite 3b. That is an excellent two room suite, one of the best in the building,' he said nervously.

The manager continued. 'I am sorry, signore, all the four and five room suites are booked out and there is no record at the counter to indicate that he wanted a four room suite. He is on his own you know.'

'Very well, it had been plaguing me. Thank you for your attention. Arrivederci.'

Near midnight Benini entered the Excelsior Hotel. He walked up the first flight of stairs and looked for directions to Berresford's room. There was no light shining under it. Laughter came from down the corridor, as a young couple was returning from a disco. He used the locksmith device skilfully. In his other hand he held a small L shaped lever. He inserted it into the tumbler and turned it.

A Malaysian man walked past him towards the stairs. Benini turned away, took his car keys from his pocket and pretended to be opening the door. The passer-by saw none of his descriptive features as he bent down.

He picked the lock for the second time, turned the tumbler and opened the door slowly. The curtains had not been drawn in the living room. The bedroom would be the room adjoining. He moved stealthily across the room, testing each board with a limited amount of weight until he confirmed that it was not loose. Twice he sidestepped to avoid a squeak. Then he reached the door.

He turned the handle. The door had moved barely an inch when it started to squeak. He took a tiny spray can, slightly larger than a lipstick, from his pocket and gave two short squirts on the hinges. He wriggled the door backwards and forwards half an inch at a time before opening it fully. The sleeping man was snoring and noisily exhaling on each breath. The room was pitch black — the only light, miniscule at that, emanating through the open doorway from the living room.

Benini approached the bedside cautiously, his P38 Walther automatic with silencer attached aimed in the direction of the sleeping man. As a professional assassin, he knew how to use a bullet to kill without the victim uttering a sound.

Taking careful aim, he fired one shot. The body went into convulsions, jerked and then was still.

Benini cursed silently. The explosion had not been sufficiently silenced. He was using standard factory ammunition, and not· the custom loads which he himself made up with less powder, giving lower velocity and less sound. The short length of the silencer had also contributed to the noise. He had to move fast or be caught.

Grabbing the silencer he unscrewed it. The fingers moving deftly. Both gun and silencer were returned to the holster and pocket. In seconds people would arrive. Remembering his intelligence training, he put his hand into his hip pocket, extracting a small pencil torch which he shone on the bloodied body. Fury erupted. It was not Berresford. He gasped, 'you fucking shit' in Italian. His eyes wild with anger.

Berresford woke with a jolt when he heard the shot. He threw back the covers and raced to the end of the bed, then crept slowly over to the door to the hall and cautiously inched it open. The face . . . Berresford had seen the face before, where, where, oh God, his mind reeled, his heart thumped, he couldn't go out. That face, the figure hurrying down the corridor then out of sight. He wanted to yell out, fear gripped him, the thief who hit him in his library! The Texan! My God what's he done.

He ran to the Texan's room. The door was open. He pushed it open further, turned on the light and saw the bedroom. His mind racing, he turned on the light. The horror hit him. The man's face, or its remains, was a bloodied mess. I've killed him, he thought. Why. How did they know? My bed, he's in my bed. Good God, I've got to get out of here.

He ran back. In 3b he was safe but only momentarily. Questions would be asked. All hell would break loose. He had to go.

Within minutes he heard anxious voices. They were in 3a, the Texan's room. More running, louder noises. Berresford heard the words 'dead', 'police'; there was panic.

Berresford phoned the lobby. 'Please prepare my bill.

I've had an urgent call and must leave. Thank you.'

A car load of police arrived, raced in wild panic through the front doors, hand guns and sub-machine guns drawn. The yelling started. A woman guest was screaming in French. A drink waiter was knocked flying by the first policeman climbing the steps two at a time.

Berresford beckoned the doorman to call him a cab.

'I'm late, quick.'

'Where to sir?'

'Airport, please.'

As soon as he was safely in the taxi he informed the taxi driver that he was not going to the Airport, but to the Hotel Quirinale. He had left no message for Capriglo. He hoped he would contact Tom Brady.

The Hotel Quirinale porters were not busy and took his two cases immediately to his room. He was exhausted, shaking. The horror of the previous minutes — they seemed like hours to him — and the maniac killing gnawed away at him, images of the Texan's body, of blood everywhere. His facial expression went blank. When would the nightmare finish?

CHAPTER 16

On the other side of the city, Anto Capriglo had successfully disconnected the burglar alarm. He unlatched the lock, tripping the tumbler with a small electric device which vibrated the tiny pins until they rested in the correct places. The door opened. It took him half an hour to locate the files, which he found in one of the partners' offices on the second floor.

Plugging in a small portable spotlight, he shone in on the pile of documents to be photographed. He took the minox sub-miniature camera from his pocket and focused it on a grey card to set the correct exposure. The auto exposure would underexpose the sheets, so that manual override was essential. The electric shutter and rapid transport would make short work of photographing the documents. A tiny tripod was then unfolded to keep an even distance between paper and camera.

Two hours and many films later Capriglo stood and stretched his aching back. He hadn't rested since he had started. From the corner of his eye he caught sight of a shadow behind him. Too late. The hardened edge of Benini's hand crashed down on the back of his neck, instantly breaking the spinal cord, and causing immediate death.

Benini watched him fall; stood back, and roared with laughter. He picked up the camera and removed the films from the dead man's pockets and dragged the body down the stairs to the ground floor. He pushed through the doorway and manoeuvred it onto the rear seat of his car. Six miles away, in one of the poorest parts of Rome, he dropped the body out onto a dark corner of the street.

Back in his apartment, Benini turned on a small computer terminal, dialled a London number, connected a telephone modum, and sent a telex message to the computer main frame.

Attention A. Moffatt —
Berresford alive, whereabouts unknown. Rome break-in at accountants' office foiled, Code EL32. Telexes will be shredded and burnt tomorrow.

Benini

The room in the Hotel Quirinale was by no means the best available, thought Berresford. The bare floor boards were partially covered with an ornate carpet square. The ensuite bathroom had been last renovated some years before. But it was not the surroundings which kept him awake for most of the night. He anxiously waited for 9 a.m. when he could telephone Tom Brady.

Berresford's voice was nervous, unsteady. 'Hi Tom. Berresford here, have you heard anything from Capriglo?' His hands were sweating.

'No, I haven't and nor will you be hearing from *him* again.'

Sweat beads formed on Berresford's brow, the horror returned.

'What's happened?' he said with some alarm. '... tell me ...' he asked impatiently, but dreading the answer.

'Someone must have killed him last night. He was found in a heap in a small street in the slums, neck broken. I tell you ... these men don't give a damn about life!'

Berresford felt dolorous and responsible. What would he do now?

'He's not the only one dead, Tom. They hit a man

they thought was me at the hotel last night . . . a Texan.'

Brady sensed Berresford's feelings. 'People are going to ask questions.'

'You can bet on that. He was in my room, we swapped.'

Brady spoke cautiously. 'There must be more than company fraud involved in this . . . It's not looking good . . . Where are you ringing from?'

'Not from the Excelsior, that's for sure. I'm staying at the Hotel Quirinale, in room 22 on the second floor. I'm not using my name, I'm booked under Mr Forrest. Tom . . . I'd like to take you up on that offer to get me to Paris; . . . as quickly as possible. Is it still on?'

'Sure.'

Berresford sighed in relief. Then, after some silence:

'Tom! What do *you* think?'

'Someone is desperate to get rid of you,' came the slow reply.

Berresford sat on the bed, pushed back the covers. the face in the corridor kept flashing, those eyes and dark hair. He'd never forget the callousness of the murder. Brady went on talking.

'Michael, I've got a few things to clear up over here. I'll make it about lunch time, stay put, don't leave the room under any circumstances.'

The line went dead.

Berresford's room had become more hideous. It was not the furniture or the poor view of the youth hostel over the road, it was the lack of air conditioning. It was stinking hot. He sat on the bed facing the door and lit a cigarette. The curls of smoke rose to the ceiling. The noise of a vacuum cleaner droned from a room nearby.

Two windows up towards the street, a young couple were peering down the side street, pointing and chatting excitedly. Leaning out a little further Berresford could see the object of discussion. A small Fiat had had a minor collision with a motor bike. The man in his thirties, driving the bike, was arguing furiously with the girl in her early twenties.

'If that was my only problem,' he thought. 'Stuff Turnstile and the Von Kessel Dossier! Why does it have to be me?'

He closed the shutters, thrusting the bolts into the windowsill, and pulled across the drapes. The bed was soft and inviting, offering peace in a time of turmoil. Berresford yawned loudly. He laid his head back on the two softest pillows then cuddled the largest one, and fell into a deep sleep.

CHAPTER 17

The operations in Turnstile had been somewhat upset by the various Berresford incidents. Never had one man caused so many problems. Benini and Farwood were the subject of strenuous criticism from Moffatt. Telexes signed 'The Telex' sent out commanding messages, dictating policy and correction.

The police in Australia wanted Berresford for questioning in connection with Mrs Patterson's murder. His car had been seen outside her house prior to his telephone call to the police.

Investigations in Rome were underway into the death of the Texan. Why was he in Berresford's room? Where was Berresford? The Italian police needed answers.

On the other side of the ocean a presidential sub-committee had still not solved the problem of the multitude of corporate bankruptcies. The CIA had put its feelers out in many countries, searching for answers.

Hours passed before Brady arrived at the Hotel Quirinale. He took the lift to the second floor and knocked on Berresford's door.

Berresford awoke from a deep sleep. He dragged himself out of bed and approached the door cautiously.

'Who's there?'

'It's Tom. Tom Brady.'

Almost reluctantly, Berresford opened the door. He emitted a sigh of relief.

'If it hadn't been you, this could have been it...' he said despondently.

'Come on, come on, buck up... Get your things together. I've got the car parked just around the corner, half on the footpath,' Brady replied. He explained, 'I've discreetly checked through the agency. The police have the Italian equivalent of a Warrant of Apprehension out on you regarding the murder at the Excelsior. We'd better get going Michael.'

'Can't I rest? Let's go tonight?'

Brady's mood changed instantly. 'Get hold of yourself! You're in real trouble. I'll stick my neck out for you, but there is a limit. We must go. When we get moving you'll feel better, you can rest in the car.'

Berresford realized his error.

'I'm sorry Tom... so many things have happened... I think it's catching up with me.'

'Forget it, it's them. The last thing you want is to be cornered by the local constabulary. You'd be far too vulnerable. Press, publicity on your whereabouts, you'd be a dead duck.'

'Alright, alright.' Berresford grumbled, and dragged his jeans over his legs.

'Put on something comfortable, we've got a long way to go.'

Within minutes he was out of the Hotel. But for the rest of the day, he was sullen and unresponsive. It was not until that evening that he regained sufficient interest to enter serious conversation with his friend. They spent the night at a nondescript hotel, leaving early next morning to complete the last leg of the journey.

The monotonous drone of the car engine lulled Berresford to sleep. Tom Brady was still alert. In the distance he could see the outer suburbs of Paris. He reduced speed as he approached a blind intersection.

With his right hand he struggled with a Michelin touring map. He glanced momentarily at it, trying to ascertain his present location. Suddenly a Citroen came into view from his left, travelling at over 120 kilometres. Brady braked abruptly to avoid a collision. The offending car began blasting its horn the moment it entered the intersection. The jerking car and wailing horn abruptly interrupted Berresford's sleep.

'What was that? Where are we?'

Before Brady could answer he continued. 'How long to the airport?'

Brady did not answer immediately. He had just put a long Panatella cigar in his mouth. Removing it he spoke in a serious tone.

'Michael, you've gone through goddam hell the last few days. Why don't you rest up a bit? Stay downtown in a small hotel and give yourself a break.'

'I don't know...' Berresford replied, shaking his head. 'Maybe a stay for a couple of days will give me time to think. Your idea of staying over makes sense. Any suggestions?'

A large truck was overtaking them, its silver container glistening in the sunlight. The diesel motor roared as it changed gears; dense smoke created by the huge engine puffed into the air from the exhaust stack. Brady waited until the noise subsided. He lit the cigar he was chewing, then proceeded to think aloud.

'Now let's see. It wouldn't be smart to stay at one of the bigger hotels, they might track you down. Some of the smaller ones are pretty grotty. We need something in between. The Boulevard St Michel area, that's it. Do you know that area, Michael?'

'No, I'm lost in Paris.'

'Very close to the St Michel Station, it's in the university area. There are a number of hotels to choose from. I've stayed there myself, the first time I came to Paris. By mistake I went to the Hotel California; thought it would be a big American chain operation. The hotel Claude Bernard on the Rue Des Ecoles, it's pretty neat. I'll stop at the next public phone and check you in, O.K.?'

'Make sure it's got a bathroom, Tom. I travel light and sleep naked.'

'Sure,' was Brady's only reply.

At the hotel Claude Bernard, Berresford and Brady had finished lunch. The light conversation had not drifted back to recent events. Berresford had just ordered coffee when Brady posed the question.

'That document on Von Kessel and the bank, I would like the agency to take care of that for you Michael.'

Berresford was annoyed and emphatic. 'The hell you will, it's trouble. I would like to handle it my own way. The German copy's in the bank and safe, this translation is the only one around.'

Brady was offended. 'I'm sorry you've taken that attitude, Michael. I was only trying to be helpful. Can I have a quick look at it?'

'O.K. but no copies.'

Berresford smiled, dabbed his lips with his serviette and explained. 'If they are connected, I want control of the situation. I can't take the risk of the investigation going off half cocked.'

'O.K. Michael, let's leave it at that. But if you change your mind...'

There was twenty minutes of silence while Brady studied the document intently. He then looked at his watch and handed the dossier back to Berresford.

'If you don't mind I'll have my coffee and see about garaging my car. I'll leave it here for a few days. I'll fly back this afternoon and come back and get it next week, if you're still here I'll look you up.'

'Thanks for all you've done, Tom. I'd like to...' Berresford opened his black leather wallet.

Brady interrupted, gesturing with his open hand that money was not required. 'Enough, come on.'

After Brady had gone, Berresford returned to his room, kicked off his shoes, threw back the covers and lay stretched out on the primrose sheets. In his hand he held the battered visiting card of the German professor. It was the card that Mrs Patterson had given him before her death.

CHAPTER 18

It was the time and the place for Michael Berresford to
rest. The curtains were not drawn and the afternoon
sunlight streamed into his room. Below at street level
there was an active procession of people on the
pavement. Tourists, university students, local folk
meandered past the long array of shops.

Fleeting thoughts of recent events occupied his brain
in glimpses of reality and fiction. Faces, events, places.
Cala. Cars passing, too close — pull over! He rolled
over in bed, avoiding the imaginary car.

Half an hour passed. His eyelids began to flicker.
Someone was calling, the voice was foreign. There were
noises; unfamiliar sounds.

The maid entered the room and was surprised to see
Berresford asleep on the bed. Her apology made him sit
upright, small beads of perspiration forming across his
forehead. A shock of brown hair lay untidily across his
face.

'Yes?' He said, almost without thinking.

The attractive French girl, with her white apron
offered a brief apology. Her words were too fast for a
precise translation. Berresford endeavoured to rectify
the problem. She understood the meaning of his
gestures and left the room, quietly closing the door
behind her.

The professor's card was still lying on the bed.
Berresford picked up the telephone and called through
to reception.

The girl spoke good English. She said her name was Christine. This gave Berresford the confidence required.

'Christine, could you possibly obtain a phone number of an old acquaintance of mine who lives in Berlin? My French is not good enough to obtain the number from your French operators. Could you kindly send the bellboy up for this man's card. It gives his last address, which I believe is still current. When you obtain the number would you be so kind as to write it on the back?'

'My pleasure, monsieur.'

Minutes later Berresford had the professor's number. He calculated that it would be almost 6 p.m. in Berlin. He asked Christine to place the call.

When the phone rang back, a young female voice was answering the call, opening with salutatory remarks in German.

'Excuse me, do you speak English?' Berresford requested.

'Yes, sir. Who is calling?'

'I would like to speak to Professor...'

'I am very sorry,' she answered curtly. 'My father left here a little time ago, we have no forwarding address. He is old, sick, perhaps dead. I am terribly sorry.'

Berresford sprang back.

'Please don't hang up! The matter is urgent. I have come from Australia after speaking with an old friend of his. Your father was working, investigating in fact, some people referred to in some old papers my friend took with him to Australia. Do you know anything about this?'

The girl hesitated. She didn't speak for a few seconds. 'Your name again, please?'

'Berresford, from Melbourne, Australia.'

'Please be so kind as to leave me your number. I will ring back later, someone is at the door.'

Berresford's mind raced... It was clear to him that

the last remark had been invented. Should he give his number? Was it safe? An instantaneous response was required.

He gave her the number, the hotel and his room number.

'Please ring me back within the hour. I will be leaving shortly.'

'Yes, Mr Berresford, I will do that.'

A series of clicks followed, then silence.

Berresford paced the room. Had he exposed himself? He was being hunted, that much was clear to him. He had lit his second cigarette when the phone rang again.

'Mr Berresford?' The same young female voice on the line.

'I am calling from a public phone box, we cannot be too careful. My dear father has been persecuted. He has tried to help his old friend in Australia, who is now dead, and I believe, so is his wife.'

Berresford was surprised. How did she know? He listened intently.

'Mrs Patterson wrote my father a letter. She told him that you may contact him. When she didn't respond to his reply he made some enquiries and learnt of her death. He had already seen the signs. You were being watched and investigated. So he has left here and we admit his whereabouts to no one. He's living in Cologne, I will give you his address. I will also ring him and tell him that you will be in contact with him. He is an old man, Mr Berresford, please be kind to him, and also patient. His address is 149A Rheinalle Strasse Bad Godesberg in the city of Cologne. Best of luck.' A click and the phone was dead.

Berresford scribbled the address on the breakfast menu, the nearest bit of paper to him. A barrage of questions flew through his mind. What had he found? What was the connection? Was it possible that Turnstile was involved with the German business? Nothing was clear. He lit another cigarette, slowly inhaling the soothing smoke into his lungs, walked to the window and glanced at the street below. The view was absorbing, but offered little relief from the anxiety created by the conversation.

Within ten minutes he had booked a seat on the next flight to Cologne. The desk clerk arranged for a cab to De Gaulle Airport.

Berresford found the flight uneventful and uninspiring. The air was clear and the views below were spectacular, but they created little diversion from the thoughts of what the professor may say.

The plane bounced in three resounding bumps as it landed. A little over half an hour later Berresford had found a taxi to take him to Godesberg. The taxi driver had at first found Berresford's English unintelligible. Then he wrote the address on the back of an envelope and the driver immediately acknowledged the request.

A variety of housing designs gave an interesting insight into the quality homes in Cologne. The taxi stopped opposite a two-storey white brick villa with large timber slats stained dark brown. Vine-like creepers had attached themselves in numerous places along the brick exterior. A herringbone brick path led to the large timber front door with a sturdy chain and bell pull.

Berresford jerked the chain. A distinctive clang from the bell inside was clearly audible. A minute or so later a young man answered the door.

'My name is Berresford, is Professor Stuller at home please?'

The young man answered in guttural English, deeply soaked in a German accent. 'If you will excuse me, please wait here, I will see if he is home.'

Berresford had not dismissed the taxi. The driver was reading the evening paper, waiting patiently on the other side of the street.

A fragile old man came to the door. He was tall; but

he would have been much taller in his youth, thought Berresford. His face beamed a friendly smile as he spoke.

'You are Berresford, yes?'

'My pleasure professor.' Berresford extended his hand, which the old man took and shook vigorously.

'You have not dismissed your car already,' the old man said looking at the car on the opposite side of the road.

'Yes, that is my car.' Berresford confirmed.

'Please, we shall go somewhere else and speak. We have visitors in the house, if it pleases you.' The old man was kind and reassuring.

'Where ever you choose professor. I've come a long way to see you.'

The old man retreated a few steps and seized a walking cane from the hall stand. He pointed it towards the car, beckoning Berresford to move. 'As you people say: let's go...'

Berresford courteously let the old man take his time down the steps, across the street and into the seat of the waiting car. He hurriedly opened the rear door on the opposite side and slid into the seat.

'Where to professor? I don't speak German. Please instruct the driver accordingly.'

It was almost three miles to the quaint Bavarian restaurant. Its huge baronial doors had large black metal straps with huge bolts. Stone steps led them to a grand foyer. The old man left his stick in the cloak room and shuffled his way through another two huge doors at the other end.

A waiter in Bavarian costume courteously opened the doors and ushered them into a spacious lounge with an array of rustic timber tables and chairs, and bright red and white table cloths hung diagonally across the tables.

The old man muttered something in German. The

head waiter nodded his head in agreement and ushered them to the far side of the room. It opened on to a corridor, then another room with numerous cubicles separated by plush red velvet curtains.

'We can talk privately here, Mr Berresford.' Patiently Berresford waited for the old man to shuffle himself into a comfortable position on the cushion placed on the singular solid timber seat. Berresford sat on the opposite side of the table.

A jovial drink waiter appeared. The old man beamed a kindly smile and ordered schnapps then looked to Berresford for a request.

'Scotch, water and ice, please.'

The old man rattled the request off quickly in German. The service was prompt. The old man proposed a toast.

'To my dearly beloved friends who have passed before me, and to you, the one accepting the challenge of good over evil.'

Berresford smiled. He clicked glasses with the old man, at the same time questioning his own sanity in pursuing the problems of others. Surely he had enough troubles of his own? It was after the second drink of schnapps and the discussion on the flowers in his garden, the weather and Berresford's flight that the old man embarked on the point of the discussion.

'You have read the Von Kessel report already? You know I have a lot more to tell?'

Berresford nodded, not speaking.

He reached in his pocket for a packet of cigarettes, offered one to the old man, who shook his head in disapproval. 'But go ahead please, I have no objection.'

The waiter reappeared and he ordered more schnapps. Berresford asked for another scotch.

The old man continued. 'I received Helga's letter, sent only hours after you left her. When I wrote back I received a reply from her solicitors.'

He leaned across the table, his eyes watering as he

141

whispered to Berresford. His grey bushy eyebrows lowered and the steel blue eyes below them focused alternately on each of Berresford's eyes.

'The son Rudolf is a fanatic, Berresford. He will stop at nothing. We have uncovered a hornet's nest. I worked in Hitler's SS with your fellow director, Patterson, during the war. I have been hunted by the Jews, but never found. Yet I did them no harm. I am a pacifist, I have never been aggressive to any man. The infidel, Von Kessel, stole money from his shareholders. He bled the cash from my homeland, spirited it into the Bolshevik Revolution in Russia, and I have proof.'

He raised his voice, waving with his index finger at the ceiling. 'This son of a pig is alive in England. He has multiplied his wealth, now worth a king's ransom, and he has the help of foreign governments.'

The old man leant back against the seat resting momentarily before proceeding. Berresford leant forward. 'His name, his name. Who is he? Is he connected to Turnstile?'

'The knight is old and alive,' the old man replied, nodding his head.

The background noise, at first unnoticed, was reaching a crescendo. Through the open doors to the adjoining rooms the Bavarian singers yelled at the tops of their voices as the traditional drinking song neared the end. Berresford craned his neck out of the cubicle to catch a glimpse of the festivities. The drums rolled, the cymbals clashed, the singers shrieked 'skoll' and the band leader demolished a stein of beer to the merriment of the cheering crowd.

Berresford returned to the conversation with the old professor who had again leant back against the seat.

This time his head was resting back slightly on a timber rail in front of the curtain separating the seat behind him.

'But his name professor.'

Something was wrong with his eyes. They were set in

a glazed stare. He was staring above Berresford.

Berresford looked towards the ceiling at the imaginary point of focus. There was nothing to take his attention. The next glance to the old man's face brought him to a horrifying conclusion. A small rivulet of blood was dripping from the corner of his mouth. The man was dead. He reached over and touched his shoulder. The body slipped into the corner of the cubicle.

Berresford forced himself up the edge of the long seat and pulled back the curtains of the adjoining cubicle. Two glasses lay on the table, but it was empty. There was money on the table. He looked towards the door and saw a thickly set man passing through the large double doors.

Think! Get your wits together, he thought. He would have a lot of explaining to do. There were more important things to be done now.

Berresford had cashed some travellers cheques at the airport. He opened his wallet, guessed at the final bill. He placed the notes conspicuously on the table.

His head was reeling. His breathing was rapid, and the sweat poured profusely from the pores of his skin. Somehow, he had to leave without attracting attention.

At the main doors leading to the entrance foyer, the head waiter, not aware that Berresford could not speak German, asked him politely if anything was the matter. Berresford guessed correctly, put his hand over his mouth and patted it a couple of times, as if he was ill.

He walked through the doors and into the street. As the doors closed behind him the yelling started. The taxi cab was still waiting. Hurrying but not running, he reached it and climbed into the back seat.

'The airport, the airport!'

The driver responded. 'O.K. O.K.', to please the foreign tourist.

'Quickly please, quickly.'

The taxi set off speedily towards the airport. It was

almost midnight when he arrived back in Paris. The flight had been comfortable with little turbulence, but Berresford's mind had been plagued with the Von Kessel legacy, *'Life will never be the same again.'*

CHAPTER 19

Berresford was not anxious to return immediately to the hotel. He asked the taxi driver to stop near the St Michel station. He wanted to walk . . . and think. When would the killing end? Why didn't they kill him? Surely it would have been easy. Why just the professor? They'd tried to kill him before. These questions revolved endlessly in Berresford's mind. It was not logical. They had tried to kill him in Rome, so why not in Cologne? There was no reasonable explanation.

It was a warm night. He had memorized the direction of the hotel. Walking up the Boulevard St Michel is normally a pleasant experience for tourists, the broad street being lined with bookstores and sidewalk cafes. Perhaps because it was uphill, and he was walking with an unusual briskness Berresford noticed the sound of someone walking with a similar gait not far behind. He increased his brisk clip almost to the point of running. The footsteps behind increased too. He slowed down to a walk, the steps slowed too. He did not glance back. It was only three streets to the Rue Des Ecoles. A turn left and he would enter the street of his hotel . . . a street of hotels.

When he turned the corner, he glanced back. The figure behind was wearing a dark trench coat and a floppy hat. The face in the shadows. Berresford felt a visceral pumping. The blood surging with the adrenal infusion activated by an unconscious brain directive that the body was in mortal danger. He had already made his decision. He would not go directly to the hotel Claude Bernard, but to the hotel next door, the St Jacques. His mind racing, he struggled to engineer the safest escape.

He crossed the street. His pursuer did likewise. On reaching the hotel St Jacques he nonchalantly walked through the front door and took a seat in the foyer. His pursuer did not follow him into the hotel. So far so good, he thought. He went to the reception desk. Someone would speak English.

'Excuse me, I have an irate ex-girlfriend following me. I am staying at the hotel next door. I do not want her to know that I am staying there. Is it possible for me to go from the rear of this hotel and perhaps come in the back door of the hotel Claude Bernard?' Berresford hastily pulled his wallet out and extracted a twenty-dollar US bill. He thrust it into the hand of the clerk. 'Please . . .'

'This way monsieur.' The lad giving the wan smile of one whose cup is overfull.

It was easy, perhaps too simple, Berresford thought. Within five minutes Berresford was safely in his room. He turned on the lights. Something was amiss. His suitcase had been moved a few feet from where he had left it. The bed, still ruffled, was not the same. The chest of drawers had been moved. In the bathroom, his bag of toiletries had been disturbed. The mirror! There was writing on the mirror. 'Oh, God help me,' he moaned loudly, terror in his voice. The message was short and written carefully, the words neatly formed in straight lines.

Burn the report, return home and destroy the copy in the bank. Also your pursuit after Turnstile is futile. This is your last warning. There are others less patient.

The signature was a large V. K. Shocked and totally bewildered by the discovery, Berresford screamed his thoughts aloud.

'How in the hell could they trace me here? How could they possibly know that I placed the original in the bank? Why didn't they kill me? They tried to in Rome. Are they the same people after me? There must be more than one.' His face drained of colour, his eyes wild. He thrust his hair back with his hand in an automatic reflex. He staggered to the small refrigerator. Scotch. He threw some ice in a glass and filled it to the brim with water. The omniscience of his pursuers, that intimate knowledge, frightened Berresford witless.

'I've got to think, I've got to think,' he continued out loud. 'I'm hounded on two fronts. One wants to kill me for the dossier; the other one for my knowledge of their illegal operations. They must be separate, but the coincidence!'

His thoughts were now silent. The coincidence was one in a million. Berresford had no desire to stay in the hotel any longer. He packed his bag, then rang the cashier and asked for his bill.

The next call was to the bellboy. He gave him the money to pay the cashier. He would leave the hotel by the rear entrance and walk to the station, hopefully unseen. His thoughts became vocal again.

'And get my arse out of here!' he yelled. He was near breaking point.

He arrived at St Michel station some twenty minutes later. No one had followed him; or, if they had, he had not seen them. He took the train to the next station, then hailed a cab to De Gaulle airport. It was time to go to London. He could not give up now.

On the flight to London Berresford made a concentrated effort to discover how the assassins had found him and had tracked down the professor.

In the end there was only one conclusion. The professor's residence now occupied by his daughter and son must have been bugged.

The old man had fled to escape his pursuers, but they

had left behind unseen traps in electronic gadgetry that eventually would lead to his discovery. The phone call he, Berresford, had made would have provided them with his phone number in Paris, and the name of the hotel. The rest would have been easy. Having discovered that he was at the hotel, they would have followed him to Cologne. It was not a busy night at the Bavarian restaurant. It would have been easy to book the adjoining cubicle. The assassination was done noiselessly, a silenced low calibre bullet at the base of the skull, or perhaps a steel spike thrust into the same place. And following him back to Paris would have been a cinch.

CHAPTER 20

As the wheels touched down on the tarmac at Heathrow Airport, Berresford was aware that this was the last chapter in the saga. Good sense told him that a mistake now could mean that he would never leave London alive. Having been cleared through customs and immigration formalities he hurried to the exit.

'Where to Gov.?' The quaint little English taxi driver requested.

'A Knightsbridge Hotel. Haven't chosen one yet.'

Over an hour later the driver informed Berresford that Knightsbridge lay directly in front of him. He pointed out to the driver his interest in being near the Turnstile building. The driver knew it. A recently constructed four-storey building, it was on their right-hand side two hundred yards in front. Berresford had already made his decision. Directly opposite the Turnstile building the Sheraton Hotel towered over Turnstile and surrounds.

'The Sheraton Hotel please driver.'

This would make ideal headquarters. The building appeared familiar to him. The form of architecture and the similarity of the facade to other Sheraton hotels was apparent.

Berresford hurried to the reservation counter. His hands trembled, his eyes constantly searching the faces of nameless people. He was in the heart of enemy territory. Searching the faces of strangers with piercing eyes resulted in return stares. At last it was his turn in the queue.

'Yes sir, can I help you?' The courteous request came with a smile from the attractive assistant behind the counter.

'I don't have a reservation. What I require is a two-bedroom suite, with separate lounge, overlooking Knightsbridge.' He gestured with his right hand in the direction of the front door.

Flicking through the cards the girl confirmed that one such suite was available. It was fortunate, since there was only one suite with two bedrooms per floor.

'What floor is it?' Berresford asked anxiously.

'The seventh, sir. Is that convenient?'

'Tremendous, exactly what I want.'

'Your name sir?'

Berresford had rehearsed the answer. He would use neither of the identities provided in his passports.

'Forrest is the name. D. S. Forrest.'

The girl passed Berresford the registration form and offered him a pen on a silver beaded chain attached to the desk. Not looking up, Berresford hurriedly filled out the form. Speaking softly but clearly, Berresford asked her if he could see the duty manager.

A minute later the manager appeared at the desk. Berresford leaned over towards him.

'I have a matter to discuss of great confidentiality. Can I speak to you in your office please?'

The duty manager ushered him through to his office. The door was conspicuously marked with the notice, 'Private'. He asked Berresford to take a seat and closed the door behind him.

'What can I do for you sir?'

The clean-cut young man in his early thirties was most obliging. Berresford had a simple request, but one which was unusual. He explained.

'It is essential that my stay in London is conducted with the utmost secrecy. For reasons which I cannot discuss it is not possible to provide you with my identifying papers, but I am quite prepared to pay cash in advance, say one thousand dollars or more if you like. I have booked a suite on the seventh floor, two bedrooms.'

'How long are you staying sir?'

'Two, perhaps three months. I am quite prepared to settle cash every week, or with my cards when they arrive.' The last suggestion was a lie. Berresford could not supply any cards or papers in the name of D. S. Forrest. Garreau's words, however, were clear in his mind. *Retain maximum flexibility. Don't form habits that the enemy can follow. Pay cash in advance at hotels, continually changing the name wherever possible. You'll find this easier to achieve in American chain hotels or in small low grade hotels on the periphery of the city. To them cash is the attraction.*

The assistant manager looked at Berresford with a quizzical expression on his face.

'You're not in any trouble, are you sir.'

Berresford was emphatic, appeared annoyed. 'Of course not! I'm sure you're doing your job, but I resent that.'

The young man was quick to apologize. 'I am sorry sir, it is my job you know. It's alright as far as I'm concerned, but it will have to be confirmed with our manager tomorrow.'

'Leave a message for him and I'll ring down tomorrow morning and make an appointment to see him.' Berresford felt exhausted and looked it. He completed the registration card and handed it to the young man, then counted out a thousand American dollars in large denominations.

'I'll bring you back the receipt,' the young man said energetically, leaving the room.

On his return Berresford was told that his bags were already in his room. The duty manager offered to show him the suite.

The rooms were ideal. The second bedroom would

be required for the surveillance equipment which Berresford had yet to purchase. He would explain about the equipment to the manager tomorrow.

'I hope you have a good night's sleep, sir. We'll hear from you tomorrow.'

The young man left, closing the door behind him. Berresford turned off the light, walked to the window and drew the curtains.

The four-storey building of Turnstile Investments was almost directly opposite. From this position he could clearly see the front and side of the building. The main entrance was in sight and surveillance of both the Turnstile workforce and customers could be done at ease.

The next morning, Berresford had been observing the people arriving at Turnstile for almost two hours when the phone rang. It was the hotel manager.

'Is that Mr Forrest . . .'

Berresford was in luck. The accent positively, undoubtedly, west-coast American. On occasions like this Berresford's American accent became more pronounced than usual. He needed his fellow country-man's sympathy.

'Hello, yes, this is Forrest.'

'My name's Thompson, the hotel manager. What can I do for you?'

'I would like to meet with you, but not in your office. My employers do not want me seen at this stage. I would be greatly obliged if we could meet anytime convenient to yourself in my suite on the seventh.'

'Sure, that's no problem. My secretary is just brewing up a coffee. More like we get back home. Would you care to join me? I'll send some up and see you, in say five minutes?'

'O.K. That would be fine; it would be greatly appreciated.' As he came through the door, the manager, in his mid-forties, appeared a little overweight. But he had a round, ruddy, cheery face.

'Glad to meet you Mr Forrest. The coffee's on its way.'

'Sure, take a seat.' Berresford ushered him into the living room and pointed to the most comfortable chair. He pulled out the small table between them, anticipating the coffee tray coming shortly. Extending his hand the manager smiled.

'Please call me Brett.'

'Mine's Michael,' Berresford said, shaking his hand vigorously. The manager's smile faded. His eyes indicated that something was amiss.

'But I thought . . .'

Berresford stopped him.

'Oh yes, my initials when I signed in are not the same. This is why I want to explain. I am doing some important surveillance work for an agency. I need your permission to fill the spare bedroom with various surveillance equipment to watch people in the street below. All hush hush. My name is not Forrest but it will have to do. They are preparing new papers for me.'

Berresford spoke convincingly.

'Intelligence, I expect.' The manager beamed. Hotel life was exciting.

'Brett, I can't tell you that. If you asked me if I was CIA I would have to say no. But that might not be the answer. I need your help.'

'Don't worry about it. The money's fine. I can tell by your clothes you can afford to stay here. What else can I do for you?'

They were interrupted by a knock on the door.

'That'll be the coffee,' the manager said, streaking towards the door. Any knock, every knock made Berresford nervous. He was in the enemy camp. But his fears were unfounded this time. The coffee was placed on the table by the waiter. When they were on their own Berresford continued.

'Brett, I said I need your help. This is a covert

operation. I'll have to level with you.'

Berresford wormed in his chair.

'Is it possible to have this room serviced only by people who can keep their mouths shut?' Without giving the manager any time to answer he continued. 'The surveillance equipment I'll be using is very sophisticated. I don't want gossip to get around the hotel. Perhaps we could leave the second bedroom unserviced. There'll be less questions asked that way. The other matter that concerns me is my name and description. Could I trust your desk clerks to refuse to confirm that a person of my description is staying in the hotel? I can assure you it is essential. My life may depend on it.'

'God, do you really mean that?' The American manager was intrigued; he was loving it.

'We are really on to something, but my instructions are to work alone. So I'm vulnerable. I'll need your help, Brett.'

'You can rely on me.'

The manager poured the coffee.

'As far as I'm concerned, Michael, you're not here.'

'What about room staff, can they be trusted?'

'I'll do a little shuffling around. I've got one guy whom I've known for eleven years, well before I came here. I'll tell the others it's VIP treatment and keep him to serve your room. The one that just delivered the coffee is another one who's totally trustworthy. I'll go back and make up a list so that I can get the roster right. I can fix this easily.'

Berresford took out his wallet. 'I realize Brett that a lot of this work you are doing for me will be done out of hours.'

'No, no. I don't need that,' the manager said, shaking his head vigorously.

Berresford insisted. 'The agency pays, not me. Take it, you might have to tip the staff.'

The manager gave a broad smile. 'Michael, I like the

cut of your jib and I trust you.' He pushed the money away. 'You keep that. If it's in our country's interest, it's in my interest. It's my pleasure to help you. Tip the staff if you want, nothing for me. I'm very pleased to be able to help you. Is there anything else, Michael?'

'Let me know if anything suspicious happens, people asking questions about a person answering to my description, anything.'

The manager looked a little perplexed. 'What about the police?' He had changed his tone, speaking slowly.

Berresford decided to lie. 'They're not a problem, they're on our side.'

'I get the message.' The manager finished his coffee and let himself out. Berresford remembered Garreau's words. *Build up allies, contacts. In a crisis you'll need them.*

The conversation had given Berresford the confidence he badly needed. For the first time in days he felt relaxed. He did a tour of inspection of his suite.

The living room was eighteen by sixteen feet with a three-piece lounge suite, a coffee table, a small bar fitted with a refrigerator and shelves for glasses. The two bedrooms were much the same size, on each side of the living room. Both bedrooms had access to the hallway.

CHAPTER 21

Berresford looked at his watch and did a mental calculation.

It would be just after midnight in Australia. Garreau surely would be home now.

He wouldn't ring him direct. Garreau had given him explicit instructions as to how contact should be established if there was any doubt of his phone being traced and he knew it had. He would ring a number that was manned 24 hours a day and leave a message for Garreau. Garreau would return his call on a diverted and untraceable line.

Again fortune was with him. The hotel was equipped with direct dialling facilities, including international calls. He dialled the number. The girl at the other end answered curtly.

'Your message please.'

Berresford commenced as directed.

'Code Foxtrot Sierra Zulu. Import 1. Staying room 701 Sheraton Hotel London, opposite Turnstile. Under D. S. Forrest. Call back please.'

He gave the girl the telephone number. '999.'

This last number was his call sign. Berresford was surprised when it only took four minutes for Garreau to return his call.

The bedside phone rang. Berresford pushed back the bed clothes and sat on the edge.

'Hello, Michael. Are you O.K.?'

'I'm fine, but I've had a rough time I can tell you.'

'I have no doubt,' Garreau said emphatically. 'You have really stirred up a hornet's nest. They traced the number of the car when you visited Mrs Patterson and you are wanted for questioning in relation to her murder. You are also wanted for questioning by the Italian police in relation to the Texan's murder in your hotel. And that's not all. The West German police want you in connection with the murder of the old professor in Cologne. What in the hell's happening?' Garreau was shouting.

Berresford bounced back with equal enthusiasm.

'What do you think is happening. I've been followed and I've beaten an attempt to assassinate me. That was the Texan: he got what was meant for me. It's really getting hot,' Berresford yelled back. 'And you tell me you're excited.'

Garreau's voice softened. 'Hang on Michael, I'm on your side. But why didn't you contact me?'

'Couldn't, too risky. They've had me tapped at every move. But I'm certain I wasn't followed here.'

'Who, how many?' Garreau resumed yelling.

'Take it easy will you, Ian. I was following the lead I had on the Von Kessel Dossier which I got from Mrs Patterson. Somehow they, whoever they are, traced my call to the professor's daughter. They got him before he was able to tell me anything worthwhile.'

'I take it you got nothing on Turnstile in Rome?'

Berresford exhaled smoke from his cigarette. 'They had the drop on me. How I don't know. It wasn't sheer guess work, they tapped into our telephone calls. When can you get me a scrambler?'

'Soon.'

'There is one aspect I can't understand. They tried to kill me in Rome but they let me go in Cologne. Why? I guess there may be two parties after me. I can't be sure. In fact I just don't know anymore, and the phone worries me.'

'Hold yourself together, Michael. You'll get the

scrambler within a couple of days. The London agents can supply one as soon as I can establish a compatible code for our two machines.'

'Ian, how did you go with the additional company searches?'

Garreau responded enthusiastically. 'It's great, really great. The organization is far bigger than we ever anticipated. Heaven knows how big it is, but in Italy, Australia and London they have a string of companies. Each board controlled by them has a small number of directors in different combinations.'

There was silence for a number of seconds. Berresford thought that they had been cut off. 'Are you there Ian, are you there?'

'Yes, Michael. The more I think about that Von Kessel report, the more I want to have a look at it. How about sending me a letter over giving me authority to collect it from the bank?'

'No way, definitely not. It'll only cause trouble. You don't want to be involved.'

Garreau was annoyed. His voice became commanding as he hissed through his teeth.

'Michael, you listen to me. No one will know that I have it. I can work on it while you're busy engaged on Turnstile. Now don't be ridiculous.'

Berresford was obstinate. 'I'll have no part in it.'

'Berresford, you've being ridiculous.' It was rare for Garreau to call Berresford by his surname. 'Michael I want you to write to me and give me authority to pick it up from the bank.' He yelled. 'I'm not asking you, I'm telling you. I've done everything I can to help you, at least subscribe to this one request.'

Berresford did not answer at first. It was true: he could not have survived so long without Garreau, and he still needed his support.

'Alright, I'll post it today. I'll send it to the safe post box you gave me.'

'That's better,' Garreau said cheerfully. 'Yours is

definitely the only copy left, isn't it?'

'Yes, the only one. But I've got too much to do to worry about that at present.'

'Good idea, leave it alone. Get your surveillance equipment set up. Now you're thinking,' Garreau said with encouragement.

'What about Cala's accident? Any more on that?'

'Nothing, drawn a blank. The local police have given it considerable investigation from all the aspects you and I discussed. No, I don't think we can pin anything on anyone. It will go down as an accident, unless you can turn up something over there.'

Berresfords lips tightened. 'You bet I will.' Weary, he lay back on the bed and continued the conversation. 'The manager of the hotel is American and is very cooperative.'

'Good.'

'He thinks I'm a CIA agent and has told the staff in the event of any enquiries about me to say they have never seen me.'

'Good work. Anything else?'

'No, that seems to be it. Might give you a ring tomorrow.'

'Best of luck, Michael.'

Berresford replied despondently, 'Thanks, I'll need it,' and hung up.

Michael Berresford relaxed momentarily. He lay back on the unmade bed, his head resting on his hands. He stared at the ceiling, but the peace was not to last long. The violence of the previous days crept back into his consciousness, stirring him, causing him to leap off the bed and stride to the window.

He stared at the Turnstile building. Three people were entering it on the ground floor. Two were together, obviously; the third was nonchalantly climbing the four steps. Someone else was emerging. Berresford grabbed the narrow window sill with both hands, pressing his head against the window. 'My

God,' he said, 'it looks like Cala.'

Pangs of pain gripped him; he stared at the figure walking down the foot path. 'I must get my surveillance equipment, binoculars, a telescope.' He turned away from the window as he continued, aloud. 'I must be going mad, I'm seeing things.' But for a moment he was sure it was Cala.

CHAPTER 22

While Berresford was busily engaged in ordering surveillance equipment, one of the world's most powerful men was considering Turnstile's fate too. The supreme leader of the USSR was relaxing in the commodious living room of his apartment in Kutuzovsky Prospekt. He was enjoying a short break, having just returned from Hungary. The next meeting would take place in ten minutes in his living room. It was a secret meeting. It had to be. It concerned the most sensitive internal arrangements.

The Premier glanced around the room, furnished in unusual luxury, even for him. Many of his furnishings had been given to him by the Hungarian Government to show their gratitude for his efforts in 1956. He rose from his large padded leather chair and walked over to the cupboard, which also served as a bar. His hand hesitated for a moment and then settled on a bottle of Stolichnaya Vodka. He smiled as he took out a small drinking goblet —classical early Russian silver. It was neatly engraved on one side with a village scene. On the other side lay an engraved inscription: 'To my friend, commemorating your appointment to the Politburo. Leonid Brezhnev 11 April 1973.'

A tall, professional looking man, the Premier was known for his cultural excellence and reserved manners. He had advanced considerably in the party. Brezhnev had engineered it all. Brezhnev had carefully nurtured him through the infighting and prejudice of the upper echelons of the Soviet Government Central Committee and Politburo to eventually become his successor. As he poured the ice cold vodka into the silver cup, the Premier reflected on the words of his friendly predecessor. *We all have enemies, never forget that. The KGB will always be your strength, but beware of the military intelligence of the GRU. They have unseated premiers before.*

The GRU, or Glavnoye Razvedyvatelnoye Upravleniye, was the Russian Chief Intelligence Directorate. The Premier could remember the way his ageing leader had spoken slowly, nodding his head for emphasis as he had made the various points. Khrushchev had created the KGB in 1956 because of defections from the GRU, Brezhnev had explained. *You might think the GRU has been pushed into the background. Not so, they control the largest operation in world defence intelligence. Also they control the plan for the destruction of the western monetary system. If the Turnstile operation fails, blame them. If Turnstile succeeds, keep it close to hand, take it over if necessary. It must lie under the direct control of the KGB.*

Three distinct raps on the front door echoed down the wide central corridor leading to the entrance foyer. The Premier's three comrades had arrived for the meeting. In turn he greeted his powerful colleagues with the traditional kiss on each cheek. The president of the KGB was the first to speak.

'How was Hungary, Sir?'

'Excellent. A worthwhile mission, but I'm afraid I am a little long in the tooth for their over-generous hospitality.'

The man behind him spoke. 'A far cry from the rubbish we're being dished out in Poland.'

The Premier nodded, but did not reply. It was the third man's turn to say something.

'I am aware of the importance of this meeting,

realizing how tired you must be after your journey.'

'Yes, take a seat gentlemen. The meeting won't take long. I'm sure you have plenty of other commitments. I'm sorry the meeting was called at such short notice.'

He invited them to sit in the most comfortable seats. The Premier elected to sit on the piano stool, and proceeded to address them informally.

'Turnstile is currently manipulating 732 public companies around the world. It is successfully bleeding their funds to safe havens. As you know the GRU are charged with the duty of making sure that this is accomplished. An American, Berresford, a suspected CIA agent is close to infiltrating the operation. We must prevent him from succeeding. All credit must go to the KGB. The GRU are to muff it. You're to see to that. This is our chance to undermine the GRU. We cannot afford to miss this opportunity. Files will be sent to you. Find Berresford, use any methods to ensure the GRU don't get him first. Kill where necessary. Make Berresford the scapegoat. Make sure the GRU bungle it, then I will use my power to pass control of the Turnstile companies to the KGB. I want your best English-speaking men assigned to this task force. That's all gentlemen.'

His steel grey eyes conveyed his menacing message. 'Are there any questions?'

Each of the men shook his head. All three were despondent. The assignment was a grave responsibility.

CHAPTER 23

Tom Brady, like many CIA operatives, was plagued with an enormous pile of paper work. The morning's mail and dispatches occupied a sizeable part of his desk. Skilled in management, he had separated the important items from the others, shuffled them in order of priority, and set himself to deal with them systematically.

It was just before a lunch he had arranged with his attractive blonde secretary and he was looking forward to it. He realized the importance of a dispatch from Washington, marked 'secret'. He placed it on top of the pile. One part he read twice.

> The continuing spate of bankruptcies in the USA is currently being investigated by a select committee. It has become apparent that many of the failed companies have lost heavily to foreign countries. Speculation has arisen that it may be influenced by a powerful organization set up to disrupt the western economy. Motive could be political. All agents are to report any evidence supporting this claim. Particular attention should be given to foreign banks suspected of illegal activities.

It then detailed the method for transmission and collection of the information. He locked away his classified files and went to lunch.

Mario's restaurant was only thirty yards from the Via Veneto. Spotted white marble stairs at the entrance led to the basement level. The food was exquisite and the service attentive and friendly.

Under normal circumstances Cynthia was charming company. But her witty and entertaining remarks failed to keep Brady's mind from Berresford. No matter how hard he tried, his mind kept returning to the Von Kessel file, to the German Bank, and Berresford.

'You're not listening to me, Tom!' said the attractive young lady.

'I'm sorry, squirrel.' Brady looked up abruptly.

'I really don't think you've heard a word I've said throughout lunch.'

'I'm sorry, I've got something on my mind.'

'Another woman no doubt.'

He laughed and slumped back in his chair. 'No, no, the last thought in my mind.' Brady tapped a biro pen on the table. 'Ten million US dollars in 1917. What would that be worth by 1932, with interest?'

'You're kidding.'

'No, I'm serious.'

Her smile faded. Her agile mind went to work quickly. 'Fifteen years at say four per cent, oh say sixteen million?'

'In the hands of a clever and unscrupulous business man, what would that be worth today?'

Smiling she threw her hands back and pushed herself well back in her chair. 'Wow, you even pick my brains at lunchtime now.' Again she returned to serious calculations.

'If they were really smart and avoided disasters . . . it could compound to a billion plus, easily.'

'That's what I've been thinking. Let's enjoy lunch. You're going to have a busy afternoon typing a report for Washington.'

'The Von Kessel Dossier.' He thought aloud.

'If only I'd a copy of it. If only I knew where he was.'

'What was that Tom?'

'Doesn't matter. Let's have dessert.'

CHAPTER 24

Farwood put away his listening device. He resumed his position in the driving seat and drove the inconspicuous truck away. No further information could be gained from Garreau's phone calls. He had no further lead as to the whereabouts of Berresford. The instructions from 'The Telex' were clear.

Almost two days had passed and Berresford had not rung. Ian Garreau was not surprised. He had instructed Berresford before leaving to minimize his calls until the scrambler had been set up at either end, rendering the conversation unintelligible should the phones be tapped. It was mid-morning when he cleared the post office box. Berresford had been prompt. The authority to remove the Von Kessel Dossier from the bank had arrived.

By five o'clock the dossier had been translated and typed up in English. He returned home and was greeted by his wife at the back door. The children were playing on the back verandah. Garreau was still on holidays and Mandy enjoyed him being around the house.

'Kick your shoes off, settle yourself down in the loungeroom and I'll bring you a nice cold beer.'

'You're on,' he said as he opened the kitchen door to the hallway. 'I'm just dying to read this and I'm as dry as a chip.'

The lounge suite was old and cumbersome, yet very comfortable. He left the original in the envelope and put it on the floor beside him. The translation was clear and accurate. It took almost half an hour to read it. He remembered Berresford: Those who read it, their lives will never be the same. It was true, he thought; and it may also apply to me.

It was customary for Garreau to play with the children after dinner before putting them to bed and kissing them goodnight. But that evening he hurried through his roast duck and apple sauce, which Mandy had made especially for him.

'Mandy, I'll skip coffee. I've got an urgent dispatch to send. I'm going down to the club. I won't be home till late.'

Mandy was furious. Her remarks were cutting.

'For heaven's sake, Ian, you're on holidays. And if it's that silly thing of Michael's, leave it until tomorrow. You're not home often, haven't you got any consideration for the children? It's alright for you, I have them all day.'

'Hang on, something's come up. It's important, and it is about that document.'

'I don't give a damn about your document!'

Then he noticed that Mandy had changed before dinner. She was wearing a dress which she had only worn once before. He became conscious that she was wearing his favourite perfume. He left his chair and went round to where she was sitting, giving her a small kiss on the cheek. She lightly pushed him away. Garreau realized that she was close to tears. She had been under a lot of pressure through Berresford's ordeal. This was the kind of pressure he was used to, but it was almost unknown to her.

'Darling, I have to go. I mean, it's very important. I never realized what he had in this report. It is that special.'

The children had become silent. Both had stopped eating. Mandy burst out.

'Go on, take your damn papers! Don't come home at all tonight if that's what you want. I'm used to it.'

Garreau was already half-way to the door. He snatched his car keys from a hook on the wall.

'I'll be home as early as I can.'

Twenty minutes later he was at the so-called 'club'. The place had no telephone number which Mandy could call, nor any address that she had ever been given. He sat down and encoded to the Head of Operations in his department. When he had finished it he carefully checked the dispatch back with the original.

Michael Berresford, an American living in Australia for last ten years has located a document on one Rudolf Von Kessel. The document starts in 1932 and in the main finishes in 1944. Describes dealings of now defunct German bank, Die Drehkreuz Bank A.G. Berresford had been investigating corporate criminal activity with a company known as Turnstile Investments London, possibly a connection. I was helping him as a friend in conducting his enquiries. Have just read this report tonight. Request clearance to continue or is there mutual ground. If so await your further instructions.

On matters of such importance it was Garreau's standing orders to wait for a reply. Three hours later it came.

Document important, classified security 1. Dispatch it as per standing instructions. No copies! Attach with it detailed report of Berresford's and your activities to date. Congratulations. This will be of great service to our country. Don't encourage Berresford further, at least not until we have made contact. No doubt new instructions will come out for you shortly from my office. Heed them carefully. You will note that your counterpart referred this to higher authority. All further communication should be directed to me. Do not discuss at local level.

Then came a long code number. Garreau sat back in the

chair, turning off the complicated transmitting and receiving equipment in front of him. He whistled quietly, then chuckled to himself. 'Higher authority', it said.

'I've made it. Christ, he's got to be one off the top.'

CHAPTER 25

The second floor of Turnstile Investments Limited was busy as usual. Moffatt was most agitated. He had been forced to interrupt his discussion with Benini four times to take phone calls from stockbrokers. When he had finished he stood up and walked to the window. Without turning round he spoke quietly.

'Berresford has only one way of unearthing our operations now. That is to infiltrate this office. How this meddling amateur can upset such a large operation is totally beyond my comprehension and how such an experienced operator like you can't get rid of him is equally surprising. No doubt he'll head for London if he's not already here. Quite obviously he'll interview some of our staff. What do you think, Benini?'

Turning around, Moffatt looked directly into Benini's expressionless face.

'I agree with everything you have said.' Benini proceeded, speaking in a most cultured English tone tinged with a slight Italian accent. 'He will come near this office and endeavour to observe which staff arrive here each morning and sort out those who belong to our organization. He therefore will have to come within one hundred yards of this office. I must take up a position nearby where I can capture him. With a bit of luck I will get him first up.'

Moffatt replied. 'Since you two have never seen each other; Berresford will not know your identity.'

Benini gestured with a shrug of his broad shoulders

and parted his hands. 'That's not altogether true. He had a fleeting glance at me at his home when I recovered the telexes. I will make arrangements today to station myself opposite Harrods, where I can cover both the station entrances and the front of the building.'

'And how will you do that, Benini?'

Moffatt sniffed audibly. He could smell the after-shave that Benini was wearing.

'Money, of course, speaks all languages. If I pay enough, anyone will let me stand inside their shop. I need a good cover and full view of the street. I have already selected the place which is most appropriate.'

Moffatt frowned. His lips tightened in anger as he raised his voice in an invective attack.

'Well, do something. This fellow gives me the creeps. Follow him and fix him.' Moffatt jabbed the air with his forefinger.

Benini now asked the questions. 'How's Farwood going with his friend, Ian?'

'We know his identity. He's some sort of sleuth investigator named Garreau. He lives in Frankston.' Moffatt turned back towards the window again, and continued as he peered out into the street.

'I have ordered Farwood to eliminate him immediately. He has telexed back and informs me that he wishes to keep him alive for a day or two to intercept his communications with Berresford, particularly in order to get his present whereabouts.'

A telex was just coming in on the machine. When it stopped chattering Moffatt tore off the message. He read it and yelled with rage.

'Berresford and Garreau are now using scramblers. These boys are getting too smart for their boots. Both must go as quickly as possible, Benini. When Farwood finishes Garreau, I'll get him over here to help you.'

Benini was not flustered. His voice became soft and melodious.

'I don't need Farwood. All I need is to sight Berresford, then he's mine.'

Moffatt's index finger was pointing again. 'Now look here, Benini. We don't pay you hundreds of thousands of dollars to tell us what to do. You do as you're told. When Farwood comes, he joins the team.'

'Very well, Mr Moffatt. As you have instructed. If there is nothing else, I will take my leave.'

'That's all.' Moffatt said sharply. He moved his hand as an act of dismissal.

Benini rose and turned to the door, which he opened and closed carefully behind him. Moffatt returned to his telex machine. He sent a scathing note to Farwood to speed up his efforts to eliminate Garreau.

CHAPTER 26

Although it was still summer, a chilling north wind had brought out the overcoats and hats this evening in Dzerzhinsky Square, Moscow. The noted British defector, Kim Whiting, late of the propaganda agency 'Novosti' (a division of the KGB) and now assigned to the GRU, was just finishing his meal of caviar and smoked salmon. With him sat his superior at the GRU, General Yevgenni Ketrovranof.

Ketrovranof was a tall, ageing general, currently senior Vice-President of the Soviet Chamber of Commerce. A Soviet specialist on western business activities, he was considered to be one of the most gifted officers in Russia. Although better known for his quick wit and jovial attitude, his business acumen and understanding of western world finances was of paramount importance to the Politburo.

On leaving the officers' club the two men walked without comment across the square to the spacious headquarters building. A committee, formed ostensibly from GRU, had called a meeting to discuss 'Operation Depression'.

The two men entered a small room, whose ceiling height was almost as high as the room was long. Already seated around a large table were four other senior personnel from the GRU. The meeting was due to commence at 8 p.m. Having glanced at his watch, Ketrovanof began to speak:

'Well gentlemen, since this is a special meeting there

is no formal agenda. You have been called here today to discuss one item: the problems relating to Turnstile in London. I do not want this meeting to develop as the one we had last week did. It is important that we show our leaders that the GRU is the supreme intelligence body in Russia. The KGB can never equal a project like "Operation Depression", by virtue of which we are well on the way to destroying the western monetary system.'

Ketrovanof's large hairy hand thumped the table repeatedly. 'Our second objective, the Siberian gas pipeline, is under construction and ahead of schedule. We are ready to set the OPEC parties warring with each other in the Middle East in a way that will totally destruct all Middle East oil supplies. But not before our pipeline is finished. Our control of energy supplies in Western Europe gives us the power to create higher fuel prices. Nothing must be permitted to stop the plan. So please forget your personal prejudices and get down to facts. Comrade Kovoski, the GRU's most decorated officer, will now address you on the latest developments concerning the problems associated with Turnstile, London.'

'Thank you Comrade.' Vladimir Kovoski was a man of small stature. He had thick black hair which swished over his eyebrows and which gave him a haunting appearance. He proceeded.

'Gentlemen, for some considerable time now we have been watching the activities of Turnstile in London with interest and satisfaction. They have contributed greatly to the downfall of the western monetary system. You must see that nothing impedes the progress that has been gained to date. Intelligence reveals that an American, Michael Berresford, is apparently in England with the sole purpose of discovering the extent of operations of Turnstile and of "The Telex". He has an early German file which we must recover and destroy since it could link the USSR to the knight. It is

174

for this sub-committee to consider immediately what measures we should take to eradicate this imbecile. I would like to recommend that the GRU handle it in our usual way. Our operatives are already stationed in London and ready to eliminate him on sight.'

Kovoski's voice screeched; his fist was clenched as he continued. 'Two, we believe that it would be in our best interest to use our top men in the GRU to back up "The Telex" in the event of Berresford being able to infiltrate Turnstile. For this we would look to you, Mr Chairman, to kerb interference from the KGB, particularly the first chief directorate in the Special Operations V.'

Whiting sprang to his feet. 'Mr Chairman, don't you think that the hit should be carried out by the KGB?'

Someone yelled, 'You idiot!'

Another voice called out, 'You western pig.'

Ketrovanof raised both hands in a gesture to stop all arguments.

'Gentlemen, please! I have already made it clear. I want no discussion as to which agency is to carry out this work. This is ours.'

He thumped the table. 'The GRU is all powerful ...' his voice rose and cracked on the last word. 'I believe at this stage the GRU has a free hand to handle this matter the way we think fit. We can't let the KGB get in on the act. Are we agreed on this course of action?'

All hands were raised. The Chairman continued. 'Then it is agreed.' He turned his eyes towards Whiting. He had little regard for the traitor. As they rose the rubbers on the legs of the chrome chairs squeaked around the room. They filed out the door one-by-one into the cold Moscow air.

CHAPTER 27

Berresford had chosen a firm dealing in both surveillance equipment and photographic equipment. He proceeded to ring them.

'I'm interested in buying a quantity of surveillance equipment. I will be able to sign a declaration to say it won't be used in the UK. And I would like some of your brochures, please. If you send them to my hotel straight away I will give you an immediate order. I want delivery this afternoon if possible.'

Twenty minutes later a courier arrived with the brochures. Berresford carefully studied the vast range of equipment available. The first item he chose was a telenight vision device. The brochure read: 'All in all, on the darkest night, with only starlight or a distant street lamp providing illumination, this device would give the appearance of daylight.'

The next item he chose was an electronic calculator-transmitter. This looked like any other ordinary calculator; but, according to the brochure, 'It is fully operational, therefore completely inconspicuous. The built-in electric microphone can pick up even the faintest whispered word and is powered by built-in calculator batteries.'

Berresford lit a cigarette and studied the brochure carefully. He then chose a pocket-size transmitter, and also a seven inch surveillance special telescope, with matching tripod and camera adaptor, which Garreau had recommended to him. Finally he ordered what the brochure called 'The Infinity Tele Ear'.

He perused the instructions and read, 'This device remotely monitors all sounds and voices at any location where there is a telephone nearby. The unique circuitry utilizes the existing telephone system, with very little modification, so that it can be controlled from, and transmitted to, the telephone which you are calling from — no matter where in the world you happen to be. After installation you can listen at anytime and from anywhere with no fear of detection.'

The equipment arrived late that afternoon. Berresford was pleased with his purchases. He was also alarmed at the ease with which this most sophisticated equipment could be bought.

For the first time in days he was enjoying himself. He set up the surveillance equipment and tested the results. It was still far too light to test the night telescope. However his daylight seven-inch telescope was excellent. The image was clear and the objective could be viewed and photographed at the same time.

It was half past five. Most personnel would have left the Turnstile office, he thought, as he peered through the telescope. Four men filed out one after the other, each carrying a briefcase. He adjusted the focus to get a clear image of their faces, and photographed them in rapid succession. He peeled off the polaroid sheets and returned to the telescope to see if there was any further movement. Over the next half hour, no other people were seen leaving the building.

For an amateur he was very satisfied with the quality of the pictures. He intended to photograph every person entering the building for several days. Garreau's advice had been clear: *The photos will help you separate clients from staff. Pick your mark, then infiltrate.*

Berresford looked at his watch. It was almost 9.00 p.m. No one had left the building after 5.45. His eyes were growing tired from the continued surveillance of the Turnstile building. Pedestrian traffic had eased greatly but the motor traffic down Brompton Road through Knightsbridge was still very busy. Perhaps now is the time to check out the Turnstile offices he thought. There was no indication that anyone was watching the building. He grabbed his jacket, hastily locked the door and started for the service lift.

When the lift stopped he made his way to the loading bay, which led him through the rear of the hotel to small lanes which criss-crossed their way to the streets east of Sloane Street. The smog dimming the evening light, he strolled along the pavement a little more slowly than usual so as to familiarize himself with the local geography. A cold wind had arisen, sending a chill through his lightweight suit.

The back street was one-way because of its narrowness. He walked a short distance and then turned left into Harriet Mews. A few hundred yards further he turned right into Harriet Street which took him to Sloane Street. He started to walk faster now, glancing into an occasional shop window just as tourists would.

He walked casually past the many shops and headed in the direction of Brompton Road. This he crossed and turned to the right. It led him straight to the Turnstile building in Knightsbridge.

There was still a number of people about, yet no one appeared to be taking any interest in him. He walked towards the entrance to Knightsbridge station, then turned right and walked past it.

A thickly set man in his mid-forties, wearing a light fawn gaberdine coat, was standing in front of the shop opposite him, reading a newspaper. He stared intently at Berresford when he walked past. Berresford shuddered. Had he been recognized?

He decided to continue walking. A hotel loomed up in the foreground. In the foyer, he turned and looked over his shoulder. The man in the gaberdine overcoat was following him.

A passage led to a small bar where there were a number of people. Berresford was near panicking, but he forced himself to remain calm.

The man made his way to the other end of the bar. Their eyes met. When the drink arrived Berresford drank it in two sips. He then left the bar, walking slowly at first towards the main door. He would not go to the Turnstile building now.

When he reached the first intersection he ran the first few steps to the pedestrian bay in the centre of the road. And then, without waiting for the lights, in the next break of traffic, he crossed the road. He reduced his pace and retraced his steps down past the shops in Sloane Street, occasionally glancing at the displays. His heart was pounding, his skin tingling with the surge of adrenaline through his body.

One window reflected the street behind him. The thick set man had also stopped, purportedly to light his cigarette. Berresford started off again. In panic he bumped into an elderly couple; he apologized and hurried down the pavement, crossed several more streets, then stopped outside a quaint old restaurant. He needed time to think. He went inside.

To his surprise the restaurant was much larger than anticipated. Steps rose to a mezzanine floor. He walked up them briskly, noting that it was sparsely occupied. A waiter approached.

'Table sir?'

'Yes, please. I'd like one somewhere near the balcony where I can look down into the street.'

'On your own, sir?'

'Yes, a small table please.'

The waiter chose a table from which Berresford could observe the front entrance. The man would have caught up to him by now. But no one seemed to have followed him in.

Then he saw it: part of the gaberdine overcoat in a doorway over the road. He left the table and retreated

179

down the steps, to the rear of the restaurant in the direction of the toilets. An unmarked door closed the end of the passage. When he reached it he cautiously looked over his shoulder, but no one was in sight.

The door opened to a storeroom, then into the kitchen. A chef's assistant came out.

'You looking for the toilets?'

'No, I'm trying to find the back door. An old buddy of mine just arrived, and I owe him some gambling money.'

The chef's assistant was fat and jovial. He laughed and pointed to a white door.

'That leads you to a narrow lane behind. Follow it down two hundred yards, make two left turns and you're back into Sloane Street.'

'Thank you very much. I hope I can do the same for you one day.'

His mind racing, Berresford sprinted down the narrow lane. When he reached the end he turned left towards a street lamp which illuminated the next intersection. He kept up the pace until he reached it. He slowed for the last few steps in order to turn left again. A tall building obscured his view of the street around the corner and it was not until he was on the corner itself, to his horror, that he saw his pursuer six feet in front of him.

The stocky man reached into his pocket. He withdrew a pistol as Berresford hit him in the chest with his shoulder. The two crashed to the ground. Berresford grappled with the hand holding the gun, forcing it away from him. His assailant tried to gouge his eyes, but his thick, strong fingers fell short as he lifted his head back. He thrust his knee over the stranger's arm, holding the gun, and then delivered a forceful punch with his right fist to the man's temple.

The attacker succeeded in rolling and throwing Berresford off him. Berresford sprang to his feet and dived on him. The full weight of his body was transmitted through his knee into the attacker's back. The man's ribs cracked, accompanied by a scream of pain.

'You son of a bitch,' Berresford yelled as his hands grabbed for the gun. He spun the man around, thrusting his right elbow into the man's throat. The injured man reeled back and dragged Berresford with him; then his knee crashed into Berresford's groin and sent him flying onto the ground. The two men struggled face to face. And then Berresford felt the gun, twisted it and it exploded. The attacker collapsed in a heap, muttering something in a foreign tongue. Berresford panted.

'Who sent you after me, who do you work for?'

The man replied with great difficulty, spitting blood as he spoke. 'Cannot escape, there are many of us, we will get you.'

'Who's we? You mean Turnstile? Who's we?' Berresford yelled again.

In a low guttural accent the man replied. 'Nor...nor. They won't get you...amateurs.'

He then gurgled and his head dropped. Berresford could see that he was dead. He became aware of the sound of running feet, and of the shrill scream of a bobby's whistle, as he started to run towards Sloane Street.

CHAPTER 28

In the next few days Berresford tried to establish records of the employees of Turnstile. Recording their time of departure on the back of each photograph gave him an accurate picture. However, clear pictures could not be obtained for all of the personnel of Turnstile Investments. The camera angle was such that they had to face him at the right moment. This was one problem which he had not yet overcome.

He was contemplating this when the phone rang. It was the bell captain's desk. There was a letter for him.

'Bring it up please.'

He gave the boy a tip and opened the envelope. 'Ah, Garreau' he said aloud. Inside there was a covernote and another envelope.

Garreau's covernote stated that he had forwarded Berresford a pistol with silencer and attachments. Berresford should be able to collect them at the customs desk that day. Garreau had ingeniously hidden them in two large ingots of silver-lead-zinc conglomerate. He had described them on the manifest as ore samples for metallurgical testing.

Berresford threw the unopened envelope aside and returned to the window and the telescope. The Turnstile building appeared to be empty. There were no lights shining on any of the floors. It was now 8.30 p.m. Perhaps Turnstile officers did not work after hours, but he was puzzled that there were no cleaners.

The telephone rang. He immediately turned on the

scrambler when he heard the pips for long distance.

'Hello, are you there, Michael?'

'Yes, Ian. coming in very clearly. How are things progressing?'

'Good. I'm now talking from my car via my new radio car telephone. Obviously you've got your scrambler on. Neat isn't it?'

'Makes me feel more secure.'

'What have you been doing?'

Berresford went on. 'I've got all my surveillance gear set up, as you suggested.'

'Don't say anything, Michael, that could give any indication as to where you are. And, please, under no circumstances mention the name I gave you in that envelope. Have you read it?'

Berresford put his hand in his hip pocket and removed the envelope. 'No I haven't had need of it yet.'

'Well read it tonight and destroy it. Don't forget to memorize it as it is the password to this person.'

Berresford decided to read the letter directly after the telephone call.

'Where are you ringing from?'

'For safety I've moved down to my holiday home at Phillip Island. I am parked on top of a cliff with visibility for some seven or eight hundred yards in all directions. These people are professionals and I'm taking no risks.'

'Are you on your own?'

'No, I'm only one thousand yards from my house, I can see it from here. I've got two other ASIO operatives from work staying with me to be on the safe side.'

As their conversation continued a dark blue Mercedes edged quietly up the road and halted in some trees about fifteen hundred yards from Garreau's car. Farwood turned off the scanner-receiver tuned in to Garreau's conversation with Berresford. He was greatly irritated with Garreau employing a scrambler. He had gone to considerable trouble to acquire a receiver to match the frequency of Garreau's new radio phone.

He made sure the car would be ready for a quick escape. He removed a pair of binoculars from a leather case. He then opened the glove box and took out a small transmitting device. He crept through the trees and grass, to a place where he could safely observe Garreau, and focused his binoculars on the car. He could see the driver but not clearly. Garreau had the telephone headset against his ear.

Putting the binocular strap around his neck, Farwood removed the small transmitting device from his pocket and pulled out the aerial. He looked through the binoculars again. Garreau was still speaking.

He placed his finger over a small silver button and abruptly touched the 'on' switch. Berresford was cut off in the middle of his sentence. There was an enormous bang, and then a series of beeps.

Berresford panicked. He disconnected the scrambler and then frantically searched his pockets for his personal telephone book. Then he remembered that he did not know Garreau's holiday phone number. There was nothing he could do.

Having got himself a drink, Berresford read Garreau's letter.

Below is the name of a man from whom you can enlist help if things get desperate. He works as an investigator in the Internal Revenue Department in London, under the name Nicholas Wood. That's where he can be contacted during the day. The method of contact is by telephone. Ask him where you could meet and talk about some important business. No doubt he will want to meet you in a fairly open place where there are plenty of people. When you meet him say only two things. They must be whispered in his ear. First say the words 'Garreau', and 'Khomenko'. He'll probably look at you with shock. You should then go on to say: 'the only place to discuss this will be in private and I'll leave it to you to choose the place.'

I give you his background for when you keep the second appointment. He is forty-two years of age, born in Moscow. His mother was Hungarian. On a visit to see his relatives in Hungary, they were caught up in the 1956 Hungarian Revolution and forced to escape to Holland. They eventually came to Australia. I recruited him for ASIO. He stayed in Australia between 1956 and 1973. Now he is our executor, when our National Security is threatened in the UK. Tell him these words exactly: 'In whose hands there is iniquity, whose right hand is full of bribes.' He will ask you which hand, which foot. You answer by touching his right hand only, nothing more. Any mistake and he will kill you.

He will do anything you want, kill if necessary. Never underestimate him. Now burn this. Best of luck old buddy. If you need to use Khomenko you must be in big trouble.

Sincerely
Ian

Berresford's hands were trembling. Recent events were taking a hard toll on his whole nervous system. Yet, he would not turn back.

Someone was knocking. He opened the door to his suite and the waiter brought in his dinner.

'What shift are you on tomorrow, John? I see that your name is John from your tag.'

'I am on the same shift as today, Mr Forrest. Start at two p.m.'

'Would you like to earn fifty pounds by doing a small job for me?'

'I most certainly would,' beamed the waiter.

'These papers provide the information necessary for

a customs clearance on three parcels coming in from Australia. Do you have a car?'

'Yes I have a small Austin.'

'These three items will be rather heavy. If you could collect them tomorrow morning and bring them back to me. Oh yes...on the way back please call into a hardware store and get me a two-inch chisel and a hammer.'

The waiter understood. 'I'll have the parcels back to you before lunch.'

Berresford gave the waiter the papers and counted out ten five-pound notes.

'Oh by the way, if they query the three parcels, tell them the silver-lead-zinc sample is of no commercial value. If they wish to take a small sample for testing they are welcome.'

The next morning Berresford showered, shaved and dressed in casual clothes. The sky was clear and it looked like a warm day. He adjusted the focus on his telescope to a jogger who had arrived at the entrance to the Turnstile building. Shortly afterwards two other well-dressed business men arrived dressed in pin-striped suits, then half an hour later a stream of men and women entered the building. When one person came into focus his heart nearly stopped. He shakily adjusted the focusing device and exclaimed 'My God, it looks like Cala!' As he spoke aloud he caused the eyepiece to fog up. Was he going mad? This was the second time that he had seen her. He rubbed the eyepiece with his shirt end but she had gone. Once again he spoke aloud, trying to reassure himself.

'I'm fine,' he said, 'it's just a crazy coincidence.'

But the girl reappeared as the staff streamed into the street to take their lunch hour. The impact sent intense shivers down Berresford's spine. He could not see her face, but from the back, with her hair, head, clothing, she looked remarkably like Cala.

He noted that at one o'clock four men filed out. Two of them were the very same ones who had arrived before the staff in the morning. He photographed them again. Already he could see a pattern. He could offer no explanation as to why the four business men arrived before the staff. But he was sure of one thing: one of the four leaving at one o'clock, although he was now dressed in a pin-striped suit, was the jogger.

He ate his lunch while watching the Turnstile building.

It was almost 2.30 p.m. when the girl appeared again on top of the steps. He zoomed in for a close up, focusing carefully. His face drained of colour. He whispered.

'It's Cala, they've got Cala!'

Through the focused telescope he could see her face. Yes, they were her clothes. His heart raced madly, his mind became a whirl. He could no longer think rationally. He ran to the door, slamming it behind him. Curious guests stared as the man, running wildly, pushed past them on his way to the lift. On reaching the foyer he ran through the doors and tore off like a madman down the road in the direction he had last seen her taking.

A green double-decker bus driver honked his horn as he braked to avoid the sprinting man crossing the road. He could see her: she was one hundred and fifty yards away, walking towards the railway station entrance. He increased his pace, and one hundred feet from her he excitedly called her name.

'Cala, Cala!'

Berresford fought to understand how it could have happened.

'Cala . . . Cala!'

On the last few steps of the railway entrance he reached forward to grab her on the arm and swing her towards him.

The girl had not responded to his call. Her face

187

showed fright and surprise. She stared at him. The man appeared to be in shock. His eyes told it all, there was disbelief, surprise, untold disappointment written all over his face. Gently she wormed away and released his grip on her arm.

Berresford, short of breath, stammered. 'You, you must think... must think I'm mad. I thought you... my dead wife.'

He cast his eyes downwards and wiped his sweating forehead with his forearm.

'I'm terribly sorry, it was your hair, clothes, build, but most of all your face. You could have been twins, please forgive me.' She suddenly felt kindly disposed to him. 'Don't worry.' She smiled compassionately. 'It's probably the hair, the cut is very popular. And I suppose she shopped at Jaegar?'

'Yes she did!' Berresford said softly. 'We were here some months ago.'

'Come on. I'm on my way to the post office. Walk with me, you may feel better talking to someone.'

She took an instant liking to him and in any case she preferred fellow Americans. Taking his arm she started walking towards Harrods en route to the post office. Berresford, still bewildered, slowly regained his calm. The couple crossed the busy road at the intersection, intermingling with the crowd of shoppers in Sloane Street.

'My name's Sarah, Sarah Standford.'

'I'm Berresford, Michael Berresford. Sorry I gave you such a fright. Cala my wife was killed in a car accident a few weeks ago...' Silence. 'I'm not a crackpot, you are very alike, well at a distance anyway.'

The resemblance was remarkable and the girl was delightful, quite a change from the harshness that the world had shown him in recent weeks. Suddenly he had to remind himself of the dangers that existed walking the streets in an area so close to Turnstile. He shivered at the thought.

Benini had secured a position in a small jewellery shop behind the security of a plate glass window. One hundred pounds a week cash in the pocket of the proprietor had made it possible.

Benini was becoming bored after two days of standing and looking. There was little to keep his attention. Suddenly, his eyes caught sight of the very attractive young lady who worked in Turnstile's office. She was walking down the street on her way to the post office. As usual his thoughts were perverted.

The rapid movement of a man running down the street towards her caught his attention. Berresford! His hand dived into his coat pocket and fastened securely around the butt of his gun. His left hand patted the other pocket. The silencer was there. What were they talking about? She had taken his arm, and they were moving away.

As slippery as an eel moving through the water, Benini crept to the jewellery shop's front door. He opened it and quietly slipped into the street. He merged into the crowd of tourists and shoppers, never taking his eyes off the couple as they walked some hundred yards ahead. He surmised that they had spoken before and that she was working with Berresford. He's probably fucking her, he thought.

Benini found a small lane way. He needed cover for a few moments. It was clear of people. Quickly he removed the silencer, and screwed it to a nine millimetre automatic pistol. He eased it back into the pocket of his three-quarter length coat, which had been altered for that very purpose. His hand gripped tightly around the butt. He clicked off the safety catch with his thumb and quickened his pace in order to catch up to the couple.

Benini weaved his way through the crowd and unbuttoned his coat in readiness. He adjusted his gait to match theirs, using the people in front as a cover. Benini crept forward. His first shot would be through the middle of the girl's back, the second one through Berresford's chest.

There were many jewellery shops in Knightsbridge. The one they were passing had some extraordinarily large diamonds on display.

'They hardly look real at that size, do they?' said Berresford.

'They're pitched at the Arab market, you know. This is the place where most of the diamonds in London are sold,' she answered.

Berresford glanced at the window and suddenly he caught a reflection in the glass cabinet. He froze. That face! He could see the bulge in Benini's coat, pointing towards the girl. There was no time.

'Look out Sarah!' he yelled.

Berresford slammed his body into Sarah, sending her crashing into the doorway of the shop. Then he threw himself at the assassin, grasping him below the knees. At the same instant there was a loud explosion as Benini's first shot missed and smashed through the window, shattering the thick plate glass onto the pavement.

Berresford hit the pavement and rolled violently away from the killer. Benini tried to use his free hand in an attempt to break his fall, but he tripped over a small girl and landed on her little brother. The children screamed.

Before Benini had recovered, Berresford had grabbed Sarah by the arm and crawled frantically through the open shop door. He slammed it shut, then pulled the lock release and retreated to the back of the shop.

'It's a robber. Police, police,' the little shopkeeper screamed. As he pressed a hidden button, an incredibly loud siren began wailing.

Berresford and Sarah threw themselves on the floor behind a small counter. The shopkeeper had likewise thrown himself on the carpet without really knowing why.

Benini was desperate, furious. How had Berresford seen him? He had to escape before the police arrived. He sprang to his feet and sprinted down the street, crashing between the bewildered shoppers. He reached a corner and reduced his pace to a brisk walk. A small alleyway led off the street. At the back of a restaurant he found some large trash cans. Turning his overcoat inside out, Benini stuffed the gun into the can, removed his gloves and put them into his pocket. On regaining his breath he left the lane and strolled nonchalantly towards a vacant taxi.

The pale old jeweller lay terrified on the floor behind the counter. An old man with a hooked nose and sunken eyes, he had a small pistol trained on the door, with his elbows resting on the floor. Both hands holding the gun shook uncontrollably.

A small crowd had gathered around the window outside. The shrill scream of bobby whistles could clearly be heard, intermingled with the sounds of children crying and of excited conversation. Berresford put his hand on Sarah's shoulder. He spoke softly but urgently.

'I'll see if the coast is clear. We've got to get out of here! ...quickly.'

Hysterically she replied in a loud whisper. 'Police, police, get the police!'

Berresford was annoyed that he had to explain. He didn't want the shopkeeper to hear. He hissed through his teeth. 'I can't, we can't, we've got to leave now.' With that he struggled to his feet, dragging her by the arm.

'Stay here,' he told her. He went to the door. The small crowd had formed a semicircle around the broken window. A bobby was inspecting the damage. Berresford looked carefully in all directions. Benini was gone. Beckoning Sarah with his finger he unfastened the lock. Sarah came obediently to his side.

She whispered to him, overemphasizing her words with her lips.

'We've got to tell the police.'

'No,' he said harshly.

Sarah responded scornfully. 'What sort of a person are you if you can't go to the police?'

Berresford's eyes narrowed. He was furious. 'What sort of a person are you to work for a murderer?'

Sarah's eyes widened. Her mouth opened, and her hand covered her lips in a gesture of surprise. 'The man, of course: Benini!'

Berresford responded emphatically. 'I don't know who the hell he is but he's tried to kill me before and I know he killed a Texan in Rome. Let's go,' he commanded.

'I still . . .'

He opened the door and pushed her into the street. A policeman's hat towered over the crowd. He pushed towards Berresford and Sarah. He had a strong Lancashire accent. 'You stay 'ere, no witnesses leave until 'eadquarters men arrive.'

In his best American accent Berresford replied, 'I'm sorry, we're American tourists, we saw nothing, and we have no intention of staying.' With that he pushed his way through the crowd, dragging Sarah by the arm.

Everything had happened so rapidly. Berresford was grateful for Garreau's tuition. He knew what to do and his decisions were reached quickly. The Hotel was less than five minutes away. It was essential to go in the opposite direction at first and then to double back through the back streets to the rear entrance.

'Walk as fast as you can without running,' he insisted. The hee-haw of the police car sirens drew closer.

Sarah still pleaded. 'Please let me go to the police.'

Berresford was sharp. 'You can't. I'll explain later.' She stopped. Grabbing her arm even tighter he pulled her after him. She whined. 'You're hurting me . . .'

'For God's sake woman, it's your life I'm saving.'

She stopped protesting. Intermingling with the crowd they hurried to the nearest corner, and then turned to walk briskly down the side street, which was less crowded. He remembered Garreau's words: *Stay in the crowd as much as possible. Move at their pace. Do what the man in front does, be natural.*

Periodically they stopped whilst Berresford surveyed the street. He knew what to look for. The terror was still alive. He increased the pace.

'Michael, can't we take a rest now?'

'Not yet.'

They reached another corner. A grubby old man was pushing a dilapidated wooden cart piled with used newspapers. They skirted round it, momentarily stepping off the pavement onto the road. Berresford took a quick look over his shoulder. 'I think ... we're being followed,' he whispered, desperation in his voice.

Less than two hundred yards behind him, two men dressed similarly to the one who had attacked Berresford two nights before were running down the street in their direction.

'Run Sarah, run down here!' Berresford screamed, turning off the street.

Sarah pursued Berresford down the narrow deserted lane. One hundred and fifty yards further the lane ended, turning right into a narrow service lane. If they reached it they'd be out of sight. Sarah was panting wildly. The uneven pitches made her running more difficult.

She yelled. Berresford turned. She was several yards behind.

'My shoe, I've broken my shoe...'

Her uneven gait was slowing her down considerably.

'Throw them both off, we can't stop,' he screamed at her. She was running faster now, the rough pavement tearing into her stockinged feet. Their pursuers had turned the corner, and were now sprinting in inexorable pursuit.

'Only twenty yards to go,' he shouted. The first bullets whistled past, missing their target and hitting a brick wall at the end of the street with a resounding twang. Berresford slowed down slightly. 'Get in front of me, Sarah, quick!' He kept behind her, protecting her from the assassin's bullets.

A new sound joined the clap of running feet. A powerful motor bike, Berresford thought, its motor urged in fast acceleration.

'Four yards now...' he yelled.

Too late. The first bullet hit him somewhere in the back. He felt his muscles and cartilage tear away. The second bullet hit him as he dived to the ground in the upper right leg. He tumbled over and hit the ground. It was crawling distance to safety.

The new assailant, on a powerful black motorbike, was dressed in black leather with matching helmet and smoked visor. In his hand he held an instrument of death, aimed six feet from the first pursuer. There was an enormous explosion as flames, stretching fifteen inches, ejected from the short barrel. The man's distorted head hung limply over on one side, blood gushing freely. The second pursuer turned his gun on the black jacketed attacker. The bike was now heading straight at him. He fired wildly at the bike rider. The shots, nowhere near their mark, careered into buildings further behind. With another enormous explosion, the rider's powerful .44 magnum projectile ripped into his flesh where arm meets shoulder, almost severing it from the body. He screamed in pitiful agony. The rider braked, turned and charged again. His next shot exploded into the man's chest, ripping it open.

By now Berresford had struggled to his feet. Sarah came to his aid, putting his good arm over her shoulder.

'Come on, Michael. Try... walk.' She was hysterical. They struggled and hobbled down the service lane,

which lay behind a number of old terraces. Berresford
was in excruciating pain; but was driven on by self-
preservation. Sarah was crying uncontrollably but she
still managed to drag Berresford down the lane.

The sound of the motor bike came closer. It had
reached the entrance to the tiny lane. Two steel vertical
posts obstructed the motor cyclist from pursuing them
on the bike. Sarah glanced around. He had a gun in his
hand. As she looked he lowered it, and the bike roared
off and out of sight in a split second.

Shock was setting in. Berresford yelled loudly.

'Come on. We've got to get to the back of the hotel,
the Sheraton Hotel.'

Sarah sobbed as they scuttled off. 'Give yourself up
Michael. You've, you've got to get to a doctor.'

Berresford insisted. 'Back of the Sheraton Hotel, only
a few hundred yards ... got to get me there.'

They reduced their pace to a slow walk, as they
reached the rear of the hotel. Berresford's shirt was
soaked in blood. A large red patch had developed on his
jumper, in the region of his shoulder. A bright red
streak had also appeared down his trouser leg, spilling
over his socks and into his shoe. Sarah had ceased
arguing. The dramatic impact of the last hour had
numbed her senses and she was content to follow
Berresford's demands.

Painfully Berresford struggled up some small steps.
They made their way to the service lift. As the lift door
opened two women in their fifties, members of the
cleaning staff stood aghast.

'What's happened,' they said, eyes staring.

Berresford was quick to reply. 'I was mugged down
the lane, stabbed with a bottle. I'm going to my room,
nothing serious.'

'Are you sure? I'll get a doctor.'

'No. I'll get one shortly, don't worry.'

The lift stopped on the seventh floor. Sarah was still
silent, except for the occasional whimper and sniffle.

On reaching the door Berresford fumbled for his keys, but he couldn't get the key in the keyhole. Sarah took it from him and let him inside. Berresford collapsed on the couch, barely conscious. Sarah pulled up his jumper and shirt and inspected the wound.

The bullet had penetrated the flesh under his right arm. It had cut its way cleanly through the flesh of his shoulder. Sarah was relieved. 'Michael, I don't think it's done any serious damage. Where did the other one hit?'

'Nicked my bum.'

Sarah removed his trousers. The second bullet had cut a clean flesh wound on his buttock. Her red swollen eyes caught his, and she sighed deeply. 'I think you're going to be alright, Michael, but you'll need a doctor. You saved my life out there ... I owe my life to you.' She started crying again.

Although in pain, Berresford forcefully took control again.

'Come on, pull yourself together Sarah. I'm going to need your help. And promise me one thing, if I pass out for God's sake don't leave. I want to tell you everything, I'm not a criminal. I've done nothing to be ashamed of, but there are those out there who want to kill me. Now they want to kill you too.'

The legacy of the Von Kessel Dossier had never been more apparent. The old lady's words rang in his ears. And now he knew that however he might wish otherwise, those words applied to Sarah too.

The occupation of cutting up the sheets into makeshift bandages restored her calmness. She looked at him thoughtfully.

'Michael, I've had a thought. I know an army doctor, a close friend. He could help you. He's treated these sort of wounds before and I'm sure I could rely on his discretion in not reporting it to the police.'

'O.K. Ring him, the pain's killing me. Before you do, would you kindly light me a cigarette. They are on the bedside table in my bedroom. I have to explain to you about Turnstile.'

When she returned, Berresford had already passed out.

CHAPTER 29

Berresford came to as the doctor jabbed him with a tetanus shot. The doctor also gave him some pain-killing tablets, and spoke reassuringly.

'Well Michael, you'll live to see another day.' He passed Berresford a slip of paper. 'This is my number at the hospital. If you need me give me a call.' He turned to Sarah.

'And you young lady, you look washed out. Get to bed early tonight and take one of these.'

He passed her a small bottle of Mogadons, as she showed him to the door. She gave him a polite kiss on the cheek.

'Cheers,' he said.

Sarah returned and flopped down in the easy chair at the side of Berresford's couch.

'I've had it,' she said. 'Now . . . what's next for me?'

Berresford paused a moment before he spoke. 'That's what I've been thinking about. Whom do you work for in Turnstile? I mean your immediate employer?'

'Moffatt,' she said. 'He's the boss of the first man who tried to kill us. Mario Benini. I don't know what he does at Turnstile.'

Berresford nodded. 'I know what he does. He's one of their murdering henchmen,' he said with difficulty.

'What about the others Michael? Who were they?'

'I've got no idea,' Berresford replied. 'But this is the second time that this sort of thing has happened. One group seems to be out to kill me, and the other simply kills the people whom I contact. Now, it looks like someone is protecting me! I can't explain it. I don't understand. But I do know Benini and his lot will kill either you or me on sight. They know I'm close to penetrating Turnstile.'

'But Michael, are you?' Sarah said desperately.

'I can't give up now, there's no turning back.'

'But what about me?' Sarah said pitifully.

'As I said before, I don't know. Stay here, I guess.'

'How can I? I've got no clothes, nothing.'

'That's the least of our worries. I just don't believe you could go back home without risking your life. You certainly can't walk around these streets, they seem to be everywhere. And we can't go to the police.'

'Yes, that would expose you, wouldn't it?'

'Unfortunately you're right. But I won't stop you if you go. It's your life, I've got no right to interfere.'

'No, I've just decided,' Sarah said firmly. 'I'm staying to look after you until you're better. You'll have no chance of getting them in your present condition.'

Berresford was losing focus. His speech was becoming blurred.

'No you can't do that. Get on a plane and go. Go back home.'

'But you just said they might get me.'

Berresford was dizzy and confused. 'You're right. We're cornered. Alright, you use the bedroom where my surveillance equipment is stored. I'm pretty friendly with the hotel staff. Don't forget the name is Forrest . . . you're Mrs Forrest. I'll send one of the trusted stewards out for some clothes . . .' He was barely coherent.

'It's done then,' said Sarah.

Berresford didn't respond. His eyes had closed. The pills had already taken effect. She leant over him to turn off the light. There is something about him, she thought. He is my kind of man.

BOOK THREE

CHAPTER 30

Stepping out of the black Cadillac limousine, Tom Brady felt the impact of Rome's hot weather. The Leonardo Da Vinci Airport was busy as usual.

But it was not business as usual for Tom Brady. Being the CIA resident agent in Rome had its advantages. But rarely did it involve the meeting of important dignitaries, particularly those close to the President himself.

Brady weaved his way through a maze of corridors and escalators, finally discovering the correct arrival lounge for the Pan Am flight from New York. He had been given a brief description of Bertram Hillings, President of the Security Exchange Commission.

Hillings was travelling with diplomatic sanction. He was the first passenger through, avoiding immigration and customs. Brady's alert eye recognized him immediately.

'Mr Hillings? Tom Brady.' They shook hands vigorously.

'Call me Bert,' Hillings said, 'everyone does.'

Some minutes later they were seated comfortably in the Cadillac, heading towards the Rome American Embassy. Brady was curious and expressed his feelings in his first question.

'The two reports I put in on Berresford and the Von Kessel Dossier were pretty detailed. I am surprised you thought it important enough to see me personally.'

Hillings was an executive who had made his place in

the financial world precisely through his attention to detail.

'It's the small print, Tom, that interests me: the little bits you didn't say. Perhaps you thought they weren't important. Are you free for the rest of the day, Tom?'

'My time is yours, Bert. As much as you want of it.'

'O.K. Let's get down to business right away. If you don't mind, though, I'd like to have a shower and a clean-up first. These long flights leave you awfully sticky.'

'Sure. That's fine with me. I'll organize some lunch. We can start then, if it suits you.'

'That's great Tom. A man after my own heart. No time to waste. Are you married?' The American executive looked hard into Brady's eyes.

'No. Still a bachelor.'

'I just thought I'd warn you. I believe your superiors agreed to my suggestion that you leave for London immediately after our meeting. Thought you might like to know.'

'Thanks for telling me. Yes, I'll organize a few things this morning. Do you know for how long?'

'A month, six weeks maybe.'

'Great. The change will do me good.'

The car pulled into the Embassy and stopped at the main entrance. Several steps led up to large solid timber doors. A huge American crest of painted and polished brass held a commanding position overhead, between the two enormous pillars on either side of the front door. The chauffeur took the solitary suitcase inside, and Hillings disappeared with him.

Between the reception rooms and the offices in the Embassy are two dining rooms. The small one is set aside for meetings such as this. Brady was already seated when Hillings arrived, wearing a neatly cut suit. Their menu selections taken, Hillings got straight to the point.

'Your first report on the Turnstile and Von Kessel

Dossier might have been put aside if you hadn't pointed out the Russian connection with that German bank. Were you surprised when we asked you to follow up with more detail, and commence investigations into the Berresford affair?'

Brady was pleased that his report had gone so far and into such high places.

'Yes, I was surprised. But then again you don't strike such an interesting situation every day.'

'May I speak frankly?'

'Go ahead.'

'Did you help Berresford with the sanction of the CIA?'

'No, it was personal. I could see nothing in it for us at the time. One thing Bert: I'm sorry, but at times I'll have to say "no comment". I don't want to get myself in any sort of trouble.'

'That's fine with me. I want you to level with me because the detail's important. What sent Berresford on this Turnstile rampage?'

'Two things. Firstly he believed his company was duped by Turnstile Investments Limited. Bled dry of its funds. He was able to get some evidence, papers, which implicated them in corporate fraud. These they quickly recovered. An attempt was made on his life and his wife was killed in error. That started it. Then, separately, he was given a file on the German bank and Von Kessel. The file was given to him by the wife of a deceased Director of his Company, name of Patterson. She too was killed. Berresford believed there was no connection between the two although the coincidence seemed enormous. When he arrived in Rome his mind was set on breaking into Turnstile's accountant's offices over here. He knew they had control of two companies in Italy, both based in Rome. Berresford hoped to find documentary evidence of corruption.'

The fish soup arrived. It was hot. Hillings stirred it lightly with his spoon. 'Go on Tom.'

'He arranged for a private investigator to break in and photograph the documents.'

Hillings interrupted. 'Did you arrange that?'

'No comment.'

Hillings smiled. 'Go on Tom.'

'Well, that man was murdered. Found in the slums, bashed up, wallet and watch gone, an empty bottle of brandy in one pocket. But the autopsy indicated that he had not been drinking. His neck had been skilfully broken. Possibly by a karate chop, or some blunt instrument. Other marks on his face and body were inflicted after death.'

Hillings squirmed in his seat.

'Who did it?' he enquired.

'That's a mystery. There are many unanswered questions. Berresford was clever. At his hotel he swapped suites with a fellow American. Both had half a large suite. The Texan sleeping in the adjoining half suite was shot dead during the night. I'd say he was mistaken for Berresford. Again by a person unknown. Berresford had a fleeting glance at him in the hallway and recognized him as the one who stole the documentary evidence on Turnstile in Australia.'

'These boys sure move around,' Hillings interrupted. The main course had arrived. The waiter served the roast beef. Hillings lavished butter on his jacket potatoes. 'What happened then?'

'Berresford told me he was going on to London to investigate Turnstile. He wouldn't leave me the document. But a friend of the Pattersons, an old retired professor in Berlin, had also been investigating the whereabouts of the missing funds. Evidently he had discovered where the money is today and also the recipient, perhaps Von Kessel himself or else a member or members of his family. The old professor had apparently moved to Cologne in fear of his life when he heard of the death of Mrs Patterson. Berresford somehow found him, but he was followed. They killed the old man. What he told Berresford I don't know.'

'Have the authorities developed any leads on the killers?'

'Yes, we had a break. My counterpart in Berlin has followed it through. We have reason to believe that the two men who killed the professor and were seen leaving the scene of the crime are KGB.'

'Christ!' Hillings muttered. 'How deep is this thing?'

'What are your personal impressions?'

'I've got plenty, but I'm stuffed if I can work out certain aspects: like how or why didn't they kill Berresford in Cologne; why did they try to kill him in Rome and in Australia but not in Paris? It doesn't make sense.'

'Where is he now?'

'I don't know precisely. London, I think.'

'Well your superiors will inform you that they want you to go to London to find him. What have you turned up on Turnstile in London?'

'There are no company records between 1932 and 1955 anywhere. But we know the company was formed in 1932. The Turnstile building is a miniature Fort Knox. It is virtually impenetrable by any of our surveillance equipment. Our boys discovered that penetration of the computer room, which is the guts of the thing, would cause all tapes to be erased. We are relying on finding Berresford first. He may have some answers. But we must find him before they get him.'

'Do you believe there is a connection between Turnstile and the German Bank.'

'Oh, I haven't told you that. Yesterday afternoon I was pondering over my notes. Everytime the German name came up, which for me is pretty difficult to pronounce, I just called it in my mind the German bank.'

Hillings interrupted. 'That's natural.'

'Well, it is. But I wanted more than that, and it suddenly crossed my mind. Maybe that word has a more literal meaning.'

'So?' Hillings pushed his glasses back with his index finger and leaned forward to hear.

'I rang one of our interpreters and asked them if Drehkreuz had any meaning.'

'And did it?'

Brady's face went into a deep frown. He hadn't touched his beef.

'Yes?' Hillings asked impatiently.

'The word means Turnstile.'

CHAPTER 31

Benini sat in his Rome flat sulking over the Sloane Street debacle. Everytime he thought of Berresford he broke out in a verbal outburst.

'Figlio di puttana!' he yelled. 'Figlio di puttana!'

He opened a second bottle of La Crema Cristi. The flat in Rome was his home base. Tax free remuneration from Turnstile provided more than adequate funds to meet his expensive tastes. The floor had been resurfaced with hand selected white marble. Most walls were covered with an off-white velvet. As he sat drinking he mentally tried to compose a telex describing the latest events. He dreaded Moffatt's reply.

'Figlio di puttana, Berresford!' he yelled again as he walked over to a mahogany cabinet which housed the computer terminal. He carefully placed a small black felt mat on top of the cabinet, then fastidiously centered the terminal on top.

His head ached with annoyance as he tapped out his version of his attempted elimination of Berresford. His assumption had been obvious and correct. Berresford had managed to infiltrate the staff of Turnstile at the highest level. Moffatt would be furious, he thought.

He had elected on his own volition to leave London and return to Rome. He had not sought a clearance from Turnstile. It was the first time he had made such a move without authority. It worried him, as he sat impatiently waiting for a reply. He knew it would come in the next few minutes.

The phone started ringing. Six rings. The sign. He looked at his watch. Only thirteen minutes, he thought. It seemed like hours. He called London and reconnected his machine to the designated memory bank of the computer.

Seconds later the little machine was tapping out a message in telex form.

Attention M.B.

Your futile efforts are exasperating! Your idiotic attempt yesterday beyond belief. Return immediately. Find Berresford and the girl. Complete mission forthwith or I'll pass you back to AE.

The Telex

A shiver went down Benini's spine as he read the words. He took a gold Cartier lighter from his pocket and burnt the message in a large crystal ashtray.

Moffatt had borrowed the cryptonym AE from the CIA; it meant Russia. He would be on their hit list if he failed again. The connection between Turnstile and the Russians had always baffled him.

His feet slapped across the marble on the way to his bedroom. Even the luxurious massive round bed with its black mink bedspread and its memories of outrageous orgies failed to humour him. Benini began packing his bag, his face full of murderous fury.

Waiting to meet Tom Brady at Heathrow airport were two other CIA agents. He knew them both from the CIA training farm in Williamburg. Brian Anderson was chief of the station (the CIA London Head-quarters) and was the first to speak.

'Hi Tom, great to see you.'

Brady's cheery black face lit up with delight.

'Hi there old buddy. How's the fishing?'

'You know Kevin Winfield, don't you?'

'Sure I do. And what have you been doing Windy?' Brady said cheerily to Winfield.

'Not much, I've just come back from the US.'

Fifty minutes later their brown Jaguar arrived back at the Embassy. They set up a meeting in a conference room. Brady opened the conversation.

'Well, gentlemen, fill me in.'

'There's not much to tell, Tom,' Anderson began. He pushed himself back in the staid timber chair, resting both hands on the edge of the table. 'We're sure Berresford is in London. But where, we're not sure. Yesterday there was a commotion in Sloane Street. A person unknown fired two shots from a silenced pistol at somebody we presume to be Berresford and some girl. The girl's not yet identified. An old jewish jeweller with eyes like a hawk picked out Berresford from twenty photographs.'

'Who was behind the hit?' Brady enquired.

'The description doesn't match any of the Russians we know, but they might have brought in someone new from another country. It might even have been a person employed by the Turnstile show itself.'

'Have you been able to prove any connection between Turnstile and the Russians?'

'None. A complete blank as far as we can see,' Anderson said authoritatively. 'But it's pretty clear that the Russians want Berresford for what he's got on Turnstile.'

'How smart is this Berresford?' Winfield asked, speaking for the first time.

'He's one hell of a smart boy,' Brady replied. 'It seems that there has been a number of attempts on his life, and that he's escaped unscathed. He's either winning through a surprise approach because he's an abject amateur, or this guy is far more skillful than you would first believe.'

'He's got to be staying somewhere,' Anderson muttered.

'Have you checked the hotels in the Turnstile building area?' Brady interrupted, turning to Anderson.

'Of course we have. First thing we did was check every hotel and lodging place within a couple of miles of the Turnstile building. And what a job that was! But it was done, and efficiently.'

'What other measures have you taken?'

'We're setting ourselves up on the fourth floor of the Sheraton Hotel. We have the Turnstile building under visual surveillance, and a team of boys on the street. We've got to have a break sometime or other.'

Brady nodded his head thoughtfully. 'Yes, and I only hope it's not too late.'

At the same time in a small cold room of the Russian Embassy, eight men huddled around a large table. The leader of the GRU contingent in London was addressing his officers. He delivered the conclusions of the lengthy meeting sarcastically and abruptly.

'I want to make it clear. Berresford is notoriously dangerous to the Turnstile operation. We have lost three men in a week. The file on him is obviously a load of garbage. I cannot concede that an amateur can take out three trained field officers in such a short time and remain alive. You can take it from me that there will be questions asked, not only of me but of all of you, if you fail in the task of eliminating this humbug in the next few days. He must be found and killed. The KGB are itching to step into this operation. It is your duty to see that this doesn't occur, by expediently eliminating both Berresford and Moffatt's secretary. There is no room for error. We must protect Turnstile so that it can continue to damage the western monetary system. The financial power and influence of Turnstile is unquestionable. It's the largest single conglomerate of its kind in the western world. We need control of it, we need it to continue to strip funds from the filthy, greedy rich. Your lives are not important in achieving this. We must stop Berresford from infiltrating further into the world of the old man we know as The Telex.'

CHAPTER 32

Sarah had been up for over an hour. Berresford was still sound asleep. She ordered coffee and toast for both of them. At half past eight she saw Moffatt in his track suit jogging to the office as usual. At around nine o'clock the employees arrived. Everyone but her, she thought. Looking at the building now sent shivers down her spine. Berresford would wake shortly. She had many questions to ask him and knew that he had many to ask her.

She hurried to the bedroom. Berresford was sitting up in bed. His face was pale, his eyes reflecting the horror of the previous day.

'I've been dreaming,' Berresford sounded apologetic. 'The whole bloody mess was coming before me. Distorted faces, bloody bodies. I can't stand it. I'm just not used to this terror and carnage.'

'How do you feel this morning?'

Berresford shrugged his shoulders. 'My shoulder's killing me,' he moaned. 'Come on, Sarah, sit by the bed. I've got stacks of things to ask you.'

'Michael, do you mind if I order my clothes and cosmetics first? I'll have them by late this morning if I order them now.'

'Sure,' he said. 'Go ahead. Forgive me, how thoughtless.'

Sarah hurried to her room for the list, Berresford's brown silk robe fluttering around her slim body. She had a very attractive body. The swell of her breasts was tantalizing under the soft fabric, the movement of her nipples on the robe made them stand out, a silhouette of her figure was apparent with the glaring sunlight shining through the window behind her. The last thing in Berresford's mind was a sexual encounter, but somehow this girl stimulated him. She returned seconds later.

'By the way, you missed my old boss Moffatt.'

At the mention of the name Berresford sat bolt upright. 'What!' he said excitedly. 'He's the director of the whole operation!'

Sarah smiled. 'No, he's not. There are four at his level.'

'What do you mean?' demanded Berresford. 'Then who is behind Turnstile?'

'Someone else, I guess. No one knows.'

'What do you mean, no one knows?'

'Well, I'm pretty sure Moffatt's never met him.'

'It can't be, it's got to be Moffatt.'

Suddenly Berresford's confusion returned. 'What in God's name is going on?' he asked aloud.

Twenty minutes later, at the breakfast table, they were ready to talk.

As Berresford unfolded his napkin the questions began.

'Well, little lady, tell me all — in fact everything you know about Turnstile.'

It had been a long time since Sarah had enjoyed breakfast with a man. She put some jam on her toast.

'Well, let's see; where do we start? I suppose I've had a unique experience in working at Turnstile. They have a crazy way of employing people. No one is ever employed for a period of more than six months. I've established that from discussing it with the girls at tea break. They don't tell you that it is a temporary position when they put you on. I think I'm unique, because I've worked there on two occasions. The first time was for six months two years ago under Redford, one of the four bosses. When I went back to the same employment agency, they didn't recognize me. And for a reason which I don't know myself, I didn't state on the application form that I'd worked there before.'

Berresford nodded without speaking.

'So I was employed again, this time under Moffatt.'

'Tell me more, Sarah.'

'It's a four-storey building and Turnstile occupies it all. The operations appear to be divided into four divisions. There is a divisional leader, like Moffatt, on each floor. Each morning the management arrives before the other staff. Only the personal secretaries get to see their chief. He leaves after they go to lunch and if he's out for a long lunch he doesn't return. The girls leave before the management leaves.'

Berresford looked at her intently. 'That's damn crazy.'

'I know, I agree, but if it wasn't for their crazy system they would have woken up to the fact that I've worked there twice.'

'How many companies do they have interests in?'

'My first boss, Redford, employed me as his stenographer and personal secretary. On that floor we controlled 127 companies.'

Berresford stopped eating and whistled. Sarah continued.

'That's right, 127 companies. On Moffatt's floor he has a few more, but some of them are smaller. Probably ....138, I think.'

'What interest do they hold in them, and what size are these corporations?'

'It seems they have shares varying from a few per cent up to forty per cent. In all cases they have control. As to the size of the companies, there's nothing under a few million dollars and many of them have hundreds of millions in market capitalization.'

'You're kidding,' Berresford exclaimed, in disbelief. 'For a secretary you understand the business world pretty well!'

'My first job was with an accountant. My shorthand was good and they gave me important assignments, so I learned a lot of the jargon and workings of corporate business.'

'Go on, I'm fascinated,' Berresford said with enthusiasm.

'One thing that interested me is that the directors in the companies we control on the first floor are the same as those involved in the companies on the fourth. I think there'd only be thirty or forty directors all told, but they spread themselves through all those companies.'

'What about the other two floors in the building?'

'I've had lunch with some of the girls working on those floors and I'm reasonably sure that the set-up is the same for all four managers.'

'I don't get it,' Berresford said with some annoyance in his voice. 'Who in the hell is running the thing?'

'Someone from outside. On one occasion I was in Moffatt's office taking dictation. The telex machine was chattering away. Being curious I read over his shoulder and saw that it was signed The Telex. All four managers sign as The Telex anyway, but I was surprised on this occasion. This day the other three managers were out. I said to Moffatt, "Have you been sending telexes to yourself?". He was very annoyed that I noticed.'

'What happened then?'

'He said something rather strange. I'm still not quite sure what to make of it.'

'Quick, what?' Berresford said impatiently.

'He said "forget it. The old knight would go out of his brain if he heard you say that".'

'Old knight? You mean a knighthood knight?'

'I guess that's what he meant.'

Berresford was puzzled. Sarah was being most informative but the facts didn't fit.

'Well, let's see. There must be over five hundred companies involved. Is there anything else on this old knight?'

'Yes, we have a closed circuit television in each of the managers' rooms. It's a two-way affair on speech evidently, and one-way in video. Perhaps the old man's plugged in.'

'What makes you think that?'

'One day I walked into Moffatt's office and he was in the middle of a spirited conversation with someone. The closed circuit television camera was working. I heard him use the name Sir James, but that's all. I foolishly remarked, "Oh I've always wanted to know a knight, we don't have them in America. What's his name?" His answer rocked me.'

'Oh?' Berresford exclaimed.

'He said, "It's none of your business but for the record I don't even know the rest of Sir James' name myself".'

'What's that supposed to mean?'

Sarah shrugged her shoulders. 'Be blowed if I know. Damn strange if you ask me.'

'How many countries are involved in the consortium do you think?'

'I guess about thirty. They're all over the place, but there is a lot of financial activity in the tax haven countries: Lichenstein, Panama, Switzerland and so on.'

'That makes sense,' Berresford said slowly. 'I wish to hell I knew who the old knight was.' He threw his teaspoon on the table. 'I'll get them!' As he stood up to leave the table, he almost knocked over the coffee pot in the effort. Sarah helped him back to the bedroom.

CHAPTER 33

'Michael...Michael...Are you awake?' The soft feminine voice drifted through the half open door into Berresford's bedroom, arousing him from sleep. He yawned loudly, speaking as he expelled a lung full of air.

'Oh, what time is it?'

'Eight o'clock, sleepy head. I've been up for an hour.' Sarah stood in the doorway. Her body was scantily covered with a semi transparent blue negligee. The outline of her shapely legs and narrow waist was clearly discernible.

'How do you feel this morning, Michael?'

'It's the best I've felt all week. I think it's healing really well.'

'I'll be the judge of that,' she replied.

Berresford yawned again and rolled out of bed, dressed in a short pair of pyjama pants with nothing over his bandaged shoulder. He walked towards his bathroom door, and gave her a slight tap on the bottom as he passed.

'My, my, you are feeling better!' she said, smiling.

He emerged fully dressed.

'Hey there, what's all this mean?' she asked, still smiling.

'I've been holidaying long enough. It's time I got to work.'

Sarah frowned. 'You're not going to try to break into Turnstile, are you? I thought you'd given up that idea.'

'I mightn't break in, but I think I know the man who can.'

Sarah broke into a mild panic. 'You're an idiot, Michael. I've told you, the place is a veritable fortress. The outer walls are composed of reinforced concrete and granite, then there's a space and virtually another building inside, built of the same material. All the windows are one inch bullet-proof glass. You must have noticed you can't see in, even with your strong telescope. It is surfaced with one-way mirror material on the inner glass. The roof is feet thick of steel and concrete.'

Sarah gushed on, unabated.

'But that's not your biggest problem. The computer and all the computer banks are in the basement. I've seen it, I went down with Moffatt about six weeks ago. The anteroom before entering the computer room is guarded twenty-four hours a day. The door to the computer is over a foot thick and electronically operated. The anteroom was as far as I got. Moffatt said that only one person could be in the computer room at one time. He dictated notes on the erasure system for the computer tapes in the event of penetration.'

'What was that?' Berresford was suddenly interested. 'You never mentioned that before.'

'You never asked. He dictated a letter to an electronics firm. They installed electronic erasure devices in the event of burglary.'

'What were the details?' Berresford said excitedly.

Sarah looked at him, perplexed. 'I'm sorry. I just can't remember.'

'Which firm? You've got to remember which firm.'

'I'm sorry . . . I write so many letters. Maybe I'll think of it later.'

'Well, that settles it,' Berresford said emphatically. 'I'll bring Garreau's man in. He'll know what to do.'

'Who is he?' Sarah demanded. Berresford was taken aback.

'His name is Nick Wood and he works for the Internal Revenue Department. I can't tell you any more than that.'

'And why not?' Sarah was now defiant.

'I'm sorry, Sarah. That's what I was told by Garreau. I believe he is a man with considerable ability. We need him, Sarah. I want both advice and expertise.'

Sarah gave a sigh.

Berresford exploded. 'Well what in the hell else can I do? What can you and I do against them? Take Benini for example. What do you know about him?'

'He's smooth and handsome.'

It was Berresford's turn to be furious. 'For God's sake, Sarah, he's a bloody murderer! He tried to kill both of us. What a stupid thing to say.'

'I'm telling you what the girls in the office say. You asked...'

'I don't care about that. What about his modus operandi? Do you know anything about that man?'

'Very little. He's very close to Moffatt. He often calls without an appointment and leaves a short note. They're always open for me to read, but they never make any sense. He writes some odd sort of code, numbers and things.'

'How does he sign?'

Berresford was trying to remember the telexes that he had read between Turnstile and the Accountant's offices in Australia.

'He always signs the notes. I think it's the Italian equivalent of Mr B.'

'What's that, Sarah?' Berresford said quietly.

'Sig. B. Capital S, and capital B.'

Berresford's face went white. His lips trembled, he had to avert his eyes.

'It can't be,' he said, barely audible.

'What's up Michael? Are you alright?'

He spat the words through clenched teeth.

'The bastard's the one who was screwing my wife.'

He left the room, slamming the bedroom door behind him.

He sat on the bed and thumbed through the pages of the Government section of the telephone directory. He found what he was looking for. Seconds later the telephone operator came on the line.

'Good morning, Internal Revenue Department,' a woman's voice advised with obvious monotonous repetition.

'Mr Nicholas Wood, in the Investigations Section please.' Berresford now could contain himself. He was on the move again. A phone was ringing.'

'Wood speaking,' came a deep voice in clipped English.

'You don't know me, so my name is unimportant. I have a brief message from a friend of yours. Where would you suggest we meet?'

Some seconds passed with no reply. Berresford was not sure if they had been disconnected.

'Are you there? Are you there?'

'Yes, I am here,' the man said slowly. 'Do you know our address?'

'It's in the phone book,' was Berresford's curt reply.

'Stand on the steps at 12.30, in the lunch hour, today. Give me your description.'

His voice was cold and calculating. Berresford was not sure whether he should proceed, yet his intent on revenge forced him on.

'I'll be wearing a light grey suit. I'm well built, with brown wavy hair. I'll be wearing a white shirt with a plain blue tie.'

'Enough!' The phone clicked. The man had hung up.

Berresford returned to the living room. Sarah was nowhere to be seen. Then the muffled sounds of a woman sobbing gave him the answer.

He ran into her bedroom. She was lying on the

unmade bed, sobbing unceasingly into the pillow. He knelt on the floor next to the bed and stroked her back.

'Darling, darling, I'm terribly sorry, what in the hell have I got you into?'

She couldn't catch her breath to answer.

'Come on, come on.' He put his arm around her, pulling her towards him, kissing her on her reddened wet cheeks. 'It's going to be alright.' He sat on the bed and pulled her up towards him, holding her face against his. 'Come on darling, snap out of it.' His voice firmed to a commanding tone. Taking the corner of the sheet he dabbed her face dry until she stopped sobbing. Between her sniffles and coughs he explained.

'I think the world of you, I wouldn't do anything that would hurt you.'

'What about you? They'll kill you.' She started sobbing again.

She put both arms around him and kissed him tenderly. She blurted the words out between the tears.

'They'll kill you, Michael. I don't want to lose you . . .'

'Come on pretty lady, go and clean yourself up. We've got some talking to do.'

They sipped their coffee quietly. Both realized that a new strength had developed between them. Berresford's hand rested on the table; it took the pressure off his wounded arm. Sarah put her hand over his as he started speaking.

'I'm meeting Garreau's man at lunch time. He'll help us. Garreau assured me that if anyone could help me he would.'

'But how are you going to get out, Michael?'

'I've thought that one through . . . I'm going to ring a hire car and chauffeur shortly and have him meet me at the back of the hotel. I'll go down the same way that we came in the other night. Don't worry, Sarah, it'll be O.K.'

'Oh, Michael,' she said, grabbing him on his right

arm with her two hands. She was trembling. He put his arm around her affectionately. 'Do what you think is right, Michael.'

Michael spoke in a soft, affectionate tone. 'Go and lie down, have a rest. I'll join you for lunch, after I've spoken to Nick Wood.'

CHAPTER 34

The hire car chauffeur was waiting behind the hotel. Berresford gave him the address.

'When you get there I want you to drop me off at the main steps. Find a parking spot within seeing distance from the steps. I won't be long.'

'Righto Guv', she'll be apples.'

When they reached the steps and stopped, Berresford checked his watch. The trip had been slower than expected due to bad traffic. It was now 12.27.

He had three minutes to be in position. He turned to the driver.

'Don't worry about opening the door, I'll be alright. Now stay in sight, please.'

He mounted the steps and took up the position described by Khomenko. It seemed more appropriate to use the man's real Russian name. The minutes ticked away. Berresford became nervous. At 12.39 a dark, thick-set, middle-aged man with black wiry hair approached. As he was walking past, and directly opposite him, he spoke.

'Follow me,' he said as he kept walking.

Berresford followed him as casually as possible up the steps and through the swinging doors. He turned left into the main foyer where many people had gathered. Khomenko sat down on a bench seat beneath a window. Berresford sat next to him and waited. Not looking around Khomenko pulled out a newspaper which he had been carrying underneath his arm.

Without turning towards Berresford he muttered softly.

'Who sent you?'

Berresford, not so skilled at such surreptitious methods, leant towards him, half turning his face.

'Garreau. You're Khomenko.'

It was as if he had been hit with a bolt of lightening. He didn't move an inch. But the tension of his fingers as he held the paper gave him away.

'Not here,' he said softly.

'I know,' said Berresford.

'Where are you staying?' Khomenko enquired.

'Sheraton Hotel, Knightsbridge.'

'I know it. The main dining room is on the top floor. Be there at 4.30 this afternoon in the men's toilet.'

With that Khomenko folded the paper and walked away. Berresford, still sitting, was stunned. He hadn't expected the meeting to go like this. There was something about Khomenko — something evil, sinister. Yet Garreau had spoken of him with confidence. He would be a useful man, alright.

'Cor, that was quick Gov'.' The driver chirped.

Berresford turned the key in the door. 'It's me,' he said, pre-empting the question.

'Oh Michael, thank God you're back. The phone rang twice while you were out. I didn't know what to do, I didn't answer it.'

'You did well. No one else knows I'm here. It's possibly the accounts department downstairs. I am due for my first payment. I'll get them to send the bill up.'

Before he had finished speaking Sarah gushed out. 'What happened? Will he do it? Will he help us?'

'I don't know. I'm meeting him at 4.30 here.'

'Here?' She was surprised.

'Upstairs in the dining...'

He hadn't finished. 'You can't! You can't expose

yourself like that!'

'Let me finish!' He said indignantly.

'I'm sorry Michael.'

'I'm meeting him upstairs on the dining room floor, but in the men's toilet. I won't be seen.'

The service lift was unoccupied at twenty minutes past four. The stainless steel doors opened on the top floor. Berresford cautiously peered out, his finger still on the 'open' button.

The lunch crowd had gone and the tables had been reset. It was too early yet for customers. Finding the men's toilet, he pushed the door open. The lights were on. He checked the cubicles.

On the furthest wall from the entrance door were two electric hand driers. His hands were sweaty, and he turned towards them. The roaring sound of the dryer replaced the absolute silence of the enclosed space.

His hands were almost dry when he felt it, the sharp razor edge of a Khukri knife, the famed weapon of the much feared Ghurka soldier. Its boomerang shaped blade was pressing against his throat. He froze, not daring to move. He could feel its super fine edge cutting his skin. Tiny drips of blood ran down his neck, soiling the collar of his shirt.

'Now Mr whoever you are, how do you know my name? I suggest you don't try to move or I'll have you in two parts.'

Berresford had never felt such terror. His mind was blank; he could barely remember his own name; his whole body had stiffened with the thought that death was so close.

He stammered. 'My...my name...is Berresford, Michael Berresford, friend of Ian Garreau.'

'Go on,' Khomenko said with a deep throated whisper.

Then Berresford repeated in parrot fashion the passage from Garreau's letter which he had been instructed to repeat verbatim.

'Which hand, which foot?' Khomenko simply asked.

Berresford touched his right hand, but remembered not to point to either foot.

'Very well Mr Berresford. You realize that what you have told me gives me every reason to kill you? My cover is blown.'

Berresford was terrified. 'Yes, I know that... but I need your help. I had to take the risk.'

Khomenko pushed Berresford's shoulder slightly so that they could look at each other. He had a deadly appearance. Yet the man was ambivert, neither backward nor outgoing.

'Well, it must be terribly important to you Mr Berresford. You must be in great trouble, if Garreau sent you to me.'

Berresford took two deep breaths. He was trying to relax, to let his body fall limp. He had been totally taken aback by the Russian.

'Where is your room?' Khomenko's tone dry.

'On the seventh floor.'

'Anyone else there?'

'Yes, but I have a suite. We can talk on our own. I have instructed the girl...'

'Oh you have a girlfriend?'

'Not as such. She's part of this, she's on my side.'

Suddenly the Russian became aggressive. The knife was still in his hand. His eyes pierced icily into Berresford's.

'She knows nothing, I hope.'

Berresford raised his voice. 'For God's sake. Garreau told me that I mustn't tell anyone. No one knows.'

The Russian gave a sardonic smile. 'Lucky for you. Let's go to your suite.'

They were on their own in the lift.

'I'll introduce you by your English name, if you want.' Berresford offered.

Khomenko nodded.

Berresford was alarmed again. Had he made the right choice?

Without knocking he turned the key and walked in. On seeing him, Sarah winced. Her fingers rushed to cover her open mouth as she stepped back quickly towards the window.

Berresford had forgotten that there was blood around his neck. He spoke quickly. 'It's nothing dear, absolutely nothing. Come on, I'd like you to meet our friend. Nick Wood, this is Sarah Standford.'

Khomenko smiled. Yet there was no humour in the smile. It was purely a mechanical action.

'Where shall we sit?'

'Here, over here. Take this chair. Would you like some coffee?'

'Can you get some expresso?'

'Yeah, sure. I'll ring up the coffee shop and have some sent up. Sarah will you do that while I start telling Nick what's happened to date?'

Sarah looked at her watch. It was eleven minutes to seven.

Berresford had been talking for hours. Khomenko was simply listening. Sometimes he asked a question or made a brief comment. The low table in front of them was littered with coffee cups. The room stank of stale smoke from the ashtrays. Suddenly the Russian stopped Berresford.

'The surveillance equipment which you bought, may I inspect it please?'

'Yes, of course. It's in Sarah's room.'

The door was shut. Berresford knocked and went in. Sarah was changing her dress and was dressed only in her knickers and pantyhose. Khomenko politely excused himself, turned his back to her and inspected the equipment. Berresford was surprised at the coolness of the man.

'He's as cold as ice,' he thought.

227

Khomenko nodded his head with approval as he inspected the various pieces. Sarah gathered her clothes and hurried to the bathroom.

'Most impressive, Michael. The equipment is up-to-date. It's as good as you'll get.'

He returned to the living room, sat in the same chair and lit a cigarette. The strong tobacco filled the room. Leaning back in the chair he puffed the smoke quite audibly towards the ceiling and began to summarize the situation. Berresford took a seat on the couch opposite him.

'To date Michael,' Khomenko spoke in a more relaxed tone, 'you have been both clever and lucky. Whoever these Turnstile people are, they are certainly ambitious, powerful and dangerous. My advice is that we should first eliminate half of our problem.' He stopped as if waiting for Berresford's approval.

'Yes, yes, go on.'

'I will take out Benini,' the Russian continued. 'Then I am prepared to help you get the computer tapes, but you must follow my advice to the letter.'

'Yes of course.'

'You have been clever enough to stay off the street for a week. I suspect that they have staked out Sarah's flat. It would be easy for them to obtain her address from the Turnstile records. Bring the girl in here. I want the address and description of her abode.'

Raising his voice Berresford called. 'Sarah, Sarah, Nick wants to speak to you.'

Sarah entered, her face pale. She smiled nervously.

'Sit down, Sarah. Don't be afraid, I'm trying to help Michael solve your problems,' the Russian said softly. 'In my opinion your flat will be under surveillance. I need your key and a few details.'

She pointed towards her room. 'It's in my handbag.'

'You can get it in a moment. What's the address?'

'Redcliffe Street, West Brompton, number 346.'

Khomenko wrote nothing down. His memory was

sharp and accurate. He was trained.

'How many stories?'

'Seven. It's built in red brick and served by two lifts.'

'You've anglicized the elevator I see.' The Russian gave out another mechanical smile.

'Oh yes, they wouldn't know what you were talking about if you said elevator here.'

'Is there a caretaker?'

'Yes, on the ground floor adjoining the lift on the right hand side. He's old and he usually goes to bed at about eight o'clock. The foyer is lit twenty-four hours a day. You need a key to gain entry to it after eight o'clock.'

'What does your flat consist of? Describe it.'

'You leave the lift on the fourth floor — the lifts are side by side — my flat has a door on the opposite side. It's the third down the corridor on the right.'

'Do you turn left or right when you leave the elevator?'

'Left, and the door's on the right.'

'Do you have a balcony?'

'No, there are no balconies.'

'Describe the interior please.'

'You enter into the living room. There is a small kitchen on your immediate left, and a door between the kitchen and the living room. There is a second door on the left which leads to a small hallway. The toilet and bathroom are in one room at the end, the door is straight ahead, and on the right-hand side is my bedroom.'

'So it's a small hall? Six feet square?'

'No, even smaller. I'd say six feet by four. It just breaks the toilet from the living room.'

'Thanks Sarah. Now the key.'

She returned with the key to her flat and another to the main entrance.

Khomenko turned to Berresford. 'Now your gun, where is it?'

'Under my pillow.'

'Give it to me, and also your silencer please.'

'But . . .'

Khomenko's eyebrows raised. 'You were going to say that you will be left unarmed? I've already thought of that.'

From his pocket he withdrew an article wrapped in a large handkerchief. Taking care not to touch it, he placed it on the table. Pulling back one corner, he unveiled a snub nosed .44 magnum Smith and Wesson revolver.

'I don't have a silencer. I'll take great care of yours, you can have it back tomorrow and keep this one.' He pointed to the huge heavy calibre revolver, its stainless steel body gleaming.

'I still don't understand,' Berresford said.

'You don't have to,' was the curt reply. 'If there is anyone there tonight I don't want to use a noisy weapon.'

Berresford nodded in approval.

Khomenko appeared quite anxious to get on with the job. He removed the magazine and put it in his pocket. Then he checked to see that no bullet was left in the breach. He tucked the gun behind his belt and the silencer into his coat pocket as he moved towards the door.

The moment the door closed Sarah ran to Berresford and threw her arms around him, pressing her body against his. She was trembling. Berresford put his arms around her and whispered reassuringly.

'It's alright darling, it's going to be O.K.'

CHAPTER 35

Khomenko drove past Sarah's flat in Redcliffe Street for the second time. It was just after 3 a.m. He had seen enough.

'This will do,' he said to himself as he parked the car in a side street. He adjusted the gun, attached the silencer and loaded it. It was clear that the place was under surveillance. The small Austin car that had been seen whilst passing the flat had tinted windows. The windows had fogged up from the warm breath of the occupants.

'Ah,' Khomenko had said softly to himself.

The car was facing in the same direction in which he was walking and he could vaguely make out the shapes inside. Both men were obviously sitting in the front seat. The car was parked thirty yards from Sarah's flat on the opposite side of the street, facing towards the entrance.

'No fucking imagination,' he thought. His fingers felt the contoured grip of Berresford's gun. He checked to make sure that there was no obstruction to prevent the gun from being drawn quickly.

When he reached the car, he tapped loudly on the passenger side window. Both men had drifted off to sleep and awoke with a start. The surprised passenger wound down his window and stared at Khomenko.

'What's up?' he demanded. Khomenko bent down, staring directly at the passenger. There was barely a few inches between their eyes. Khomenko's Russian was clipped, aggressive.

'What in the shit are you doing?' he said authoritatively. 'I want a word with you two.'

Both driver and passenger were bewildered.

'Unlock the back door.'

They did so automatically. He slipped in the back of the car. 'What time do you ring Petrovich?' he demanded.

The driver emitted a sigh of relief. 'Oh, you are one of us. I just couldn't think what in the hell was going on.'

'Any sign of the girl, or Berresford?'

'Not a thing.'

Khomenko changed the subject to food. He was describing a new discovery as his right hand closed around the butt of the pistol, his forefinger poised for a split second pull. The weapon came out, carefully concealed behind the seat.

The driver and passenger both relaxed and started looking ahead while talking. It was tiresome twisting around to speak to the back seat passenger.

Khomenko knew he had to be quick. He positioned himself in the centre of the back seat. His left hand steadied him as his right hand uncoiled and raised the long nosed gun to stop on the centre of the driver's neck, one inch below the skull. His forefinger hooked on the trigger, his finger curled and pressed; the muffled explosion caught the passenger unaware. Too late! Khomenko had positioned the gun on the second victim and fired again. The two inert heaps slumped forward, motionless.

Khomenko slid out and walked casually towards the red brick building. He turned the key in the security door on the ground floor and carefully surveyed the empty foyer. The two lifts were on his right as Sarah had said; the caretaker's door was also on the right-hand side, four yards further on.

When the lift doors opened on the fourth floor, he went to the left and checked the door numbers. 'Where can I put it?' he thought as he walked along. 'Ah, perfect.'

Between the doors of the various apartments were hung colourful prints of stately homes in England. He stopped at Sarah's door; the picture was three feet to the left. He wet the suction cap of a small black object about an inch square, a five-inch aerial wire hung from it's centre. He pressed it firmly onto the gloss painted wall behind the picture and returned to his car.

The voice was clear, perhaps a little too loud in the miniature earpiece plugged into Khomenko's ear. He could clearly distinguish Farwood's harsh English accent. Who was he talking too? Ah ... yes ... he was talking to Benini. An hour later he pulled out the ear plug and started the car. He yawned, he was tired, he hadn't been to sleep all night but it was worth it he thought. He yawned again, started the car and drove off. He laughed. It was a derisory laugh, the mocking sound made with Benini and Berresford in mind.

CHAPTER 36

'I don't care how long it takes! Don't leave until you've got two pictures of them, side on and front. I'll patch it back by facsimile through to Washington this morning.' Tom Brady was now yelling into the phone. 'I don't care what sort of a story you concoct! Just get them, and don't come back without them!' He slammed the phone down.

Brian Anderson had just entered Brady's office. 'What in the hell's going on?' he asked.

'Two Russians who arrived on a trade delegation two days ago were found murdered. Sitting in a car in West Brompton.'

'How were they killed?'

'Both shot in the back of the neck. A thoroughly professional hit job. It was done at close range but there were no powder marks. The killer obviously used a silencer.'

'KGB?'

'Don't know, that's the bloody problem. We're having trouble getting photographs from the police. Do you think it's connected with Berresford?'

'Got no idea.'

Tom Brady was annoyed. There were too many missing pieces in the jigsaw. Nothing was clear.

'Anymore on Berresford and the girl?' he asked Anderson.

'Nothing, a complete blank. It's as if the bastard vanished in mid-air.'

'Maybe he's dead?'

'Could be. I'll check my snoop and see if the GRU have still got an order out to kill him.'

'How long will that take?'

'About twenty-four hours. I'll start the wheels rolling now.'

'Thanks Brian. Sorry if I snapped at you, but it's so bloody frustrating.'

'It sure is Tom.' Anderson said as he left.

It was three o'clock in the afternoon before Khomenko woke up. He immediately rang Berresford, who asked him straight away.

'How did you go last night, Nick?'

'Nothing, drew a blank. I can't get them on my own, I need some bait.'

Berresford exploded. 'What in the hell do you mean? You mean the girl.'

'Exactly.'

'I won't be in it. Forget the whole thing,' Berresford said firmly.

'She'll come to no harm.'

'Well I won't be in it anyway.'

'Listen,' Khomenko demanded. 'If you want to stay alive you'll do what I say. If you want the girl to live another week you'll do what I say. You've got no alternative. I can assure you there is no risk.'

'Are they watching it?'

'Better than that. One is sleeping there. Benini must be close by. I think I heard him speaking on a walkie-talkie. He's probably in another room. I've got to take out the man in the flat, and entice Benini onto the scene. It sounds like they're professionals so we can't afford any slip-up. I'll get them tonight.'

'Then what?' Berresford was arrogant, if not rude.

'Then it's Moffatt's turn.'

'Moffatt?'

'Yes. If you and Sarah are right, he jogs to work every

morning, we'll make our snatch tomorrow.'
   'Snatch?'
   'Yes. You and I are going to kidnap Moffatt.'

The alacrity of Sarah's thinking stunned Berresford.
'But Michael, I don't mind. We've got to stop them
someway. I hate it as much as you, but it's no good
having Nick if we don't take his advice. You said he's a
pro.'
   'I don't like it Sarah. I won't have it. I won't have
your life placed in jeopardy. I got you into this.'
   'Let's not jump to conclusions. Let's hear him out
tonight. We can always back down if we don't like his
plan.'
   'Alright, but I don't like it.' Berresford was pacing
the floor.
   'And for God's sake stop pacing. Put that cigarette
out, that's three in a row.'
   He took one last puff and put it out.
   'I'd love a drink,' she said with a change of tone.
   She smiled as she sat on a stool at the small bar, and
stirred the glass with a plastic spoon. Berresford
reflected on Khomenko's schedule. Moffatt was to be
next.
   'Do you think we're going too far Sarah? The Moffatt
business, I mean.'
   'For God's sake, Michael. We're in it, we've got to get
out of it. He's obviously involved with the murders and
we both know he set up the attempted assassination on
us.'
   'Damn him, but where will we take him?'
   'Haven't you got any faith in Nick?'
   'Yes. I suppose you're right, he must have a plan.'
   'You can always opt out if you don't agree with it.'
   'I suppose you're right.' Berresford surveyed the girl
sitting opposite him. His imagination recreated the
bare breasts that he had seen when Khomenko had
barged into her room the day before. Intuitively Sarah

sensed his interest.

'You sexy old bastard,' she said. 'Come here.'

Without hesitation Berresford left his stool and joined her on the other side. She stood up, put her arms around his shoulders and pressed her body against his, giving him a light fleeting kiss. His arms folded around her. She held him back a little and looked at him. Then, snuggling in close to him, she kissed him passionately. His hands explored her back, her waist, and lightly brushed over her bottom. He could feel where her pants started and finished as they both slipped down onto the floor.

A few miles away a heated meeting was taking place in a small room in the Russian Embassy. A group of people were hunched around a round table. The leader poured cold fury on his subordinates.

'You incompetent pigs! Two more dead in a week, that's five in all,' he roared. 'And you call this man an amateur. Not only is he a skilled professional, I could give him a job training you, you incompetent lot.'

One person at the table dared to question his superior. 'But how did he get behind them in the car and hit them so accurately?'

This only increased the rage of the senior officer. He waved his hands wildly. 'How in the hell do I know? Berresford's a genius, but the top brass won't believe that. The files show that he is an amateur in these operations.'

'What do we do now?'

'Well, it's no good staking out the flat. He's been there, done that. We must comb the streets. He'll show eventually. I have no doubt that he's going to make a crack at Turnstile. I want the four managers at Turnstile under constant surveillance. Never let them out of your sight, particularly Moffatt. He's the one responsible for the Berresford affair in the first place. And Berresford knows that too.'

237

'Shouldn't we be in the building.'

The leader looked at him with scorn. 'You incompetent arse. Of course we can't go inside. We are never to have any visible contact with Turnstile.'

'How long have we now?'

'We have three days, only three days to the weekend, after which the KGB will take over. We will lose control of the project, through your bloody incompetence,' the leader snapped again.

'We're doing our best,' the officer said.

'The hell you are! Find him. Now *get out* all of you!'

Brian Anderson sat back at his desk. As head of the CIA station in London, he had a number of useful contacts with the other side — agents that had turned. His best contact in the GRU was the Russian double agent, Madeleine Kater. Intensive investigation by the agency had discovered her weaknesses: money, sex, and alcohol. The CIA provided two of the three, and then she turned.

She lived in a small duplex. The other one of the pair was owned by an undercover company controlled by the CIA. Anderson knew the phone call would come through any moment. The cue was to ring her, ask her for her number and then say 'sorry wrong number.' And as soon as possible, Kater would ring back from a public telephone box.

He was jolted by the shrill, ring of the telephone. 'Hello. Is that you?' He recognized her voice, soft and surly. 'Be short, there are a few people about.'

'Right. Have they found Berresford yet?'

'No.'

'What about the girl?'

'Not her either. No trace.'

'Any other news?'

'Yes. Two of our operatives were hit watching her flat.'

'You know the girl then?'

'Yes.'

'Could you pass over a photograph tonight, in the cellar?'

'Sooner if you wish.'

'I'll come myself. I'll leave now. Write down her full name and address and any other particulars you have on her. If you get interrupted leave it down in the basement. I'll pick it up from there.'

'O.K.'

'Have you got any news on the Russian involvement in Turnstile?'

'No. They've told me nothing. It seems we are protecting the organization but I don't know why,' she lied.

'Pity,' Anderson replied. 'Keep me posted won't you.'

'Have you got a job for me?'

'What do you mean?'

'If we don't succeed in getting Berresford in the next three days, they'll pass over the Turnstile operation to KGB.'

'How do you mean, pass it over?'

'I don't know that either. I just know that we won't be doing anything anymore. They've threatened to pull us out and send us home if we don't bring Berresford in.'

'That bad?'

'That important.' Her reply was quick. 'Leave some money for me too, please. I'm also low on champagne, cognac and scotch.'

'Oh, alright,' he said with a laugh.

'I can see one of our people just turning into the street. We're not supposed to use public phone boxes for private calls. I'll have to get going, I'll leave it in the basement.' She hung up.

Madeleine Kater was thirty-four. She was a slim, very attractive brunette.

Anderson had blackmailed her into coming over to the west as a double agent when he told her he had a watertight case of prostitution against her. It would have resulted in her being brought to trial.

She was being most useful, he thought as he left his office. His driver let him off at a station entrance. He bought two tickets going in different directions. He had a car waiting at each end. It was standard procedure.

Twenty minutes later he had the photograph and notes. Madeleine Kater did not appear in the cellar of the duplex but she had deposited the material for him.

'Very attractive,' he whistled as he looked at the photograph in the light. They had a lead at last. Now they knew who the girl was and what she looked like. Tom Brady would be pleased.

CHAPTER 37

'Wake up...come on, wake up, Sarah.' Berresford leant over Sarah, whose naked body was partially covered by a sheet. It was still hot, even though it was one a.m.

'What was that, eh?' Sarah turned over. In the half light she could see Berresford, blurred at first. She rubbed her eyes to accustom herself to the light. 'What time is it?'

'It's one o'clock. Nick is picking us up at the back of the hotel in half an hour. You've got to get up and get dressed.'

'Are we going, then?'

'Yes. Nick rang at about 11 o'clock and talked me into it. You were asleep.'

'Oh,' Sarah yawned. She sat up, the sheet only covering the lower part of her legs. She hooked an arm around his neck and kissed him. Berresford's large powerful hands held her at the top of the shoulders as he quietly pushed her back.

'Not now Sarah. I haven't been able to sleep. This is certainly not going to be any picnic. Come on, get dressed.'

Sarah took a deep breath, stepped out of bed and went towards the bathroom.

'You'll keep,' Berresford said softly, and proceeded to change.

'Where did you get those revolting old clothes?' Sarah whispered to Berresford as she came out.

'Nick sent them over earlier this evening. The porter didn't bring them up until after you went to bed.'

Sarah chuckled. 'I've never thought of you as a council workman.'

They arrived early at the meeting place at the rear of the hotel. Berresford was solemn, concerned and frightened. 'I'd do anything to change places with a street cleaner right now.'

'Come on, it's not that bad.'

Berresford's next remark indicated his reluctance. 'I'm not going to let him use you as bait. The plan's got to be foolproof, or you're not going in.'

'Michael, we've already discussed that,' Sarah said in a serious tone. 'We've got no choice.'

'Well I . . .' The conversation was interrupted by the whirring motor of the Jaguar as it pulled up only feet from them. Khomenko, wearing a dark brown track suit, gave the orders.

'Get in.' He leant over and opened the back door for them.

'Keep down till we're clear of the hotel.' The automatic gears changed to second and then to top. Khomenko's breath was foul. He had been eating garlic. Sarah found it nauseating.

'You can sit up now,' Berresford said softly to Sarah.

'Nick, I don't want Sarah placed at risk.'

Khomenko cut him short. 'There is no risk. I told you, I don't make mistakes. Now this is what you'll do.'

Khomenko stopped the car thirty yards from the corner of Sarah's street. Berresford broke the silence to reduce his nervousness.

'It's hard to believe that a street cleaner would be working at two o'clock in the morning.'

Khomenko pulled on the parking brake. 'Well here they do. The labourer brooms the rubbish from the gutter towards the centre of the road. The mechanical street cleaner comes by at half past two, spraying water on the pavement, its large scrubbing brushes picking up the refuse. I've paid the man off who does this section. He's left you his broom resting against that post.'

Khomenko pointed to the corner. 'I want you to work down the street. Be in front of the flats at quarter past two. Check your gun now.'

Berresford followed obediently.

'Hopefully I'll have them both before we leave the lift. You're only there as a back up. I'm sure you won't be needed. Come on, Sarah, get going. Remember exactly what I've told you.'

Sarah nodded. She slipped her hand over Michael's squeezing it momentarily.

'Here goes,' she said.

'Be careful, darling,' Berresford whispered after her.

Khomenko gave her two minutes. 'O.K. now take up your position on the broom.'

Berresford was alarmed. 'Don't you think Sarah's got too much lead?'

Khomenko was cold. 'No. I'm jogging, remember.'

'Of course.'

Berresford had already commenced sweeping before Khomenko left the car. The Russian quickly broke into a jog and turned the corner in the direction of Sarah's flat.

Sarah reached the security door and opened it, leaving the key in the lock as arranged. The lift was on the ground floor. She pressed the button and went up to the fourth floor. She stood outside the lift, waiting.

Khomenko jogged to the entrance and opened the door. He stepped in to the vacant lift. When it arrived on the fourth floor, Sarah was standing there. Khomenko nodded to her. The doors closed but the lift remained on the fourth floor. Sarah hurried to the flat's entrance. She had difficulty in getting the key in the lock. Her fingers were fumbling, her hands shaking. She turned the key.

Farwood was asleep in the lounge chair. He was awakened by Sarah entering the room. To her horror she faced Farwood, a gun in his hand.

He spoke through his teeth. 'Move out of the way.' He pulled her by the arm away from the door. His gun on the ready, he checked the hallway in both directions. 'No one,' he thought. The gun then trained on Sarah. 'Where is he? Where's Berresford?'

In sheer fright Sarah stumbled and stuttered. She had some difficulty in remembering her lines.

'Ah . . . Berresford is outside.'

'Is he coming in?'

'He's parked in the car up the street. If I'm not back in ten minutes, he will call the police.'

'Good,' Farwood said emphatically. 'Get into the bedroom.' He shoved the gun barrel painfully into her ribs.

'Lie face down on the bed with your hands behind you. One squawk out of you and you're dead.'

Farwood picked up the walkie-talkie from the small table near the door. He pressed the call button. Benini's voice barked back through the speaker.

'Yes?'

Farwood pressed the speak button. 'It's John. I've got the girl, Berresford's outside in a car. He's given the girl ten minutes to get back or he'll go to the police. I think she's bluffing.'

Farwood kept his gun trained on the girl. He did not hear the padded footsteps of the jogger. The handle of the door in the hallway turned silently then inched open.

Khomenko entered, his weapon drawn. Its twelve inch curved blade glittered in the light streaming from the bedroom. Every footstep, every move he made carefully calculated. With his back to the wall, he edged towards the open bedroom door. He could hear Farwood talking to Benini, only three feet away from him.

Perhaps Farwood smelt his garlic breath. Or perhaps it was the rustle of his clothes. No matter, it was too late for him to retaliate. As Khomenko's left hand grabbed Farwood's forehead, the large curved blade, razor sharp, slashed through cartilage, flesh, gristle and bone. The Khukri knife had done its job. Farwood's head was almost completely severed except for a few strands of flesh at the back of his neck. The lifeless body crashed to the floor.

Sarah screamed, and screamed again. She sprang off the bed and ran to the living room, her fingers pressed tightly against her face. She shook in terror, moaning, sobbing. Khomenko methodically wiped the blade on the bedspread, stepped over the body and confronted Sarah in the living room.

'Get yourself together,' he ordered. 'Snap out of it. There is one more to go.'

Sarah couldn't speak. She was in shock.

'Stay here,' Khomenko said. He returned to the living room and picked up the walkie-talkie. He looked at his watch. Twelve past two. Only three minutes left. He had to move quickly. He pressed the talk button.

'It's Berresford. I'm coming to get you, Benini.'

Benini was stunned. He failed to understand how it could have happened. How could Berresford have taken Farwood so easily? He grabbed the machine-gun, slid the bolt into firing position, and rushed to the door to assault Berresford and the girl when the lift stopped on the ground floor. To reduce the risk he lay flat on the floor.

Berresford, following the directions given by Khomenko, swept his way quietly along the street and arrived in front of the flats at precisely 2.15 a.m. To his horror he saw Benini rushing from the caretaker's door and positioning himself on the floor, machine-gun in hand. He dropped the broom and felt for his weapon.

The darkness around him was in his favour. The brightly lit entrance foyer provided plenty of

245

illumination on his target. The glass door and the glass panels on either side meant that Berresford had to seek refuge in the shadows of the shrubs near the entrance step. It was split second timing now.

Benini's eye was on the lift. It had left the fourth floor.

Three, two, one. His finger itched to press the trigger.

Berresford saw his chance. The .32 calibre Walther was extremely accurate, but unpredictable through the plate glass. In a two-handed stance, using the shrub as protection, Berresford lined up the sights on Benini's head. At this distance he could choose any inch of his body.

He fired three shots rapidly. The first shot missed its mark completely, due to the deflection of the glass.

Benini rolled violently to his right and trained his machine gun in Berresford's direction. Twenty rounds of nine-millimetre ammunition went past his hidden attacker, as Berresford's remaining shots landed where he had been. The lift stopped and the door opened. Benini fired another burst towards Berresford, sprang up and ran in retreat to the caretaker's entrance.

Khomenko sprang forward in a burst of fire. He ran to the caretaker's door, shot the lock and sprang back a few feet to miss any potential fire power from Benini. It didn't come. Seconds passed. Berresford joined Khomenko.

'You go the left, I'll take the right,' Khomenko ordered, as they burst into the caretaker's flat.

Too late! An open window. They both ran to it, stumbling over a suitcase on the floor. The noise from the gunfire had deafened them temporarily. They didn't hear the car but they saw its lights. Benini, once again, had escaped.

A small crowd of people had gathered around the front of the building. Almost every light was on in the block.

Police sirens wailed in the distance.

Khomenko eased the Jaguar's speed down to just below the limit. The traffic lights ahead turned to green. In the back, Berresford was consoling Sarah. Half a mile from the Sheraton, Khomenko broke the silence.

'O.K. You two, keep out of sight. We're almost back at the hotel.'

Berresford responded mechanically by pushing Sarah down. The car stopped.

'Get a good night's sleep, Michael,' Khomenko remarked drily. 'I'll be picking you up at a quarter past seven in the morning. I'll wait for you here.'

Berresford was numb, confused. 'What was that? Where are we going?'

Khomenko scoffed at Berresford's remark. 'Don't tell me you've forgotten? In the morning we're taking Moffatt.'

Berresford nodded, suddenly remembering. Sarah was still in shock. Her eyes were red and swollen, her cheeks pale, her chest was heaving, periodically giving a muffled sob.

Berresford helped her into his bed. She had not spoken since witnessing the horrific death of Farwood.

'You going to be alright?' he said, tenderly. He was not sure how much more he could take. He badly felt like a drink and after some consideration grabbed a bottle of scotch and took it to his room. Sometime later a fragile voice broke the silence.

'I can't sleep. When is it going to stop Michael?'

He stood up unsteadily and helped himself to another drink. 'Try to sleep, darling. I'll join you shortly.'

CHAPTER 38

The clear morning sun streamed through the numerous leadlight panes of his study window. The bevelled edges of the tiny panes acted as prisms, splitting the spectrum of light and projecting tiny, multi-coloured lines across the papers on his massive antique desk. The fragile, grey-haired old man stretched his sinewy hand to activate the television monitor.

Since his birth in 1900, Von Kessel had witnessed enormous technological changes, many of them taken for granted by younger people. The closed circuit television eliminated the necessity for him to leave his Belgravia mansion and to venture to the Turnstile offices in Knightsbridge. As he depressed the switch, Moffatt's office came on the screen. He adjusted the remote camera's lens to focus on his 38-year-old protege.

'Good morning, Andrew. What do you have to report this morning?'

The old man's voice was clear and brittle. His English was polished, flawless, perhaps a little clipped — a remnant from his German background.

Moffatt turned towards the camera as he spoke, his face faintly hinting a smile.

'Oh, good morning, Sir James. I was just in the process of recalling messages from the memory bank for the southern hemisphere.'

'Anything urgent?'

'The only matter of urgency, Sir James, is the

outcome of Benini's disposal of Berresford. I'll call you back after I have studied a read-out of his report as transmitted to the main frame last night.'

'Only if there is a problem, Andrew. While you are checking the latest on Berresford, give me a rundown on our latest banking manoeuvres in Argentina. Telex it through to my computer terminal, please.' Moffatt smiled. The old man had never quite adjusted to computer jargon. Messages relayed from terminal to terminal, to him, were still telexes.

The old man impatiently flicked the television monitor to standby. His eyes returned to the overly large vase of dark red roses standing on his desk. He leant over, his small, thin nose inhaling the refreshing fragrance. His mind went back to the beginning of his banking career in England, when he had been forced to take an English name.

The Cotterslowe family had lived in Berlin since 1882. It had been lucky for him that they had no close relatives in England, although they were British nationals. The whole family had been annihilated in the First World War. Von Kessel had discovered that the son's body had never been recovered. And the Cotterslowe family's hereditary title had made the name instantly attractive.

On Von Kessel's arrival in England as Sir James Cotterslowe, his youth, education and financial resources had greatly contributed to his immediate success. Having founded Turnstile Investments Ltd, he later sold his shares to nominee holders to keep his interests secret. He had officially resigned as director in 1944. From that time on he controlled Turnstile from behind the scenes through carefully chosen puppets, whom he paid well. Moffatt was his favourite.

Von Kessel was a tireless worker and rarely slept more than four or five hours a night. He was well aware of the problem that Berresford presented and it was he who had recommended that the man be assassinated.

As he wriggled a pair of gold wire-bound reading glasses onto the bridge of his nose, his attention focused on the petals of the roses. He discovered two blooms that were not perfect, and which in fact had started curling at the ends. With the care of an expert florist, he carefully removed the two blooms, ceremoniously trod on them, and then threw them into a small, inlaid timber wastepaper basket.

A door closed with a resounding, hollow thud, the large metallic latches hitting their counterparts. Crisp, sprightly footsteps stopped at the entrance to his study, followed by three slow knocks.

'Come in.'

His faithful, elderly valet appeared, carrying the morning newspapers and some fresh yoghurt. The latter was placed on a small silver tray, accompanied by a linen table napkin and a silver spoon.

'Will that be all, Sir?'

The old man replied slowly, his eyes greedily fixed on the yoghurt — his favourite morning snack.

'That will be all, Charles.'

Before the doors were quite closed behind the valet a new noise had disturbed the silence: a loud buzz. A small indicator light illuminated on the desk in front of Von Kessel. He activated his television monitor. After Von Kessel had focused it Moffatt's face was closer to the camera now than earlier. It distorted Moffatt's appearance.

'What is it Andrew?' The old man barked...He knew there was trouble coming.

'I have just read the communique from Benini, Sir. Farwood's dead. Berresford is still free...'

'What!'

'Yes. Berresford killed him. About that bank...'

'This is more important to me than any bank takeover in Argentina...more important than anything!'

'What should we do, Sir James?'

'Eliminate the meddler immediately, at all costs. Use any method. This man is a far greater threat than ever you anticipated,' the old man snapped. He picked up the bowl of roses and emptied the contents into the wastepaper basket. He pushed the newspapers off the table, letting them fall to the floor as he angrily turned off the television monitor.

Moffatt was not smiling any more. He had a lot of thinking to do, while getting ready for his customary morning run in the park.

Berresford was first to wake, surprised to be feeling so good after so little sleep. He was also surprised to find that he had been sleeping cuddled up to Sarah's back. Their naked bodies had held on to each other. He slid his arm out from under Sarah's shoulder. As he did so she came out of her drowsiness.

'Rub my back, please darling,' Sarah whispered as she rolled over to lay face down on the bed.

Berresford hesitated for a moment but was overcome by her tantalizing request. He pulled the bed clothes back and knelt on the bed beside her.

Sarah's shapely trim figure was lightly suntanned, except for the outline of a very brief bikini, which stood out in bold contrast. Gently at first Berresford started massaging with his thumbs and fingers around her neck, taking any tenseness from the muscles. Slowly and thoroughly his hands massaged deeply into her flesh to the base of her spine. With the edge of his hands he lightly chopped across her buttocks in scissor-like fashion, sinking deep into her flesh, his strong fingers worked on towards the top of her thigh.

Sarah breathed deeply. She was wide awake now, and relaxed, as every muscle was skilfully worked over by Berresford's hands.

'Now for the light treatment,' he whispered. He lay down beside her. Using one hand at first, his fingers glided over her skin, featherlike, touching her spasmodically on parts of her back, her waist and legs. Then, without warning his heavy finger ran straight up her spine, thrusting firmly against her. Moments later he walked his fingers firmly down the centre of her spine. Every nerve in Sarah's body was in tune to his seductive touch.

Berresford was breathing heavily, the excitement of touching her body rising by the minute, throbbing for relief. Sarah rolled over, smiling. She looked him over quickly, her eyes hesitating at first to take him all in. She whispered, expelling all the breath from her body in one sentence.

'Oh . . . you're so big. Lie down, Michael, it's my turn.'

Berresford lay down on his back and closed his eyes. She started round his neck, then ran her fingers in rhythmic circles around his chest. Her delicate young fingers massaged his stomach, then his thighs, by-passing the huge stalk standing in between. Sitting back on her heels she rubbed every portion of his legs to his toes, slowly returning with lighter touches to the apex of his thigh. Momentarily she held his testicles like pieces of fruit, bumping his erection as if accidently. He was ecstatic and moaning softly. Unconsciously he was thrusting his thighs upward, the two cheeks pinching in on the sides.

Sarah lay down beside him on her side, put one leg over his and began fairy-like kisses across his lips. Berresford responded passionately, his mouth opening to hers, her tongue exploring every sensitive spot in and around his mouth.

Sarah's hand returned to his thighs, lightly touching the long thick penis until she had hold of him. Her gentle strokes soon made him wet. She stopped, took her leg off his and lay next to him, her legs inches apart. His hand glided over her blond pubic hairs, his finger delicately touching her folds and then gently penetrating her.

She threw her arms around him and kissed him

passionately. No longer could she wait. She climbed on top of him, placing him into her. Her wet body fully consumed his as he gently massaged her breasts, causing her nipples to harden with excitement. He brought the bright pink centres to his lips and started to kiss them as Sarah started a slow rhythmic movement to coincide with his upward thrusts.

Berresford could no longer hold back. He gripped her two shapely cheeks near the base, pressing in on every upward movement, gripping his body in hers. Seconds later the release began.

Sarah bit her lip.

'Oh . . .'she gasped. 'Give it to me, I want all of you darling.' Her breathing desperate.

Grabbing her tiny waist he pulled her in close to him, whilst his body expanded and filled her.

'One more,' she moaned, then lay on top of him, both spent.

They kissed lightly, as if they were kisses of thanks. Then she lay down beside him, his arm around her shoulder.

'I love you darling,' he said, looking into her eyes, so full of contentment.

'I've loved you from the first moment I met you,' she said tenderly. 'I'll order some coffee and toast, we'll celebrate,' she continued excitedly, smiling happily while moving towards the telephone.

'Make it champagne.' Berresford purred swooningly.

Half an hour later, with champagne, expresso coffee and toast on a tray, they were sitting up naked in bed, chatting excitedly on any trivial subject. Their happiness was like that of children opening their Christmas gifts.

Berresford padded into the living room to get some cigarettes. The packet on the bar was empty so he fossicked around and found a new pack. When he returned Sarah had put the trays on the floor and was kneeling on the bed, her head near the pillows. She was furiously brushing away the crumbs off the bed. The sumptuous sight of her svelte figure, bottom in the air, sent a thrill through Berresford's body. He stubbed out the cigarette, his piece already erect and wanting.

'Don't move,' he said softly, as he slid onto the bed. His fingers dug into her narrow waist, filling her wetness as he guided his body in and out of hers. Sarah had her head on the pillow, slightly twisted. Her hand reached back and grabbed his knee as he thrust into her.

'I want it all,' she whispered as they both reached a climax. He fell back on the bed, and reaching for her pulled her close to him. They kissed with tenderness hitherto unknown to either of them.

'I never want to let you go,' he whispered.

'And I could never live without you,' she answered.

During the next half hour the world of horror stood still as they took comfort in each other.

Then suddenly an awareness of time hit Berresford. Khomenko would be furious if he was late. He scrambled out of bed and started searching for his clothes.

It was exactly a quarter past seven according to Berresford's watch. Khomenko was waiting with the motor of the Jaguar running. 'Get in and get out of sight,' he barked. He pushed the gear lever to drive and the car leaped forward.

'Do you know what time it is, Berresford?' he yelled. 'Seventeen minutes past seven. This exercise calls for split-second timing. Another minute and you could have fucked the whole thing up, if you haven't done it already!'

'I'm sorry I . . .'

'I'm not interested in excuses. Shut up and listen. There is a bottle of ether on the back seat and some gauze. When we stop I want you to soak it completely. We'll grab him in the park. I know the route where he jogs every day. It won't be difficult.'

'Sounds easy,' remarked Berresford ironically.

'The shit it is!' Khomenko growled. 'He's got two GRU bodyguards.'

'What!' Berresford asked.

'Two bodyguards.'

'Well, what'll we do with them?'

'They're too lazy to run with him. They drive around the park, keeping him in sight. There are three places where he's out of view for a few seconds. I picked the easiest one. I'll nab him as he runs through the park and bring him back to the car with a gun in his ribs. Put these handcuffs on him.' He threw a pair of handcuffs into the back seat. Two minutes later he stopped the car at the edge of the park.

'Have those cuffs ready. This whole operation depends on timing. We've got to nab him in under a minute.'

Khomenko strolled casually towards a row of large shrubs. In the distance Moffatt's light blue track suit stood out conspicuously. The rhythm of his running was punctuated by his stopping for a few seconds and doing an assortment of exercises.

Khomenko walked slowly, timing his steps with calculated precision. In his pocket his hand gripped a .38 Smith and Wesson revolver, purposely not loaded. Moffatt approached him unsuspectingly, and then ten feet away, started a new round of exercises. Ideal, thought Khomenko. He walked past, turned abruptly, jabbed the gun savagely into Moffatt's ribs. Moffatt grunted loudly in pain.

'One wrong move, and I'll blow your back out,' Khomenko warned. He grabbed Moffatt by the arm and steered him towards the car. 'That way,' he commanded. 'The brown Jag over there.'

Berresford prepared the ether swab. He wound the window down so as to avoid being anaesthetized. The cuffs were open. It was not until he had reached the car door that Moffatt recognized Berresford from the photographs that he had been given.

'You . . . you,' he kept repeating.

'Get in,' Khomenko ordered.

Berresford swung the door open and grabbed Moffatt by the hand. He clamped the metallic shackle to his wrist.

'Give him the other one,' Khomenko uttered through his teeth. Moffatt was bewildered. He offered his hand without a struggle. Khomenko joined them in the back seat, Moffatt wedged in the middle.

'Put him out.'

Berresford forced the pad across Moffatt's face as he kicked and struggled against Khomenko's powerful arms. Seconds later he lay still.

Khomenko sprang out of the car back into the driver's seat.

The motor was still running.

'Keep him under, Michael. We can't have him coming to until we get there.'

'Where are we going Nick?'

'I've rented a small house on a five-acre farmlet in Essex. We'll interview him there.'

Berresford shuddered. He could easily imagine what Moffatt's interrogation would be like.

CHAPTER 39

Sarah had just finished her makeup when there was a loud knock at the door. She jumped nervously and anxiously searched for her watch amongst the jars and tubes on the bathroom bench. Ten o'clock. It would be the maid. Never had Sarah been so on edge. When Michael left she had an appalling fear he would never return and then what gruesome end would they plan for her. The chain tightened between the door and the jamb as Sarah made a tentative assessment. The maid's white uniform with the hotel insignia on the pocket filled the gap, her face seemed familiar.

It was the eyes that upset Sarah initially. Deep daunting brown orbs with dark surrounding rings that stared in a sinister hypnotic fashion.

'I clean room now,' the woman said in English soaked in a deep Spanish accent. 'I suppose so.' Sarah replied mechanically somewhat dominated by the woman and she released the security chain. From that moment the maid took over. She jammed the door open and pulled the service trolley opposite the opening.

'Please close that door.' Sarah requested to no avail. 'Now' she insisted, her nervous tension increasing. The maid shrugged her shoulders twisting her face in a sarcastic expression and made no attempt to close the door.

Sarah closed the door noisily and now was annoyed and frightened.

Seconds later the maid opened the door again,

jamming a wedge tensioned against the spring hinge. It sent Sarah into a mild panic. Moving to close it she saw the thick set woman open the door to the bedroom where the surveillance equipment was kept.

'No, not that room.' Sarah yelled. The woman spun around to see Sarah's trembling finger point towards the bedroom where she and Michael slept. A cheeky smirk crept over the maid's face as she retreated.

'She's one of them.' Sarah thought. The maid went into the other bedroom. As soon as she was out of sight Sarah rushed to the phone and dialled the desk. She had to get rid of the stranger. No sooner had she started dialling when the maid returned to the living room, linen draped over her arm and hand. She rushed towards Sarah. A gun, she thought as she ran screaming towards the door; knocked over the service trolley and sprinted towards the lift.

The thick set maid hung up the phone and hurried to the door to be met by another member of the hotel staff.

'Are you O.K., what was that all about?'

'I'm alright,' the maid said in Spanish. 'It's that stupid English woman, she's mad. I wish I could speak more English, I would have understood what she was raving about.'

Sarah pressed the 'down' button repeatedly. At last a lift arrived. When the doors opened at 'lobby' level she realized she did not know where the executive offices were situated. Panic stricken she hurried, almost ran towards the arcade of shops.

Madeleine Kater combed the lobby, bars, restaurants and shops in the Sheraton as her Russian superiors had ordered. She was on her second round that morning when she saw Sarah hurrying past. The girl stood out conspicuously against the slower moving tourists. Madeleine opened her handbag and grabbed the hyperdermic gun loaded with anaesthetic, jostling the bag on her knee.

She wrapped a scarf over her hand and weapon, and went scurrying after Sarah. Two more steps and Madeleine threw her weight into Sarah's back knocking her to the floor, Madeleine was on top of her.

'Get off me, what are you doing!' she yelled. The syringe gun plunged into Sarah's arm, the contents wre despatched in a split second.

Sarah screamed. 'You bitch, you rotten bitch.'

Madeleine sprang to her feet and disappeared, intermingling with the crowd.

Sarah was hysterical. She realized that some foreign substance had been injected into her arm. She stood up. The assailant was gone. She ran in the direction of the foyer. Ten yards later she realized her mistake; they would follow her. Panic set in. She yelled loudly, 'Michael, what do I do?'

She crashed into a young teenage girl, tripping her over.

'Watch where you're going,' the girl yelled.

'A doctor, what ... which way.' She ran to the end of the corridor, towards the back entrance, the fire escape, stairs. It took three thrusts of the handle to open the door. The clatter of her shoes on the concrete steps reverberated in the stairwell. The basement door was ahead. As her fingers turned on the handle the door above slammed again. She was being followed.

Hotel staff were unloading boxes from the rear of a truck. The drug was taking effect. It would take full effect soon, and she knew it. Run! But where, which way? She couldn't think. She clambered down the steps. The truck driver and the storeman looked at her in complete amazement. One yelled, 'Where's the fire?' The other one laughed.

She looked back. The assailant, the woman, was less than ten yards behind. Her vision blurred, the sounds around her unreal. Her head began to spin, and the sensation of floating overwhelmed her. Were her feet touching the ground? A head, a face ten times the normal size staring down at her. And then the ground, the earth, and the entire solar system exploded.

'You're paying Mario, so it may as well be the best. The restaurant at the Ritz hotel at 12.30.'

Benini's reply was soft, almost musical. 'My dear little Madeleine, it better be good. I'm heavily committed to Turnstile at the present and I'm not supposed to leave the building.'

Madeleine felt smug; she had the girl. 'I'll meet you in the lounge just along from the dining room entrance.'

'Very well Madeleine. Goodbye.'

Madeleine was sipping her second dry martini when Benini strolled over to her table.

'Good afternoon, Madeleine. You look charming today.'

Benini sat down and beckoned the waiter over. The GRU had assigned Madeleine Kater to the Turnstile company to ensure its smooth operation. Benini had been advised by Moffatt some two years before that Madeleine Kater was a Russian agent who would assist them wherever possible. As a result of Benini's previous encounter with the Russians, the idea of working with her had intrigued him.

Although the woman had provided little by way of assistance to his work with Turnstile, she had provided, on occasions, satisfaction for his lust for flesh and debauchery. Her sexual tastes, like his, were bizarre. On one occasion he remembered, she had murdered a 20-year-old girl model on the point of climax as Benini raped her. They had much in common.

He leaned over towards her. Madeleine's libidinous nature appealed to Benini.

'Well, my tight little pussy, what have you got for me today?'

Her attractive face hardened. Her dark brown eyes stared into his. 'You're in trouble, you can't find Berresford.'

He was immediately taken aback. He was not surprised that she knew about Berresford. But he was annoyed that she was aware of his incompetence. While surprise was on her side she kept going.

'One hundred thousand dollars,' she said slowly. 'The price for the girl; I have her.'

Benini's eyes opened up, wide. 'You've what?'

'Shush!' She cautioned with a finger over her lips. She bent towards him and confirmed.

'I've got the girl. She's unharmed, just drugged. She's in a small warehouse not twenty minutes from here.'

'What's she like?'

'She'd be a good fuck, if that's what you mean.'

'No, will she talk?'

'I haven't even started on her. I want some money Mario. The Russians pay me next to nothing. I'm sick of it.' She glared at him, her eyes half closed. 'You screw out of her where Berresford is, root her stupid and get rid of her. I need that money,' she said emphatically.

'I can't give you a hundred thousand. That's out of the question. Fifty.'

It's worth that to save face, he thought.

'Seventy five,' she bargained.

'Done,' he said with a sick smile. 'How do you want it?'

'This is the number of my account in my bank in Lichtenstein,' she handed him a piece of paper. 'I'll ring them tomorrow morning and confirm that you've kept your part of the bargain. I'll keep her doped up until then.'

'You're a thieving, double-crossing bitch,' he said with a smirk.

But she might have saved my bacon, he thought.

'Now you buy me lunch, you gorgeous thing, and no stinting. It's beluga caviar, pheasant, the lot. And if you don't mind, Dom Perignon champagne.'

Benini was obviously excited 'Anything you like,' he said, still smirking, his mind set in crazed ambivalence; having sex with her, then killing her and Berresford.

CHAPTER 40

'Open the gate Michael, and when you close it after me, run the heavy chain through and padlock it with this.' Khomenko passed a padlock to Berresford.

A few minutes later Khomenko stopped his Jaguar at the front door of a quaint two storey house. The garden was unkempt. Numerous trees and a hedge separated the house from the neighbours. Privacy was assured.

'Grab his arms, I'll get his legs,' Khomenko ordered. Moffatt's body was still limp.

'How did you get this place?' Berresford enquired.

'Rented it especially for the job,' Khomenko lied. He had been there before, many times. 'It's ideal.'

Khomenko propped Moffatt against the front door while he searched for the keys. Berresford looked at Moffatt's face contemptuously.

'I've never had the ambition to kill anyone before,' he said, 'but this bastard's an exception.'

The house was very old. The lofty ceilings had been painted white between the large stained beams. The floor had long since rotted out and been replaced with cement over which brown Spanish tiles had been laid.

'Michael, drag him over there to the staircase.' Khomenko pointed to the balustrade at the base of the stairs. 'I'll get some rope from the kitchen.'

He's done this before, Berresford thought. Moffatt showed signs of regaining consciousness. He groaned, moved his head slightly, his eyelids flicking.

'Get all his clothes off, then prop him up. Here hold

him while I slip the cuffs off and tie his hands to the balustrade.' Khomenko skilfully tied his hands to the handrail, testing each knot before proceeding with the next. Then he tied the ankles together in turn to the staircase.

The unconscious Moffatt looked pathetic. Perhaps it was his nakedness that made him look so vulnerable.

'Why did you want to strip him?'

Khomenko stared at Berresford for a few moments before he answered. 'It creates the atmosphere of vulnerability. He'll break quicker this way.'

'What now?' Berresford enquired. Even his hate for Moffatt could not diminish the horror which was now set in his imagination. He knew that Khomenko was capable of anything.

Khomenko didn't speak but left the room. Some minutes later he returned with a strip of white fabric some inches wide and a little over a metre long. He'd dunked the lot into a clear fluid in a yellow and red tin.

'What's that?' Berresford enquired.

'Its fibreglass. I have to move quickly; it'll go off in a few minutes.'

'What are you doing with that?'

'I'm going to fibreglass his cock and balls to the bannister.'

'You're what?' Berresford said in alarm.

'Adds to the terror.' Khomenko replied.

The job was quickly accomplished. Moffatt's testicles and penis were now bonded to a solid four-inch square post.

'He's starting to come to.'

'Very good,' Khomenko smiled. He left the room again and returned from the kitchen carrying a round two-gallon tin with an open top. The vapour of petroliferous fluids came from the tin.

'Nick, what in the hell are you doing? Tell me!' Berresford demanded.

'Shut up. I'm doing this, not you. Do you want to get

into the Turnstile building? Well this is the only way. It's a mixture of petrol and oil. When he wakes I'll light it up. He can't pull away without hurting himself. I'll singe him up a bit, he'll talk.'

'Isn't there an easier way, Nick. Surely, with your background...can't you use drugs, pentathol or something?'

Khomenko laughed heartily. 'That went out with button-up boots. You've been reading to many spy stories. It's too unreliable, Michael. In my job people are conditioned, sometimes hypnotized; it doesn't work. Keep them conscious, vulnerable, terrified. Allow them the option of leaving unscathed if they talk. It's a far more sensible approach.'

Moffatt was regaining consciousness quickly. His eyes opened to a blurry image of Khomenko and Berresford. Suddenly nausea overtook him and the contents of his stomach gushed to the floor, leaving foul smelling particles dripping down his body.

'For God's sake,' Berresford muttered.

'Be quiet. We'll do it my way or not at all. I'm in charge here.' Khomenko meant business.

It was some minutes before Moffatt could comprehend the situation.

'You pig, Berresford. I'll kill you for this, and your accomplice,' he said.

Khomenko stood several feet from him, staring at him intently, his legs apart and his hands on his hips.

'Now you listen, you ignorant, fucking swine,' he hissed at Moffatt. 'Or that pretty parchment face of yours and pretty suntanned body will be a bubbly mess of third degree burns.'

'You won't, you can't.' The shock of the situation finally hit Moffatt. They were going to torture him.

'I'll tell you nothing,' he yelled. 'You'll never learn a thing from me!' He screamed. 'You can kill me!'

Khomenko took no notice and nonchalantly lit a match and dropped it into the can. The flame barely reached the top of the can, but the intense heat went six to eight feet in the air. Khomenko tested it quickly with his hand.

'I can't stand it,' Berresford yelled. Tested beyond endurance, he pushed Khomenko back.

Khomenko lashed out with his hand, which crashed into Berresford's head. 'I haven't gone to all this fucking trouble to help you so as to put up with that bullshit!'

Berresford heard nothing. He was out, unconscious. Khomenko continued. He had a pernicious streak.

'Now look here, Moffatt, I want some answers and I want them quick, or I'll roast you to death.' He moved the can closer, the heat burning the hairs on Moffatt's legs and chest. He moved it back again.

Moffatt screamed in terror.

'Now listen, Moffatt, you cooperate and we'll let you live, which is far more than you deserve. I won't even cut your fingers and toes off.' Khomenko's hand plunged under the coat to remove the razor-sharp knife. Moffatt's eyes were wide with terror, his head shaking with disbelief.

'What do you want to know,' he said between sobs.

Khomenko pushed the flame near him again.

'Don't, don't!' Moffatt screamed. 'I'll tell you everything.'

Khomenko, still with the knife in hand, left the fire near Moffatt's face a few seconds more. Then he prised it back with his knife.

'How many companies does Turnstile control?'

'Seven hundred and sixty three,' was the instantaneous reply.

'How many years have you been going?'

'I don't know anything except for the past ten years ... Can't tell if I don't know.'

'Who is The Telex?'

'I don't know, I don't know,' Moffatt cried.

The fire came closer. He was sobbing loudly now.

'Ask me anything else,' he pleaded. Khomenko moved the fire away from him.

'Who killed Berresford's wife?' It worked again.

'Benini and Farwood. They did it, they did it!' Moffatt screamed.

'Who requested it?'

'The old knight. The Telex himself.'

'What's his name?'

'I know it's Sir James. What other name he has I don't know. I've spoken to him but I've never seen him in the flesh. It's a complete mystery. I only work for him. So do Benini and Farwood, and the other three managers.'

'How do you control your accounts, your messages? Is it in a computer?'

'Yes, yes,' Moffatt yelled. 'It's all in the computer on the tapes. In the basement.'

'What sort of security?' Khomenko was testing. He already knew the answers to some of the questions.

Moffatt gushed the words out. 'Only four of us can enter the computer room. There is a guarded anteroom before entering it. Once past the guard we place our right hand on a plate. It checks our fingerprints on the computer. If they match exactly the door opens.'

'Security, more!' yelled Khomenko.

'If any attempt is made any other way, there is a massive electrical field set around the tiny computer room. It will erase all the tapes.'

'How do I turn it off?' was the next question.

'Yes, you can turn it off. There is a row of buttons on the wall. The combination is 1356.'

Khomenko memorized the numbers.

'Is there any timing device on the door to the computer room?'

'Yes.'

'You held back.' Khomenko applied more flame. Moffatt screamed with pain, and then sobbed, 'It can only be opened between 10 and 11 a.m. or 3.30 and 4 p.m. Any other time will erase the tapes.'

'Good,' said Khomenko.

'Let me go!' Moffatt begged.

Khomenko turned to see Berresford coming to. He dragged him outside through the front door, and propped him on the front verandah. 'I'm sorry, Michael. I think it was too much for you. It's all over. We'll have to force one of the other three managers to let us in. He's in too bad a shape to do it, we'd never get away with it.'

Berresford was silent.

It was true. Moffatt's skin was badly burnt. Blisters had already appeared on his legs, chest and face. He looked a wreck.

'Well I'd better kill him,' Khomenko said viciously as he waved the Khukri blade towards the room inside.

'No!' yelled Berresford. 'No, don't. No murder, please. I could not be responsible for it.'

'Don't be such a fucking idiot!' Khomenko roared.

'I won't cooperate if you kill him,' Berresford yelled back.

'Very well.' Khomenko suddenly gave in. He returned to the room and cut one of Moffatt's hands free.

'Cut yourself free, you fuckwit,' he said, hissing through his teeth. 'You're lucky to be alive.'

'Thank you, thank you,' Moffatt pleaded. He was sobbing again.

'Cut yourself out of it — the fibreglass as well. I don't want to touch your filthy cock. There are no other doors or windows open in the house but the front one, so there's no point in trying to escape. Get your clothes on and come out to the front door. There is no phone. You can't go anywhere, but one false move and I'll blow you to kingdom come.' Khomenko tapped the large calibre revolver with its silencer and joined Berresford on the verandah. He closed the door behind him.

Moffatt hastily cut loose the other hand and then his legs. Sheer perseverence stopped him from fainting. He then had the delicate job of cutting loose the fibreglass strap.

Weakened by the ordeal, he kicked over the tin of burning liquid. The fire beneath him started to burn his legs and body. He screamed at the top of his voice, then made a quick decisive cut.

Khomenko pushed the door back against the body, his gun ready in hand. Moffatt had collapsed on the floor.

Khomenko commanded. 'Grab a rug and put the fire out, quick, before it burns the house down.'

When the fire was out Khomenko recapitulated.

'Well I'll have to kill him now.'

'No! No!' persisted Berresford. 'No. We've already gone too far. Where are the bedrooms? I'll wrap him in a sheet. He's got to go to hospital. We'll have him tried for murder, we'll get the tapes.'

Khomenko sighed and shook his head slowly, but he agreed. 'Very well, the bedrooms are up the stairs on either side.'

The malodorous smell of burnt flesh was nauseating. Berresford was sick twice wrapping up Moffatt's body. He was still alive, but bleeding profusely.

'No not in the back seat, you idiot, in the boot.' Khomenko commanded as they carried the body to the car.

'For God's sake, Nick. He'll suffocate.'

'I'll leave it open a few inches, I'll stick something in there. Don't worry he'll make it. The bloody smell'll turn me off my lunch.'

Berresford agreed. Anything to save the man's life. On the way back to London Khomenko pointed out a small hospital. He stopped, made a phone call, and then drove towards the emergency ward. Two professional police impersonators were already on their way

to take Moffatt into the hospital. They would pretend
to the hospital staff that Moffatt had been in a nasty
accident involving dangerous chemicals and that they
had everything under control.

CHAPTER 41

Her lunch with Benini over, Madeleine Kater returned to the Sheraton. She would nab Berresford as well, she thought.

Berresford was visibly shaken by Moffatt's torture. He had not said a word since leaving the hospital. Khomenko stopped at the rear of the hotel.

'We're here,' Khomenko boomed. 'It's clear, you can get up now.'

Berresford scrambled from the car and hurried up the steps near the loading ramp, and ran across the basement floor. He pulled the door opening into the hallway which led to the service lift.

It was sheer luck for Madeleine that she was in that part of the hotel when Berresford returned. Normally, with Madeleine's extensive training, she would not have displayed any sign of surprise when she confronted Berresford. However, the martinis and champagne consumed at lunch-time took their toll. Berresford could not help reading her face as she stared at him, mouth agape, ten feet away. The shock was instantaneous and mutual. Berresford was the first to react.

I won't use the lift, he thought, quickly turning towards the stairwell. He flung open the door and ran up the first flight of stairs. Madeleine Kater scuttled after him. Berresford pulled out the magnum that Khomenko had given him and slipped back the hammer. He clapped his feet up and down in the same place on the concrete landing, simulating the sound of a person running up the stairs.

Confused by all the wine that she had drunk, Madeleine did not detect the difference. She ran up the stairs, turning onto the landing.

'Freeze,' Berresford roared. She stopped dead in her tracks. His gun was trained at her head. She put her hands on her head and slid down to the floor, her legs buckling beneath her and rested with her back against the wall.

'Who are you, you bitch? You're from Turnstile aren't you?' Berresford spat out the words with vehement contempt in every word.

Shocked by the confrontation with Berresford, Madeleine's face spoke bewilderment. She stammered. 'I'm a friend. I'm trying to help you.'

'Lies,' Berresford hissed. 'Lies!' he repeated.

'I've just been talking to Sarah.'

'What?' Berresford exploded, trying to clear the chaos in his mind.

'Yes. She's staying at my place now.' Madeleine was stalling for time. The shot of adrenaline caused by the unexpected situation helped her regain her faculties. Her right hand was reaching for something. A small .38 calibre two-shot derringer, strapped to her leg under her skirt.

The gun was in her hand and partly raised when Berresford fired. The explosion in a confined space was thunderous. Berresford was momentarily deafened by the sound.

The bullet penetrated Madeleine Kater's ribs, her heart and lungs. Her stricken body toppled over on the floor. Berresford's face contorted with revulsion as the blood gushed in pulsating streams from the gaping hole in her chest.

He realized he had no time to waste if he was to remain undetected. He tore down the stairs and ran down the corridor to the service lift.

He arrived at his room panting and slammed the door after him, then frantically called Sarah. His hearing was still impaired. He thought that she might be answering and couldn't hear her. He ran from room to room in mad panic, then it dawned on him. Sarah was gone.

The surroundings were as unfamiliar to Sarah as were the noises. A faint pungent smell of lathe machine oil added to her confusion. A bell clanged loudly nearby indicating to workers a change of shift. The bell did it. Sarah sat up. The feeling of nausea rose from her stomach. Her face was wan from the effect of the powerful drugs and her hands trembled as she touched the tender skin bruised by the injections.

She moaned loudly. Her eyes strained to read the time on her watch, but there was insufficient light to see the tiny hands. It must be eight or nine o'clock she thought. Slowly the events that had occurred that morning came back to her.

'My God, I've been drugged.' Blood rushed to her head forcing her to lie back on the camp stretcher and rest for a few moments. 'I've got to get out of here!' she thought. 'Before that bitch comes back. She's kidnapped me!'

Painfully she rolled off the stretcher and looked around her. It was some sort of warehouse, or perhaps a small vacant factory. She could barely make out the walls and ran her hand over the uneven surface of brick.

Sarah staggered around the periphery of the building. The factory was empty. A large metal roller door led to the street. A smaller metal covered timber door was beside it. She tried the lock. The rattle on the outside seemed to indicate that it had been padlocked. Desperately Sarah tried to raise the roller door. She shook it vigorously in an effort to set it free. No such luck. Tears of disappointment and despair filled her eyes. Sarah continued to explore the rest of the factory in mad panic.

The next wall was bare, also made of brick. The roof was at least twenty feet high, and the skylight which admitted the feeble light, well out of reach. One more wall remained to be explored. This was different. It led to a room lined with asbestos cement sheets. The door to it was open. It was empty. The wall behind it was brick as well. A small skylight in the roof above provided no means of escape.

'Oh what am I going to do? What will Michael think? He must be frantic by now,' she moaned.

She returned to the camp stretcher. Her handbag was on the floor. She snatched it up and rummaged inside. She remembered that there was a small penlight torch in one of the pockets. With renewed confidence Sarah then began a more critical inspection of the factory.

The factory had been used for some engineering process. There was evidence of metal filings, and that smell of some strange oil which is usually associated with engineering. Twenty minutes later Sarah had her first break.

She discovered a broken hacksaw blade wedged in a narrow expansion crack in the concrete. At least half of it remained. Closer inspection of the two doors proved that both doors were indeed locked from the outside, probably by padlocks. But for the smaller door she thought there was a chance. The two large hinges were accessible to her and now she had the tool to cut through them.

The work was tedious and painstaking. The top hinge was only just within reach. It took almost two hours to cut it free. The door would still not open, but there was plenty of movement.

Sarah surmised that there was no guard outside; they would have heard the sawing with her hacksaw blade. She started sawing again.

The last inch took over an hour and a half due to the deterioration of the blade. Desperately Sarah tried to prise the door open. It was not made to open inwards and with all her pulling would not open enough for her to get through. At last she pushed in final desperation. It gave way with a resounding creak and she tumbled through the opening, falling exhausted to the ground.

It was a narrow industrial street. A number of small, modern factories lined both sides. Two hundred yards away Sarah spotted a telephone booth. She returned for her handbag and hurried towards it. Michael must be beside himself she thought, as she dialled the number.

The switchboard connected her to his room. There was no response. Sarah considered the various possibilities. The terrifying thought struck her: perhaps Michael was dead. Perhaps he was out looking for her, perhaps Benini had got him. She dialled for a taxi cab.

The taxi dropped her in front of the hotel. She was paying the driver when she thought of it. 'My God, how can I be so stupid. I've stepped into the lion's den.'

The lift door was about to close when a passenger pressed the open button to admit another person. Fear came over her instantly. The man in the lift appeared to stare at her. He had recognized her immediately.

He turned away from her and took something from his pocket. He tried to prevent her from seeing what it was. Sarah boldly pulled his arm back. It was a picture of her. She screamed.

'I won't hurt you, I won't hurt you. Please, please,' the man pleaded. He had an American accent.

'Who are you?' Sarah demanded.

'I'm working for the American government. We're desperately trying to get in touch with your friend, Michael Berresford. Is he in this hotel?'

'No, he's not.'

'Well, what are you doing here then?'

She had to fabricate something quickly.

'I've got to meet a friend of his.'

The man did not believe her.

'Where are you staying then?'

'We were staying in a small hotel, in another suburb. We've moved out, I haven't anywhere at present.'

She didn't want to leave the hotel but she did not want to admit that Berresford was staying there.

The man looked intently at her.

'We've set up rooms on the fourth floor. I'd like you to meet some of our men. Perhaps we can convince you that it is in the interests of the American government to find Berresford. It's certainly in his and your interest too.'

'O.K. I'll go along with you.'

A spot of luck, she thought. At least she would have a good idea of what was going on.

On the fourth floor, she was shocked to see the set-up in the suite. She wondered whether in fact the six men were CIA agents. There were rifles and surveillance equipment. One man was monitoring a telescope connected to a video camera and recorder. A table was cluttered with multifarious and complicated pieces of radio communication equipment.

None of the men were carrying any credentials. Sarah began to have some doubts. She did not respond to their questioning. They realized that they had pushed her too far when she collapsed in the chair exhausted. Caringly they carried her to the bedroom, where she slept soundly.

CHAPTER 42

Andrew Moffatt had been conscious for almost three hours. The nursing sister had refused to administer any further morphine. The pain was excrutiating. Even worse was the feeling of hopelessness.

It was the prospects for the future that drove him past the limit of sanity. Although every move brought intense pain, he struggled out of bed and shuffled to the large window. The wind was cool and refreshing on Moffatt's body as he threw the window wide open.

The scream from the nursing sister prompted one of Khomenko's fake policemen keeping guard, to rush into Moffatt's room.

'He's jumped out the window!' she cried. 'Poor man must have flipped. Better off dead anyway than the way he was.'

Khomenko's man agreed. 'No use ringing an ambulance here. We'll go and supervise a couple of your staff who can shovel him up and stick him in the freezer, till we arrange for him to go to the morgue. There will have to be an enquiry, you see.'

The nursing sister thought that they were being very callous, but she agreed.

'I'd better report the matter.'

'Don't worry, we'll look after the police side of it.'

The girl nodded.

Berresford had slept through Sarah's call. His tortured mind had completely failed to respond to the shrill ring of the phone. However, by the time Khomenko's call came he was greatly rested and answered on the second ring.

'It's Nick. Moffatt's dead, jumped out the window. Good thing, don't you think?'

Berresford replied thoughtfully. 'No, I would have preferred him to live out a life of misery. What are you doing with the body?'

'My men will take care of it. We'll incinerate him later in the day.'

Suddenly Berresford seized on an idea.

'Nick, that's it! That's all we need!' he yelled in excitement.

'What in the hell are you talking about?' Khomenko demanded.

'That's the answer, the key to the computer room I mean.' Berresford's mind was racing.

'Can't you seek Nick? All we need is his right hand, if it's not mutilated.'

Khomenko seized on the idea. 'Of course!' he said. 'Right, we'll do it tomorrow.' Berresford's brain was more alert than Khomenko's.

'No way. We've got three hours to do it.'

'Why is that?'

'Haven't you heard of rigor mortis? It sets in very quickly after death.'

'Christ!' yelled Khomenko. 'We'll have to move quick.' He immediately put the receiver down, then lifted it and started dialling again.

Mario Benini looked at his watch again, for the third time in ten minutes. Madeleine Kater hadn't rung. What in the hell was she doing? Had he been duped? The thought occurred to him that perhaps she didn't have the girl after all. He'd kill the bitch if that was the case.

He connected the computer modum to the Turnstile telephone line which led to the main frame of the computer. A search revealed a new message.

Attention M. Benini —
Take appropriate armaments to Turnstile building
this morning. You have been assigned to internal
security in the Turnstile office. Moffatt has been
killed in a car accident. Full details yet unknown.
Remain on ground floor with armaments nearby.
Let no one, repeat no one, near computer room
except three managers. Your failure this time will
cause us to revert to the original threat.

The Telex.

Benini yelled the ultimate obscenities and
blasphemies. 'Porco Dio! Porca Madonna!' He
stamped across the room, kicking a chair out of his
way, leaving it broken on the floor, and started packing
his armaments.

After his conversation with Berresford, Nikolai
Khomenko was busily engaged on a round of telephone
calls. His men were protecting Moffatt's body. It would
be delivered to his flat any moment.

His next call was a most important one, to the second
in charge of the KGB in London.

'It's Khomenko, Comrade. I have important news for
you.' He told him of Berresford's plan.

'Excellent, comrade Khomenko, excellent. We can
dovetail that into our plans beautifully. You will
receive a great reward if you achieve this. Never forget
that if it fails we want Berresford as a scapegoat. I have
read all your report. One thing worries me: are you
certain about Berresford?'

Khomenko was confused. 'I'm sorry, I'm not sure
what you mean.'

'Well, are you sure that he didn't recognize you
leaving the restaurant the night you killed the professor
in Germany?'

'No chance,' was the instant reply.

'But he must have seen you on the black motorbike when you took the two GRU men out in that back street?'

'Yes, you're right. He did see me but he couldn't recognize me. My head was covered with a safety helmet and the visor was smoked. We've tested it from fifty feet. He couldn't possibly have recognized me.'

'You don't think he'd have any suspicions about the two men you took out in front of Sarah's flat with his gun?'

'None at all. He hasn't got a clue. I can assure you that he's completely in the dark.'

'Very well then. Go ahead with your plan. Plan "E" isn't it?'

'Yes.'

'Good luck.' And the man hung up.

CHAPTER 43

Berresford hurriedly unfastened the chain as Khomenko knocked at his door.

'Where in the hell have you been?' Berresford's face looked haggard. Khomenko remained quiet, cold and calculating.

'I had to arrange things.'

Khomenko's eyes descended to the brown canvas bag. A chill went down Berresford's spine.

'Oh God, you bastard, you've cut off his hand, haven't you? Is it in there?'

'Yes.'

Berresford swallowed hard. A thin callous smile crept across Khomenko's face as he spoke.

'I had to do it,' he said quietly.

Berresford was on the verge of being ill.

Khomenko raised his black bushy eyebrows. 'Where's Sarah?'

'She's not here. I don't know.' Berresford's face was still white.

Khomenko exploded. 'Fuckwit! What are you doing to me Berresford? When did she go?'

'She was gone when I came back last night.'

'Why didn't you tell me?' Khomenko roared.

'I thought she might come back of her own accord.'

'You might have blown the whole operation!' Khomenko's hand felt for his automatic pistol. He rushed for the door, inched it open then pulled it open quickly and looked down the hallway. He beckoned

Berresford over with his finger.

'Is that the regular janitor?'

Berresford took a quick glance through the open door. He nodded.

'Piss her off,' Khomenko ordered.

Berresford stepped forward and spoke kindly to the woman, he pointed out the 'do not disturb' sign he had placed on the door knob.

Khomenko was in the bathroom cleaning the hand. The palm and fingers were in good shape and still reasonably supple. He called out, 'Michael'.

Berresford stood at the bathroom doorway refusing to go in.

'We can't waste time,' Khomenko continued. 'I'll fill you in with the details. I have a small white panel van waiting at the back of the hotel with a driver.'

Berresford started to speak. Khomenko gestured with his hand that he was not to be interrupted.

'I've instructed him to drive down the street, and turn the van round so that he is on the same side of the street as the Turnstile building. He'll stop at the entrance. It's split-second timing. Run up the steps across the main foyer, take a left turn down the stairs to the computer room. I'll take care of the guard.'

Probably murder the poor blighter, Berresford thought.

Khomenko had anticipated that. 'He's one of them Michael. He's no better than Benini. After I take the guard out, you go first into the anteroom and shoot out the television monitor. Then I'll join you. You can have the pleasure of opening the computer room with the hand.' Berresford shuddered. 'There are a number of tapes. Put them all in this bag.' Khomenko pointed to the brown canvas bag on the floor. 'Most importantly, as soon as the door opens you must cut the automatic erase system. Do you know the buttons?'

Berresford repeated the code that Moffatt had given Khomenko.

'One, three, five and six. I'm sure of it.'

'Yes, that's correct,' Khomenko confirmed.

'How do we escape?'

'Leave that to me. We'll cross our bridges as we come to them. Take the magnum and a few spare shells.' Khomenko turned on the shower to give the final rinse to Moffatt's hand. He dried it carefully, then put it in the bag. Suddenly Nick gave Berresford a menacing stare. 'The Von Kessel Dossier, where is it?'

'It's got nothing to do with this or you.' Berresford said firmly.

'I want it Michael, or we don't go.'

'What do *you* want it for?'

'I think it's a job for ASIO. Now do I get it — or do we call the whole thing off?' the Russian roared, his hand feeling the gun in his pocket.

Berresford had no option. 'O.K. I'll get it. It's hidden in the service lift.'

Minutes later Berresford returned and gave the dossier to Khomenko.

'In return my friend, here is the name and address of "The Telex",' Khomenko said as he handed Berresford a piece of paper.

'What...how did you...when...for God's sake Nick, what's going on?'

'I obtained it yesterday. Kept it for a surprise. He's yours after the break-in.'

Something's wrong, thought Berresford — very wrong, but what? Where?

'Come on, let's go. The Turnstile break-in is about to begin,' Khomenko said as he moved towards the front door.

The CIA man focused the telescope on the white van as it pulled up in front of the Turnstile building. He yelled to Brady.

'Tom, come quickly, there is something happening.'

Brady dropped the photographs of the Russian

agents which the unit had collected. The five sheets fluttered to the floor. The van door swung open.

'It's Berresford!' he yelled. 'And some chap with a stocking over his head.'

Brady stared out the window and yelled orders to his subordinates.

'Cover them, quick! Anderson, get Hillings on the phone.'

'Too late!' someone else yelled. 'One of the Russians has opened up on him.'

'Take him out!' Brady ordered. Too late, the GRU operative fired a burst from his machine pistol, the first aimed at Berresford and then at Khomenko.

Khomenko dived to the ground, narrowly avoiding the bullets that whistled over him. A dapper business man dressed in a grey suit and old school tie was caught in the crossfire, he collapsed to the ground, blood gushing from his face; he thrashed helplessly on the footpath. More shots, the Russian agent reeled backwards, his arms thrown wildly. The CIA marksman made a fatal shot. Berresford clambered up the steps. A bullet, narrowly missing him, spattered against the wall and then ricocheted off with a high pitched whistle.

More shots came from the street above. Another Russian agent picked out by the CIA marksman dropped to the ground. Blood gushed through his green jumper and onto the footpath. Khomenko was on his feet running after Berresford. Seconds later they had both reached the safety of the Turnstile foyer.

'Run, run,' yelled Khomenko.

Berresford raced down the steps. He hesitated when he saw the guard, who was attempting to unstrap his pistol from the holster. Khomenko's gun roared. The guard toppled over and fell to the floor.

'Quick, you're first.' Khomenko yelled. 'The camera ...the television camera,' he repeated.

Berresford opened the door to the anteroom. One

shot from his pistol held in a two hand stance shattered the television camera to small fragments.

Khomenko slammed the door behind him and thrust the large bolt across. It would take time to break that one down, he thought.

Berresford pulled the arm out of the bag.

'Arm down, fingers up,' yelled Khomenko. 'That's it there,' he said, pointing to a white glass plate some ten inches square, about four feet from the floor.

'Press it evenly, Michael. Take your time.'

Berresford's hands were shaking. He had difficulty in holding the arm still. Ten whole seconds passed, then the computer accepted the fingerprint pattern. The mechanism responded with a series of loud clunks as the bolts receded into the huge, safe-like door. Khomenko spun the big wheel and pulled the door towards him.

'It's all yours,' he said to Berresford, smiling.

Berresford nodded and started towards the rack of tapes in front of him.

'Cut the erase circuit, you fucking idiot!' yelled Khomenko.

Berresford stopped in his tracks. To the right of the door there were ten buttons. One, three, five and six; he pressed them sequentially. A resounding snap of a circuit breaker came from a grey steel box on the other side of the room.

Some miles away in a palatial mansion in Belgravia the old grey haired man responded to the shrill bell which indicated an emergency. Someone had broken into the Turnstile computer room. In a fleeting moment he caught sight of Berresford taking aim at the camera.

The old man was a master planner. He was prepared for any contingency. He sat bent over his ornate desk and flipped up a small black cover, exposing an array of buttons. He pressed the green buttons, all four of them.

In the Turnstile building the security doors disguised as fire doors slammed shut. Contrary to fire regulations they could not be opened now without cutting tools and heavy equipment. Huge stainless steel bolts slammed into position, locking everybody inside. Only Benini escaped. He had responded to the shooting and had run down the steps towards the computer room.

On the rooftop of the building, under a four-thousand-gallon stainless steel tank containing pure alcohol four powerful instantaneous heaters commenced their task of raising the temperature to an explosive level. The numerous and methodically placed sprinklers commenced spraying the volatile fluid into the offices — over the files, the desks and the people.

The slamming of the doors, the spray of acrid smelling liquid sent the staff into hysteria. Von Kessel pressed the first red button. The top floor of the building exploded as if hit by a bomb. With the next red button depressed, the second storey suffered the same fate; and then the third. Only the ground floor and the computer room remained.

'Hurry Michael,' Khomenko yelled, 'we've only got seconds.'

The colourless, volatile liquid was pouring into the computer room. The only decoration in the anteroom was a large and ugly abstract painting about four feet in diameter. Khomenko prised it off the wall with his knife, exposing a three-feet diameter hole. It was a tunnel: an escape route.

'How did you know that was there?' Berresford yelled.

'I do my homework,' was the curt reply.

Benini aimed his powerful pistol at the lock on the anteroom door. The stainless steel teflon coated bullets smashed into the bolt mechanism, and then ricocheted madly around the small room.

'Hurry, he'll be through in a minute,' yelled Khomenko as he climbed into the tunnel.

Berresford pushed the bag of tapes in front of him and followed Khomenko down the two-hundred-foot pipe which led to a huge underground sewer. They could hear more crashes behind them.

Benini was almost through. They're gone, he thought. The room was full of the flammable fluid. The ante room door closed after him. It was too dark to see down the tunnel. He couldn't risk a shot in case it blocked his escape. He clambered into the pipe.

Berresford was almost out. He pushed the bag out and Khomenko grabbed it. The clanging of a metallic object could distinctly be heard at the other end of the tunnel.

'Hurry!' yelled Khomenko. 'There can't be much time.'

The old man's hand poised over the last button. The ante room was the chamber; the fluid and gas the explosive; the escape pipe, the barrel; Benini the projectile. There was a thunderous explosion as the ground floor, anteroom and computer room blew up simultaneously. Benini's body was thrust at enormous velocity down the pipe, his scream of terror barely audible above the overpowering noise of the exploding material around him.

Khomenko and Berresford heard the bang. They saw the flash and some object hit the wall fifty feet on the other side of the sewer. The bloody clothes and pulped remains fell in a heap into the water and effluent swirling below.

Khomenko and Berresford stood up, their ears still ringing from the enormous explosions.

'Up the steel ladder,' Khomenko yelled, pointing a few yards ahead at the sewer hatch. He leaned down and lifted the metal hatch, easing it off with a large screwdriver. Berresford was next. As he came out his eyes blinked. Khomenko laughed. 'Give me the tapes Michael, I'll be waiting for you back at the hotel.'

'Now for your moment of glory, old fellow. Go and get yourself "The Telex".'

CHAPTER 44

Khomenko's Jaguar pulled into the arrivals drive at Heathrow Airport. Khomenko got out and dutifully opened the door for the Russian official in the back seat. Khomenko waited while the Russian adjusted his coat. The tapes were now transferred to the Russian official's black leather case.

'May I carry your bag for you Comrade?' Khomenko offered politely.

'No, I'm right.'

'But I insist,' Khomenko said respectfully as he picked up the diplomat's bag.

Sarah, in shock, lay stunned on the bed in the CIA hotel room. She had heard one of Brady's men say, 'No one could have survived those explosions. Berresford's dead.' Then the phone rang.

'It's for you.' Anderson said, looking at Brady. 'It's our Consul-General.'

The hollow voice on the phone was yelling in excitement.

'Tom, great news. Vadimir Kertoff, the top man from the GRU, has defected. He's here now. He wants asylum in the United States. He says that Berresford escaped from the Turnstile building through a secret tunnel. Apparently Berresford has gone over to the Russians, but not the GRU. He's handed the tapes over to the KGB.'

'Impossible.' Brady said, bewildered.

'Well Kertoff is on our side now and I can't see any reason not to believe him. Most importantly, the Russians are on the way to the Heathrow Airport. An Aeroflot plane has been delayed for some hours, the excuse being minor electrical faults. Kertoff believes they will take the tapes back to Moscow. We've still got time to retrieve them.'

'Is Berresford with them?'

'No. Berresford has been given the identity of the leader of Turnstile. His name is Sir James Cotterslowe. He lives in Belgravia.' The Consul-General gave Brady the address. 'If you want Berresford, that's where you'll find him.'

'It's beginning to make sense,' said Brady. 'We know there has been some infighting between the GRU and KGB but I never thought it would get to this.'

'Get to what?'

'It's impossible for Berresford to have done so much on his own. He's clever, but not that good. I think the KGB could have been behind the thing all along. Perhaps they wanted to blame it on Berresford, to use him as a scapegoat. It makes sense,' he repeated.

Brady continued excitedly. 'Why would he kill GRU men to give the tapes to the KGB? Think about that one.'

Suddenly Brady realized the importance of his latest knowledge. He wanted to tell Sarah. He became anxious to terminate the conversation.

'Is there anything else I should know?'

'Yes, this is important too. The major stumbling block is the Russian official at Heathrow with the KGB man. He's top shelf, a member of the Politburo. If he has the tapes, we can't touch them or him. Nor could customs under his diplomatic immunity. What can we do?'

Brady's assessment was immediate.

'Our only hope is Berresford, if he's on our side. He could retrieve them. We can use him as *our* scapegoat

— don't you see?'

'I'm not sure,' the Consul-General replied, 'but it's worth a try. I still think he's turned.'

Brady slammed the phone down. Sarah would have to wait just a bit longer.

The CIA men at the airport were rostered on permanent duty. He passed on the information quickly and efficiently. He now had a damn good chance, and he wasn't going to miss it. He hurried to the bedroom, patted Sarah on the shoulder and said excitedly.

'He's alive, Michael's alive!' She looked at him in disbelief. Brady was quick to qualify. 'But he's in danger, we can help him.'

No need to tell her he wanted to use him, he thought. She snapped quickly to her senses.

'Come on,' Brady said quietly, holding her by the shoulders. 'We're paying a visit to Sir James Cotterslowe. Michael's gone to see him; he's "The Telex".'

'The Sir James, the old knight, that's him?' she whispered.

'You knew about him?' Brady was caught by surprise.

'Only that he was called Sir James, no more. Moffatt once told me.'

'Come on, we've got no time to lose.'

CHAPTER 45

It took less than ten minutes to get to the Belgravia mansion. Thieving bastard, thought Berresford as he walked up the marble steps to the front door, his hand in his pocket fastened to the gun.

The aged valet opened the door slowly, apprehensively. Almost as if he was expecting me, thought Berresford. He raised the gun menacingly.

'Where's Cotterslowe?'

The valet was visibly frightened, his hands raised above his head, shaking. 'In his study, sir.'

Berresford waved his gun towards the doors.

'Open them,' he commanded. The valet opened the doors slowly. The old man's face appeared grotesque to Berresford. His skin was taut, patchy, and drawn over his hollow cheeks. Wispy strands of silver hair partly covered his balding head. It was the eyes that made him so haunting. From the dark hollows two beady blue sparks shone.

'Welcome Mr Berresford,' the feeble old man muttered — his voice icy, high pitched, cruel.

No longer could Berresford contain himself. He roared. 'You evil, contemptuous animal. Murderer! Thief!'

'Tut, tut, Mr Berresford. Pull yourself together... Let's talk first. No doubt you'd like to know how it all came into being... now you'll get what you came for.'

'You try any tricks old man, and I'll blast you to hell. I'm a crack shot.'

'I know,' the old man smiled sardonically. 'In fact, Mr Berresford, you would be the most ruthless killer I've ever known. You must have killed at least twenty men.'

'What are you talking about?' Berresford demanded.

'Oh don't be so modest, Mr Berresford. How you ever accomplished what you have singlehandedly is totally beyond my comprehension.'

What was he talking about? Singlehanded Berresford had not accomplished much at all. Why wasn't he told? How long had Nick known about Cotterslowe?

Berresford had plenty of questions to ask. He was surprised at Cotterslowe's open approach.

The old man kept stalling for time, hoping the GRU would arrive to eradicate Berresford. He began. 'You've uncovered the pattern of Turnstile, a pattern linking hundreds of companies throughout the world.'

'How in the hell did you ever get control of so many companies?' Berresford asked.

'As of yesterday, Mr Berresford, seven hundred and seventy one. I have bled them of 182.3 billion dollars, now safely placed in various parts of the world, in many currencies; bullion, gold and silver, precious metals, diamonds.'

Berresford whistled. 'How...'

'How did I do it? Well, it goes back a long way, Mr Berresford. In fact, back another generation. My father controlled a bank in Germany. He loaned money to the Russians in 1917 and they repaid it to me in 1932.'

Berresford's head reeled. He interrupted, stuttering. 'Then you're ... you're ... Von Kessel?'

'Of course, Mr Berresford. Who else? You knew that ... you have the dossier on me, don't you?'

Berresford was speechless. A pattern was forming in the jigsaw. As the picture developed he sensed that Khomenko was part of it. 'Go on,' he said.

Cotterslowe continued softly.

'Being European and from a country that is now

partly dominated by the Soviet Union, my loyalties were evenly spread. Big business is dirty business. It wasn't long before I was screwed by unscrupulous Britishers. My retaliation was both forceful and effective. Having killed once, I felt no pain in doing it again.'

Digressing for a moment the old man pointed to a small ornate table near Berresford.

'Perhaps you would like a momento of your visit? You seem to like weapons. Take that gun with you, it would be an appropriate trophy.'

He pointed to the silver mounted pistol, intricately decorated and inlaid with silver, the steel stock chiselled in relief with foliage and with a figure of Jupiter brandishing a thunderbolt.

'It belonged to George II, made in 1735 by a German gunsmith named Johann Gottfried Kolbe. It's one of a pair. The other is in the Victoria and Albert Museum.'

Berresford was furious. 'You can't buy me.'

'Oh, Mr Berresford, don't be so foolish. I wasn't endeavouring to buy you. It was just a kind way of returning some of the expenses which you have incurred in tracking me down.'

Cotterslowe was stalling, Berresford thought. Yet he may never get the opportunity to question him again.

'What was your ultimate ambition, political?'

'Political!' The old man shrieked. 'You fool, more than political. I control most of the finances of the western world.' Cotterslowe stood up, waving his clenched fists.

'Sit down and answer my questions,' Berresford ordered. 'How did you start?'

Cotterslowe composed himself and proceeded in a soft, almost hypnotic tone.

'It began with my chemical refinery industries. They were most successful. However, I soon found that other people's money was more attractive than my own. So I started taking over companies, and I bled their cash into my banks. Many people are stupid, Mr Berresford. Many governments are stupid. I have been doing this for thirty years. I must say that over ninety per cent of my wealth has been accumulated in the last ten years. It's an ever expanding business.'

'But what about company auditors, accountants, valuers. Why didn't they report you?'

'I own those too, Mr Berresford. It didn't take me long to realize that in order to achieve ultimate success I must have all the ingredients. So the accountants, auditors, and many important politicians, are mine. It's all there on the tapes — their names, the payments, the blackmail. Firstly, I need to bring the west to its knees, financially. Then the Governments can no longer finance their defence budgets. Next my Russian friends will have the upper hand in military might. Countries will be on a nuclear course, everywhere. My men will take over.'

'Life will never be the same,' Berresford muttered.

'Correct, Mr Berresford,' the old man cackled. 'That is our motto. A new multi-national community will emerge. A better way of life for earth's inhabitants. You could have been part of it. You were selected. Then you ruined it all by stealing my papers and producing the old Nazi file.'

Berresford was fascinated. 'What's your biggest coup?'

'Argentina was one of my most recent successful exploits. It was a multi-disciplinary exercise in economic chaos which began a war and made me a billion dollars wealthier.'

Berresford was seething. His hands were trembling slightly with the weight of the heavy pistol. In spite of this he was intrigued by Cotterslowe's methods.

'Were the Russians involved?'

Cotterslowe was gloating. His eyes lit up at the thought of his success. He raised his finger.

'In time . . . in time . . . You see Berresford, I was able

to accomplish success in a number of directions. Firstly I needed to strip capital from my American banks; this was paid to Argentinian companies in loans. Those loans finished up in my pocket and we wrote those companies off. The financial crisis in Argentina became so acute that the military junta turned to me. I suggested a way . . . it was a simple exercise. Capture the Falkland Islands. They needed many things, all of which I could provide; military weapons, support supplies. They also needed Russia's aid to gain the military intelligence to match the Britains. I was able to arrange everything. The Russians needed the meat and wheat from Argentina and I sold it to them for a handsome profit. In return the Russians made available their satellite surveillance.'

'Where haven't you been successful?' Berresford asked.

'At one stage I almost had Mexico with the help of my eastern European friends.'

The Russians again, thought Berresford.

'Iran was a toy and a profitable exercise.' Cotterslowe was getting sick of Berresford. Where were the Russians?

'Will the tapes provide enough information to return the money to the rightful owners?'

Von Kessel's voice turned cruel and contemptuous.

'You will never know Berresford. When you took those tapes an electromagnetic device destroyed their contents.' Cotterslowe began giggling like a child, bending over and slapping the table between bursts of laughter.

'Oh, did it now?' said Berresford with a smile of intense satisfaction. Then his face changed as he stormed. 'I pressed 1,3,5,6, and turned it off.'

Cotterslowe was suddenly furious. His lips thinned to a fine line in an unconscious snarl which compounded hatred, rage and terror. His left hand trembled as it moved slowly over the desk. He had had enough of Berresford. He slowly inched his chair back from the desk.

Berresford sensed danger. Cotterslowe pressed some buttons. A glint of sunlight on the glass caught Berresford's eye. From the floor a four inch bullet proof glass shield rose up to protect Cotterslowe.

Berresford rapped off two quick shots before it was fully risen. The first shot ripped into Cotterslowe's arm just above the elbow. The second hit the old man somewhere in the chest. Cotterslowe staggered backwards as a secret panel opened behind him to reveal an elevator. He fell into it and collapsed to the floor. The door snapped shut.

Berresford felt the fluid on his face before he saw the sprinklers. He raced towards the lead light window, protecting his face from the breaking glass with his arm as he crashed through into the garden several feet below. A thunderous explosion followed, blowing the other windows into the street.

Berresford heard the flames roaring. Assorted debris blew every which way. Each piece a fuel soaked fire bomb in itself. He had to get away. As he ran up the drive a black Buick skidded to a halt at the front entrance and Brady and Sarah jumped out.

Sarah screamed. 'Michael, Michael,' as she ran towards him, arms outstretched. He threw his arms around her cradling the girl whose eyes streamed with tears. For a moment time stood still as they consoled each other in appreciation of each other's survival.

'Thank God you're safe, where have you been?' Berresford questioned softly. Pushing herself back from him she related the urgent message.

'No time ... Nick has the tapes, he's given them to the Russians. They're on their way to the airport.' Sarah gasped. Berresford, holding Sarah by her shoulders at arms length, shook his head disbelievingly. Brady butted in.

'He was a double agent serving the KGB; Michael

how could you...' Brady waved his fists in suffused frustration. 'What have you done?' Releasing Sarah, Berresford, ashen-faced, twisted in mental agony. He beat his head.

'God almight...Oh God in Heaven.' Berresford suddenly realized, 'Khomenko was engineering it for the Russians!'

CHAPTER 46

The driver of the car remained seated behind the wheel.

'What's going on? Would someone tell me what in the hell's going on?' Berresford yelled.

'Shut up,' Brady replied. He snapped at the driver. 'Get your arse into gear. You can use this thing, patch me through to Hillings.'

Without speaking the driver thumped his finger on a digital panel, tapping out a connection direct to Hilling's office. When the phone answered he passed the handset back to Brady.

'It's him,' he said.

'Have you made up with MI5?' Brady's voice was anxious, determined...

'They're on the other line,' Hillings replied.

'Good. You tell them to get their arse into gear. Don't ask them... tell them. We need that chopper... Yes, the chopper they use between Gatwick and Heathrow Airport. Now... unload them... we haven't got time...'

Brady opened up a map on the seat as he continued. 'He can put down in Ranelagh Gardens. As near as possible to the Embankment and Chelsea Bridge Road corner... We've got Berresford, there's still a chance. The Russians used him for a scapegoat, now it's our turn... Who gives a damn about the regulations, this *is* an international emergency!'

Brady's tone changed as he put the phone down. he turned to Berresford. 'You're the only one that can stop them, Mike. Our hands are tied.'

Sarah had a vice-like grip around Berresford's arm. 'He's done enough!' she yelled. 'Why can't you do it?'

Brady bellowed back. 'We can't interfere. One of them's a Politburo member, the other one's the character you call Nick.'

Berresford interrupted loudly, his hearing still deficient.

'Khomenko's got an Australian passport. The Russians can't claim him,' he shouted.

Brady explained, beads of sweat on his shiny black face.

'It's a matter of grab his bag and run. I've arranged for a chopper to take you there as soon as possible.' Brady turned to the driver. The engine revved wildly and the car surged forward. 'Hurry!' he yelled.

Sarah was frantic. 'You can't, Michael, you can't.'

'It's the only way I can clear myself, Sarah.'

The driver continued pushing the car to the limit. It swerved round the corner. Chelsea Bridge Road was packed. He forced himself in, forming a lane on the wrong side of the road.

Oncoming cars were tooting their horns. The driver pushed the button operating the electric window. The motor of the helicopter and the swish of the huge blades was quite audible.

'They're coming,' he yelled. New energy surged through Berresford's body.

The driver pulled the car to a halt on the footpath. Doors flew open. Berresford gave a fleeting kiss to Sarah.

'Good luck darling,' she said, tears in her eyes. He didn't reply.

The paging device beeped loudly. The CIA agent turned it off, then on again, thus cancelling the initial call. It started beeping again. An emergency, she thought. She rushed to the nearest telephone, situated thirty yards across the airport lounge. The operator answered the telephone on the second ring.

'Deborah M.'

'One moment, I've got an urgent call for you.'

Tom Brady came on the line. He waived the preliminaries and code. There was no time.

'Debbie, we're in a hell of a mess. A senior Russian official has come over to us. He's told us that two or more Russians will be leaving on the Aeroflot plane for Moscow. One of them is carrying a bag or case. One is fairly short, very thickset, bit of a pot, aged about sixty-five. He's wearing a dark blue suit. We're pretty sure about the second one. He is six feet two, black curly hair, deep-set eyes, wearing a chocolate brown tracksuit. I think he should be easy to pick, not many travelling overseas are dressed like that. Somehow you've got to hold them until we get there.'

Her response was quick. 'How much time do you want?'

'Ten minutes or more.'

'Wow, that's a pretty tall order.'

'It's harder than you think. The short tubby one I first described is a Russian VIP. He's a member of the Politburo and you can't lay a finger on him. So any diversionary tactics must be centred on the chocolate brown tracksuit. Get going now! We're not sure if they've arrived yet.'

'Talk to you later,' and she hung up.

Five minutes later Deborah had arranged the set-up. She turned towards her fellow agent and whispered quietly.

'They're coming. The tall one wearing the dark chocolate tracksuit, looks like he's been in a fight. The other one is obviously a diplomat, he matches the description of the VIP. I'll start when they're opposite us.'

They moved a little closer to a crowd of middle-aged women.

When Khomenko and the official were directly opposite them Deborah turned and stared at Khomenko. Then she yelled at the top of her voice.

'That's him, that's him! He raped my ten-year-old daughter. You beast!'

The Russian diplomat was stunned. He didn't understand English. 'What's going on? What in the hell's happening?' he asked in Russian.

'I'm sorry, you must be mistaken.' Khomenko kept repeating.

'Call the police,' Deborah yelled. 'You bastard!'

She turned to the women. 'He raped my ten-year-old daughter.'

The women surged forward in a crowd, like a herd of cattle going through a gate to fresh pastures. They surrounded him.

'Get the cops!' one yelled.

The Russian diplomat was bewildered. Khomenko hadn't explained what was gong on. 'Crazy bloody English,' he bellowed in Russian.

'It's not me, I've never seen her before,' Khomenko explained desperately.

Minutes later a shrill police whistle sounded in the distance. Khomenko and the official tried to push their way through the crowd.

'Get out of here,' the Russian screamed. 'Let me through,' he said in Russian, to no avail. The women had taken over.

The bobby pushed his way through the crowd and demanded to know what the commotion was about. It took several minutes before Khomenko convinced him that he was accompanying a very important Russian official, that they were on their way back to Russia, and that he was his Russian interpreter and they both had diplomatic immunity. Papers were produced, photographs studied. The officer pushed the people back and allowed them to go.

It was by no means a perfect landing. The pilot took his instructions literally. The aircraft thumped hard on the tarmac. Berresford and Brady threw their seatbelts back and headgear off, and then ducked their heads to avoid the huge rotors whirling overhead as they ran towards the man in the blue suit.

'This way!' the man yelled. The words were lost with the noise, nevertheless they understood his gestures. They weaved their way through the crowded corridors, then turned sharp left. It was obvious that only three departure lounges remained at the end of this hallway. Berresford removed his gun. From the corner of his eye Brady saw the movement. He turned to Berresford.

'Put the thing away,' he muttered. 'Wait till you get there.'

Berresford responded immediately. Two minutes later he had spotted Khomenko and the Russian diplomat. He grabbed Brady's arm and pulled him back. There were only forty yards between them and the Russians. Berresford gushed between breaths, his words abbreviated to the essential.

'The bag. Khomenko's got it . . . I can take him from here.'

'Right!' Brady hissed. 'We'll keep to the left.'

They ran off towards the Russians, leaving Berresford to set himself in combat stance. He took the gun from his pocket and pulled the hammer back with his thumb. His left hand steadied the gun in a two-hand position.

Khomenko turned, saw Berresford. The Russian diplomat fumbled for a gun and shoved it into Khomenko's hand.

Khomenko and Berresford fired almost simultaneously. As blood started streaming from Berresford's chest, Khomenko reeled back. The bag of tapes fell to the floor beside him. The deadly weapon in Berresford's hand had made it's mark.

Brady pounced on the bag in a rugby tackle, clasping

it with his hands, pulling it securely under his chest. The echoes of the gunshots subsided to be replaced by the sound of the shrill whistles of police running down the corridor, their feet clapping against the hard floor. The Russian diplomat scurried off to board the Aeroflot plane.

Brady gripped the bag at each end, jubilantly shaking it and yelled. 'We've done it, we've done it,' his face beaming.

A small crowd gathered around Berresford, who lay motionless in a pool of blood. 'Call an ambulance,' one man yelled, 'he's still alive.'

A bright orb shone somewhere in the distance, slowly taking the shape of a bed lamp. It drifted closer as Berresford regained consciousness. New shapes developed in his mind. A figure was bending over him. He blinked many times, forcing himself to focus. Slowly the image of Sarah emerged from the cloudy surroundings.

'You're going to be alright,' she whispered, grabbing his right arm. Sterile images of chrome and white linen surrounded him. Other faces were there. A white-robed doctor with a stethoscope around his neck smiled at Berresford, pleased with his work. Berresford's eyes glazed, the light faded.

'You're going to be alright darling, you did it. You marvellous man, you got the tapes.'

Sarah felt for his hand. She leant over and kissed him lightly on the lips, her tears touching his cheek.

'Darling, as soon as you're well enough they're flying us home.'

Fantasy took over. Berresford saw himself sailing on a thirty-two foot racing yacht. His hand gripped the tiller, while the bow dipped incessantly into the swell, throwing spray high into the air. A breeze from astern filled the sails with a resounding slap. The main sheet ran through the block as Berresford uncleated it. Sarah hung on tightly as he released the sheets. Over the sound of wind in the rigging he could hear her singing, as she beamed with exhilaration. She was wearing a topless bikini, tanning in the blazing sun, her hair wet with spray and clinging to her head in thin strands. Her voice carried above the wind and the waves.

'Bring it on to the wind, darling. We're going home.'

CRITIC'S CHOICE

For action-packed suspense thrillers.

CARTER'S CASTLE by Wilbur Wright	$3.95
DANGEROUS GAMES by Louis Schreiber	$3.95
THE ARAB by G. Lee Tippin	$3.50
THE CHINESE FIRE DRILL by Michael Wolfe	$2.95
THE MONEY BURN by Tony Foster	$3.95
THE CROWN OF INDIA by Samuel Fuller	$3.50
SHADOW CABINET by W. T. Tyler	$3.95
DOUBLE TAKE by Gregory Dowling	$2.95
STRYKER'S KINGDOM by W.A. Harbinson	$3.95
THE HAWTHORN CONSPIRACY by Stephen Hesla	$3.95
THE CORSICAN by Bill Ballinger	$3.95
AMBLER by Fred Halliday	$3.50
BLUE FLAME by Joseph Gilmore	$3.75
THE DEVIL'S VOYAGE by Jack Chalker	$3.75
THE STENDAL RAID by Al Dempsey	$3.95
SKYBLAZER by Peter Allen	$2.95
THE LAST PRESIDENT by Michael Kurland	$3.50

Please send your check or money order (no cash) to:

Critic's Choice Paperbacks
31 East 28th Street
New York, N. Y. 10016

Please include $1.00 for the first book and 50¢ for each additional book to cover the cost of postage and handling.

Name _____

Street Address _____

City _____ State _____ Zip Code _____

Write for a free catalog at the above address.

CRITIC'S CHOICE
The greatest mysteries being published today

THE THIRD BLONDE by M.S. Craig	$2.95
GILLIAN'S CHAIN by M.S. Craig	$2.95
TO PLAY THE FOX by M.S. Craig	$2.95
NEW YEAR RESOLUTION by Alison Cairns	$2.95
STRAINED RELATIONS by Alison Cairns	$2.95
A CHARMED DEATH by Miles Tripp	$2.95
DEATH ON CALL by Sandra Wilkinson	$2.95
SNOW IN VENICE by Frederick Davies	$2.95
MAGGIE by Jennie Tremain	$2.95
THOSE DARK EYES by E. M. Brez	$2.95
NICE KNIGHT FOR MURDER by Philip Daniels	$2.95
ALIBI OF GUILT by Philip Daniels	$2.95
SOMEONE ELSE'S GRAVE by Alison Smith	$2.95
A TIME TO REAP by Michael T. Hinkemeyer	$2.95
THE DOWN EAST MURDERS by J.S. Borthwick	$3.50
THE SAVAGE WEB by Sharon Whitby	$2.95
THE LOST VICTIM by T. A. Waters	$2.95
THE GLORY HOLE MURDERS by Tony Fennelly	$2.95
MACE by James Grant	$2.95
INTIMATE KILL by Margaret Yorke	$2.95
HOMECOMING by James Pattinson	$2.95

Please send your check or money order (no cash) to:

Critic's Choice Paperbacks
31 East 28th Street
New York, N. Y. 10016

Please include $1.00 for the first book and 50¢ for each additional book to cover the cost of postage and handling.

Name _____

Street Address _____

City _____ State _____ Zip Code _____

Write for a free catalog at the above address.

CRITIC'S CHOICE

The finest in HORROR and OCCULT